A BAD CASE
OF THE CREEPY-CRAWLIES . . .

Fisher slammed her sword into a glaring red eye.

The huge spider collapsed. Hawk just had time to see the great bulk coming down on top of him, and then the spider's great weight thrust him down beneath the sewer water and held him there.

Fisher clambered slowly down off the spider's back. She dropped into the water, and looked around her.

"Where's Hawk?"

MacReady looked at Fisher. "There's nothing you can do, Isobel," he said. "I'm sorry, but it was obvious Hawk was a dead man from the moment the spider collapsed on him. . . ."

Ace Books by Simon R. Green

HAWK & FISHER
WINNER TAKES ALL
THE GOD KILLER
WOLF IN THE FOLD
GUARD AGAINST DISHONOR
THE BONES OF HAVEN

HAWK & FISHER
THE BONES OF HAVEN

SIMON R. GREEN

ACE BOOKS, NEW YORK

This book is an Ace original edition,
and has never been previously published.

THE BONES OF HAVEN

An Ace Book / published by arrangement with
the author

PRINTING HISTORY
Ace edition / March 1992

ISBN: 0-441-31837-1

Ace Books are published by The Berkley Publishing Group,
200 Madison Avenue, New York, New York 10016.
The name "ACE" and the "A" logo
are trademarks belonging to Charter Communications, Inc.

PRINTED IN THE UNITED STATES OF AMERICA

10 9 8 7 6 5 4 3 2 1

This book is dedicated to Grant Morrison, boy genius, and The Waterboys, sui generis, without whose inspiration this book could not have been written.

THE BONES OF HAVEN

Haven is an old city, but still growing, with new houses built on the bones of the old. But some parts of Haven are older than others and have never been properly put to rest. Down below the surface of the city, the remains of older structures stir uneasily in their sleep and dream dark thoughts of the way things used to be. There are new buildings all over Haven, and some of them stand on unquiet graves. . . .

1

Hell Wing

Rain had come to Haven with the spring, and a sharp, gusting wind blew it in off the sea. The rain hammered down with mindless ferocity, bouncing back from the cobbles and running down the gutters in raging torrents. Water dripped from every surface, gushed out of drainpipes, and flew in graceful arcs from carved gargoyle mouths on the smarter buildings. It had been raining on and off for weeks, despite everything the city weather wizards could do, and everyone was heartily sick of it. The rain forced itself past slates and tiles and gurgled down chimneys, making fires sputter and smoke. Anyone venturing out into the streets was quickly soaked, and even inside the air seemed saturated with moisture. People gritted their teeth and learned to ignore damp clothing and the constant drumming of rain on the roof. It was the rainy season, and the city endured it as the city endured so many other afflictions—with stubborn defiance and aimless, sullen anger.

And yet things were not as gloomy in the port city of Haven as they might have been. The rain-soaked streets were decked with flags and bunting and decorations, their bright and gaudy colors blazing determinedly through the greyness of the day. Two Kings had come to Haven, and the city was putting on an attractive face and enjoying itself as best it could. It would take more than a little rain to dampen Haven's spirits when it had an excuse to celebrate. A public holiday had been declared from most jobs, on the grounds that the eager citizens would have taken one anyway if it hadn't been granted, and people held street parties between the downpours and boosted the takings at all the inns and taverns. Tarpaulins were erected in the streets wherever possible, to ward off the rain, and beneath them could be found street fairs and conjurers and play-actors and all manner of entertainments.

Of course, not everyone got to take the day off. The city Guard still went about its business, enforcing the law and protecting the good citizens from pickpockets and villains and outrages, and, most important of all, from each other. Haven was a harsh, cruel city swarming with predators, even during a time of supposedly universal celebration. So Hawk and Fisher, husband and wife and Captains in the city Guard, made their way through the dismal grey streets of the Northside and wished they were somewhere else. Anywhere else. They huddled inside their thick black cloaks, and pulled the hoods well forward to keep the rain out of their faces.

Hawk was tall, dark, and no longer handsome. He wore a black silk patch over his right eye, and a series of old scars ran down the right side of his face, giving him a cold, sinister look. Huddled inside his soaking wet black cloak, he looked like a rather bedraggled raven that had known better days. It had to be said that even when seen at his best, he didn't look like much. He was lean and wiry rather than muscular, and was beginning to build a stomach. He wore his dark hair at shoulder length, swept roughly back from his forehead and tied at the nape of his neck with a silver clasp. He'd only just entered his thirties, but already there were streaks of grey in his hair. It would have been easy to dismiss him as just another bravo, perhaps already past his prime, but there was a dangerous alertness in the way he carried himself, and the cold gaze of his single eye was disturbingly direct. He carried a short-handled axe on his right hip, instead of a sword. He was very good with an axe. He'd had lots of practice.

Isobel Fisher walked at his side, unconsciously echoing his pace and stance with the naturalness of long companionship. She was tall, easily six foot in height, and her long blond hair fell to her waist in a single thick plait, weighted at the tip with a polished steel ball. She was in her late twenties, and handsome rather than beautiful, with a raw-boned harshness to her face that contrasted strongly with her deep blue eyes and generous mouth. Some time ago, something had scoured all the human weaknesses out of her, and it showed. Even wrapped in her thick cloak against the driving rain, she moved with a determined, aggressive grace, and her right hand never strayed far from the sword on her hip.

People gave them plenty of room as they approached, and were careful to look away rather than risk catching the Guards' eyes. None of them wanted to be noticed. It wasn't healthy. Hawk and Fisher were feared and respected as two of the toughest and most honest Guards in Haven, and everyone in the Northside had something to hide. It was that kind of area. Hawk glared balefully about him as he and Fisher strode along, and stamped his boots unnecessarily hard on the water-slick cobbles. Fisher chuckled quietly.

"Cheer up, Hawk. Only another month or so of utter misery, and the rainy season will be over. Then you can start looking forward to the utter misery of the boiling hot summer. Always something to look forward to in Haven."

Hawk sniffed. "I hate it when you're this cheerful. It's not natural."

"Me, or the rain?"

"Both." Hawk stepped carefully over a tangled mass of bunting that had fallen from a nearby building. "I can't believe people are still going ahead with celebrations in this downpour."

Fisher shrugged. "Any excuse for a holiday. Besides, they can hardly postpone it, can they? The Kings will only be here two more days. Then it'll all be over, and we can get back to what passes for normal here in the Northside."

Hawk just grunted, not trusting himself to any more than that. His job was hard enough without extra complications. Haven was without doubt the most corrupt and crime-ridden city in the Low Kingdoms, and the Northside was its dark and rotten heart. No crime was too vile or too vicious to be overlooked, and if you could make any kind of profit out of it, you could be sure someone was doing it somewhere. And double-crossing his partner at the same time, like as not. Violence was commonplace, along with rape and murder and protection rackets. Conspiracies blossomed in the shadows, talking treason in lowered voices behind locked doors and shuttered windows. Throughout Haven, the city Guard was stretched thin to breaking point and beyond, but somehow they managed to keep a lid on things, most of the time. Usually by being even harsher and more violent than the people they fought. When they weren't taking sweeteners to look the other way, of course. All of which made it increasingly difficult for anyone to figure out why the Parliaments of both the Low Kingdoms and Outremer had insisted on their respective Kings coming to Haven to sign the new Peace Treaty between the two countries.

It was true that the Peace Talks at which the Treaty had been hammered out had taken place in Haven, but only after the Guard had protected the negotiators from treacherous assault by mercenaries and terrorists. There were a great many people in both countries who had vested interests in seeing the Peace Talks fail, and they'd shown no hesitation in turning Haven into their own private battleground. Hawk and Fisher had managed to smash the worst conspiracy and preserve the Talks, but it had been a very close thing, and everyone knew it. Everyone except the two Parliaments apparently. They'd set their minds on Haven, and weren't going to be talked out of it. Probably because they simply couldn't believe what their Advisors were telling them about the city.

Upon hearing of the singular honour being bestowed on their fair city, Haven's city Councillors practically had a collective coronary, and then began issuing orders in a white-hot panic. No one had ever seen them do so much so quickly. One of the first things they did was to give the Guard strict instructions to get all the villains off the streets as quickly as possible, and throw the lot of them in gaol, for any or no reason. They'd worry about trials and sentences later, if at all. For the moment, all that mattered was rounding up as many villains as possible and keeping them safely out of the way until the Kings had left Haven. The prison Governor came closer to apoplexy than a coronary, though it was a near thing, and demanded hysterically where he was supposed to put all these extra bodies in his already overcrowded prison. That, he was curtly informed, was his problem. So the Guards had gone out into the streets all over the city, backed up by as many men-at-arms and militia as the Council could put together, and started picking up villains and hauling them away. In some cases where their lawyers objected strongly, the Guards took them in as well. Word soon got around, and those miscreants who managed to avoid the sweeps decided it would be wisest to keep their heads down for a while, and quietly disappeared. The crime rate plummeted, overnight.

Which is not to say the city streets suddenly became peaceful and law-abiding. This was Haven, after all. But the usual petty crimes and everyday violence could be more or less controlled by the Guard and kept well away from the Kings and their retinues, which was all that mattered as far as the Council was concerned. No one wanted to think what the city would be like after the Kings had left and most of the villains had to be released from prison due to lack of evidence. To be honest, few people in Haven were thinking that far ahead. In the meantime, Hawk and Fisher patrolled their usual beat in the Northside, and were pleasantly surprised at the change. There were stretches when no one tried to kill anyone else for hours on end.

"What do you think about this Peace Treaty?" said Hawk idly. "Do you think it's going to work?"

Fisher shrugged. "Maybe. As I understand it, the two sides have hammered out a deal that both of them hate but both of them can live with, and that's the best anyone can hope for. Now that they've agreed on a definitive boundary line for the first time in centuries, it should put an end to the recent border clashes at least. Too many good men were dying out there in the borderlands, defending a shaky line on a faded old map to satisfy some politician's pride."

Hawk nodded. "I just wish they'd chosen somewhere else for their signing ceremony. Just by being here, the Kings are a magnet for trouble. Every fanatic, assassin, and terrorist for miles around will see this as their big chance, and head straight for Haven with blood in their eyes and steel in their hands."

"Come on," said Fisher. "You've got to admit, the Kings' security is pretty impressive. They've got four heavy-duty sorcerers with them, a private army of men-at-arms, and a massive deputation of honour guards from the Brotherhood of Steel. I could conquer a minor country with a security force that size."

Hawk sniffed, unimpressed. "No security is ever perfect; you know that. All it needs is one fanatic with a knife and a martyr's complex in the right place at the right time, and we could have two dead Kings on our hands. And you can bet Haven would end up taking all the blame, not the security people. They should never have come here, Isobel. I've got a real bad feeling about this."

"You have bad feelings about everything."

"And I'm usually right."

Isobel looked at him knowingly. "You're just miffed because they wouldn't let any Haven Guards into their security force."

"Damn right I'm annoyed. We know the situation here; they don't. But I can't really blame them, much as I'd like to. Everyone knows the Guard in this city is rife with corruption, and after our last case, no one trusts anyone anymore. After all, if even we can come under suspicion . . ."

"We proved our innocence, and exposed the real traitor."

"Doesn't make a blind bit of difference." Hawk scowled and shook his head slowly. "I still can't believe how ready everyone was to accept we were guilty. After all we've done for this city . . . Anyway, from now on, there'll always be someone ready to point the finger and mutter about no smoke without fire."

"Anyone points a finger at me," said Fisher calmly, "I'll cut it off, and make him eat it. Now, stop worrying about the Kings; they're not our responsibility."

They walked a while in silence, kicking occasionally at loose debris in the street. The rain seemed to be letting up a bit. Every now and again someone up on a roof would throw something down at them, but Hawk and Fisher just ignored it. Thanks to the overhanging upper floors of the buildings, it was rare for anything to come close enough to do any harm, and there was no point in trying to chase after whoever was responsible. By the time the Guards could get up to the roof, the culprits would be long gone, and both sides knew it. They were in more danger from a suddenly emptied chamber pot from an upper window. You had to expect that kind of thing in the Northside. Even if you were the infamous Hawk and Fisher.

Hawk scowled as he strode along, brooding over recent events. It wasn't that long ago that most of Haven had been convinced he'd gone berserk, killing anyone who got in the way of his own personal vendetta outside the law. It hadn't been true, and eventually he'd proved it, but that wasn't the point. He knew he had a reputation for violence; he'd gone to great pains to establish it. It kept the villains and the hardcases off his back, and made the small fry too nervous to give him any trouble. But even so, the speed with which people believed he'd gone bad had disturbed him greatly. For the first time, he'd seen himself as others saw him, and he didn't like what he saw.

"We never used to be this hard," he said quietly. "These days, every time I look at someone I'm thinking about the best way to take them out before they can get to me. Whether they're behaving aggressively or not. Whenever I talk to someone, part of me is listening for a lie or an evasion. And more and more, I tend to assume a suspect is bound to be guilty, unless hard evidence proves them innocent."

"In the Northside, they usually are guilty," said Fisher.

"That's not the point! I always said I'd never laid a finger on an honest man, or killed anyone who didn't need killing. I'm not so sure of that anymore. I'm not infallible. I make mistakes. Only thing is, my mistakes could cost someone their life. When we first took on this job, I really thought we could do some good, make a difference, help protect the people who needed protection. But now, everyone I meet gets weighed as a potential enemy, and I care more about nailing villains than I do about protecting their victims. We've changed, Isobel. The job has changed us. Maybe . . . we should think about leaving Haven. I don't like what we've become."

Fisher looked at him anxiously. "We're only as hard as we need to be to get the job done. This city is full of human wolves, ready to tear us apart at the first sign of weakness. It's only our reputation for sudden death and destruction that keeps them at bay. Remember what it was like when we first started? We had to prove ourselves every day, fighting and killing every hardcase with a sword and a grudge, just to earn the right to walk the streets in peace. Now they've learned to leave us alone, we can get things done. Look, we're a reflection of the people we're guarding. If they start acting civilised and playing by the rule book, so will I. Until then, we just do what we have to, to get the job done."

"But that's the point, Isobel. Why do the job? What difference does it make? For every villain we put away, there are a dozen more we can't touch who are just waiting to take his place. We bust our arses every day, and nothing ever changes. Except us."

"Now, don't start that again. We have made a difference. Sure, things are bad now, but they were much worse before we came. And they'd be worse again if we left. You can't expect to change centuries of accumulated evil and despair in a few short years. We do the best we can, and protect the good people every chance we get. Anything above and beyond that is a bonus. You've got to be realistic, Hawk."

"Yeah. Maybe." Hawk stared straight ahead of him, looking through the driving rain without seeing it. "I've lost my way, Isobel. I don't like what I am, what I'm doing, what I've become. This isn't what I meant to do with my life, but I don't know what else to do. We are needed here; you're right about that. But some days I look in the mirror and I don't recognise my face at all. I hear people talking about things I've done, and it doesn't sound like me. Not the me I remember being, before we came here. I've lost my way. And I don't know how to find it again."

Fisher scowled unhappily, and decided she'd better change the subject. "I know what your real problem is. You're just brooding because I've put you on another diet."

Hawk smiled in spite of himself. "Right. I must be getting old, lass; I never used to put on weight like this. I can't believe I've had to let my belt out *another* notch. When I was younger I had so much energy I used to burn off food as fast as I could eat it. These days, I only have to look at a dessert and my waistline expands. I should never have admitted turning thirty. That was when the rot set in."

"Never mind, dear," said Fisher. "When we get back home tonight I'll put out your pipe and slippers, and you can have a nice doze in your chair by the fire before dinner."

Hawk looked at her. "Don't push your luck, Isobel."

She laughed. "Well, it serves you right. Anyone would think you were on your last legs and doddering towards the grave, to hear you talk. There's nothing wrong with you that a good fight in a good cause couldn't put right. In the meantime, no desserts, cut down on the meat, and lots of nice healthy salads. And no more snacks in between meals, either."

"Why does everything that's good for you have to taste so damned bland?" complained Hawk. "And I don't care if lettuce is good for me; I'm not eating it. Flaming rabbit food . . ."

They continued on their way through the Northside, doing their rounds and showing their faces. Hawk seemed in a somewhat better mood but was still unusually quiet. Fisher decided to let him brood, and not push it. He'd had these moods before, and always snapped out of it eventually. Together, they checked out three burglaries, and lectured one shopkeeper on the need for bolts as well as locks on his doors and window shutters. None of the burglaries were anything special, just routine break-ins. Not much point in looking for clues. Sooner or later they'd catch someone in the act, and he'd confess to a whole bunch of other crimes and that would be that. After the burglaries, they got involved in a series of assaults, sorting out tavern brawls, muggings, and finally a domestic dispute. Hawk hated being dragged into domestic quarrels. You couldn't win. Whatever you did was bound to be wrong.

They approached the location of the domestic dispute cautiously, but at least this time there was no flying crockery to dodge. Or flying knives. The address was a pokey little apartment in the middle of a row of shabby tenements. Neighbours watched silently as the two Guards entered the building. Hawk took the lead and kept a careful eye on the house's occupants as they made way before him. Guards were the common enemy of all Northsiders; they represented and enforced all the laws and authority that kept the poor in their place. As a result, Guards were targets for anyone with a grudge or a mad on, and one of the nastier surprise attacks these days was the Haven mud pie—a mixture of lye and grease. Thrown at close range, the effect could be devastating. The lye burned through clothing as though it wasn't there, and if it hit bare skin it could eat its way right down to the bone. The grease made the lye stick like glue. Even a small mud pie could put a Guard in hospital for weeks, if his partner didn't get him to a doctor fast enough. And doctors tended to be few and far between in the Northside. The last man to aim a mud pie at Hawk had got both his arms broken, but there were any number of borderline crazies in the Northside, just waiting to be pushed over the edge by one frustration too many. So Hawk and Fisher stayed close together and kept a wary eye on shadowed corners and doors left just a little too far ajar.

They made their way through the hall and up the narrow stairs without incident. Mothers and small children watched in stony silence, while from above came the sound of domestic unrest. A man and a woman were shouting and screeching at the tops of their voices, but Hawk and Fisher didn't let themselves be hurried. As long as the couple were still shouting they weren't searching for blunt instruments or something with a sharp edge. It was when things went suddenly quiet that you had to worry. Hawk and Fisher reached the landing and strode down the hall, stepping over small children playing unconcernedly on the floor. They found the door with the right number, the sounds from within made it pretty hard to miss. Hawk hammered on the door with his fist, and an angry male voice broke off from its tirade just long enough to tell him to go to hell. Hawk tried again, and got a torrent of abuse for his trouble. He shrugged, drew his axe, and kicked the door in.

A man and a woman looked round in surprise as Hawk and Fisher stood in the doorway taking in the scene. The woman was less than average height, and more than a little undernourished, with a badly bruised face and a bloody nose. She was trying to stop the flowing blood with a grubby handkerchief, and not being very successful. The man was easily twice her size, with muscles on his muscles, and he was brandishing a fist the size of a mallet. His face was dark with rage, and he glared sullenly at Hawk and Fisher as he took in their Guards' cloaks.

"What are you doing here? You've no business in this house, so get out. And if you've damaged my door I'll see you pay for the repairs!"

Hawk smiled coldly. "If you've damaged that woman, you'll pay for it. Now, stand back from her and put down that fist, and we'll all have a nice little chat."

"This is family business," said the man quickly, before the woman could say anything. He lowered his fist, but stood his ground defiantly.

Fisher moved forward to speak to the woman, and the man fell back a step in spite of himself. She ignored him, and spoke softly to the woman. "Does this kind of thing happen often?"

"Often enough," said the woman indistinctly, behind her handkerchief.

Fisher frowned. "Just say the word, and we'll drag him off to gaol. You don't have to put up with this. Are you married to him?"

The woman shrugged. "More or less. He's not so bad, most of the time, but he can't keep a job because of his temper. He just lost another one today."

"So he comes home and takes it out on you." Fisher nodded understandingly.

"That's enough!" snapped the man suddenly, stung at being talked about as though he wasn't there. "She's got nothing more to say to you, Guard, if she knows what's good for her. And you two can get out now, or I'll throw you out."

Hawk stirred, and looked at him with interest. "You and what army?"

"I really think you should swear out a complaint against him," said Fisher. "Next time he might not just break your nose. A few nights in gaol might calm him down a bit, and if nothing else, it should make him think twice about hitting you again."

The woman nodded slowly. "You're right. I'll swear out a complaint."

"You lousy bitch!" The man lurched forward, raising his huge hands menacingly. Fisher turned and smacked him solidly between the eyes with her fist. The man fell back a step and then sat down abruptly, blinking dazedly. Fisher looked at Hawk.

"We'd better get him downstairs. You take one arm and I'll take the other."

"Right," said Hawk. "There's some railings outside we can chain him to until we can find a Constable to take him back to Headquarters for charging."

They got him to his feet easily enough and were heading for the door when Hawk, hearing a muffled cry behind them, looked back just in time to see the woman heading straight for him with a knife in her hand. Hawk dropped the man and stepped quickly to one side, but the woman kept coming at him, her eyes wild and desperate. Fisher stuck out a leg and tripped her. The woman fell heavily and lost her grip on the knife. Hawk stepped forward and kicked it out of reach. The woman burst into tears. Hawk looked at Fisher.

"What the hell was that all about?"

"She loves him," said Fisher, shaking her head sadly. "She might not like the treatment, but she loves him just the same. And when she saw us hauling him off to gaol, she forgot how angry she was and decided we were the villains of the piece, for threatening her man. . . . Now we have to take them both in. Can't let anyone get away with attacking a Guard, or we'll never have any peace."

Hawk nodded reluctantly, and they set about manhandling the man and the woman down the stairs and out into the street.

They found a Constable, eventually, and let him take over, then set off on their beat again. The rain continued to show signs of letting up without ever actually doing anything about it. The day wore slowly on, fairly quiet by Northside standards. Hawk and Fisher broke up half a dozen fights, ran off a somewhat insecure flasher, and helped talk a leaper out of jumping from a second-storey building. The city didn't really care if a leaper killed himself or not, but there was always the chance he might land on someone important, so official policy in such cases was to clear the street below and then just let the would-be suicide get on with it. As in many other things, Hawk and Fisher ignored official policy and took the time to talk quietly and encouragingly to the man, until he agreed to go down the normal way, via the stairs. The odds were that by tomorrow he'd be back up on the roof again, but at least they'd bought him some time to think it over. Working in the Northside, you learned to be content with little victories.

"You know," said Hawk as he and Fisher walked away, "sometimes, when I'm up on a roof with a leaper, I have an almost overwhelming urge to sneak up behind him and shout Boo! in his ear. Just to see what would happen."

"You're weird, Hawk," said Fisher, and he nodded solemnly. At which point a rush of gentle flute music poured through their minds, followed by the dry, acid voice of the Guard communications sorcerer.

All Guards in the Northern sector, report immediately to Damnation Row, where there is a major riot in progress. This order supersedes all other instructions. Do not discuss the situation with anyone else until you have reported to the prison Governor. That is all.

Hawk scowled grimly as he and Fisher turned around and headed back down the street shoulders hunched against the renewed heavy rain. Damnation Row was Haven's oldest and largest prison, as well as the most secure. A great squat monstrosity of basalt stone, surrounded on all sides by high walls and potent sorceries, it was infamous throughout the Low Kingdoms as the one prison no one ever escaped from. Riots were almost unknown, never mind a major riot. No wonder they'd been instructed not to talk about it. The prison's reputation was part of its protection. Besides, if word did get out, the streets would be thronged with people heading for the prison to try and help the inmates break out. Most people in Haven knew someone in Damnation Row.

The prison itself stood jammed up against the city wall on the far boundary of the Northside, and Hawk and Fisher could see its outline through the driving rain long before they got to its gatehouse. The exterior walls were huge, dark, and largely featureless, and seemed especially grim and forbidding through the downpour. Hawk hauled on the steel bell pull at the main gate, and waited impatiently with Fisher for someone to answer. He'd never been inside Damnation Row before and was curious to see if it was as bad as everyone said. Conditions inside were supposed to be deliberately appalling. Haven had nothing but contempt for anyone dumb enough or unsuccessful enough to get caught, and the idea was that a stay in Damnation Row would scare the offender so much he'd do anything rather than be sent back—including going straight. The prison's excellant security record also made it a useful dumping ground for dangerous lunatics, untrustworthy magic-users, and political and religious embarrassments. The city firmly believed in taking revenge on its enemies. All of them.

Hawk yanked on the bell pull again, hammered on the door with his fist, and kicked it a few times for good measure. All he got out of it was a stubbed toe and an unsympathetic glance from Fisher. Finally a sliding panel in the door jerked open and a grim-faced prison guard studied the panel shut and opening the judas gate in the main door to let them in. Hawk and Fisher identified themselves, and weren't even given time to dump their dripping wet cloaks before being hustled through the outer precincts of the prison to the Governor's office. Everywhere they looked there was bedlam, with prison guards running this way and that, shouting orders no one listened to and getting in each other's way. Off in the distance they could hear a dull roar of raised voices and the hammering of hard objects on iron bars.

The Governor's office was comfortably furnished, but clearly a place of work rather than relaxation. The walls were bare save for a number of past and present *Wanted* posters, and two framed testimonials. The plain, almost austere desk was buried under paperwork, split more or less equally into two piles marked "Pending" and "Urgent." The Governor, Phillipe Dexter, stood up from behind his desk to shake hands briefly with Hawk and Fisher, gestured for them to take a seat, and then returned to his own chair quickly, as though only sheer willpower had kept him on his feet that long. He was an average-looking man in his late forties, dressed fashionably but conservatively, and had a bland, politician's face. At the moment he looked tired and drawn, and his hand had trembled slightly with fatigue when Hawk shook it. The two Guards took off their cloaks and draped them over the coat rack before sitting down. The Governor watched the cloaks dripping heavily on his carpet, and closed his eyes for a moment, as though that was definitely the last straw.

"How long has this riot been going on?" asked Hawk, to get the ball rolling.

"Almost four hours now." The Governor scowled unhappily, but his voice was calm and measured. "We thought we could contain it at first, but we just didn't have the manpower. This prison has always suffered from overcrowding, with two or even three inmates locked up in a cell originally meant for one. Mainly because Haven has almost doubled in size since this prison was built. But we coped, because we had to. There was nowhere else to put the prisoners; all the other gaols in Haven are just holding pens and debtors' prisons, and they face the same problem as us. But, thanks to the Council's ill-advised purge of the streets, we've had prisoners arriving here in the hundreds over the last week or so, and my staff just couldn't cope with the resulting crush. We had four, sometimes five, to a cell in some places, and not even enough warning to allow for extra food and blankets. Something had to give.

"The prisoners decided this morning that they couldn't be treated any worse than they already were, and attacked the prison staff during breakfast and slopping-out. The violence soon spread, and we didn't have enough manpower to put it down. Essentially, we've lost half the prison. Barricades and booby traps have been set up by the inmates in all the approaches to two of the main Wings, and they've been throwing everything they can get their hands on at us to make us keep our distance. They've started several fires, but so far the prison's security spells have been able to stamp them out before they could get out of control. So far, no one's actually escaped. Our perimeter is still secure.

"We've tried to negotiate with the inmates, but none of them have shown any interest in talking. Pretty soon the Council is going to order me to take the occupied Wings back by force, before the Kings get to hear about the riot and start getting worried. But that, believe it or not, isn't the main problem. Adjoining the two occupied Wings is Hell Wing, where we keep our supernatural prisoners. Creatures of power and magic, locked away here while awaiting trial. Hell Wing is in its own pocket dimension, surrounded by powerful wards, so it should still be secure. But there are reported to be several magic-users among the rioters, and if they find a way into Hell Wing and set those creatures loose, a whole army of Guards wouldn't be enough to control them."

Hawk and Fisher looked at each other, and then back at the Governor. "If it's as serious as all that," said Hawk, "why are you wasting time talking to us? You need somebody with real power, like the God Squad, or the SWAT team."

The Governor nodded quickly. "The God Squad have been alerted, but at present they're busy coping with an emergency on the Street of Gods. I've sent for the Special Wizardry and Tactics team; they're on their way. When they get here, I want you two to work with them. You've both worked with the God Squad in the past, you have experience coping with supernatural creatures, and you have a reputation for salvaging impossible situations. And right now, I'm so desperate I'll grab at any straw."

There was a brief knocking at the door, and it swung open before the Governor could even ask who it was. A woman and three men filed into the office and slammed the door shut behind them. The woman fixed the Governor with a harsh gaze.

"You sent for the SWAT team. We're here. Don't worry, we've been briefed." She looked at Hawk and Fisher. "What are they doing here?"

"They'll be working with you on this," said the Governor firmly, trying to regain control of the situation. "The God Squad's been delayed. These two officers are . . ."

"I know who they are." The woman nodded briskly to Hawk and Fisher. "I'm Jessica Winter, team leader and tactician. My associates are Stuart Barber, weaponmaster; John MacReady, negotiator; and Storm, sorcerer. That takes care of introductions; anything more can wait till later; we're on a tight schedule and time's running out. Let's go. Sit tight, Governor; you'll have your prison back in a few hours. Oh, and if any more Guards arrive, keep them out of our way."

She smiled briefly, and hustled her people out of the office before the Governor could work up a reply. Hawk and Fisher nodded to him and hurried out after the SWAT team. Jessica Winter led the way down the corridor with casual confidence, and Hawk took the opportunity to surreptitiously study his new partners. He knew them all by reputation but had never worked with any of them before.

Winter was a short, stocky woman with a determined, friendly manner that reminded Hawk irresistibly of an amiable bulldog. She was in her early thirties and looked it, and clearly didn't give a damn. She'd been through two husbands that Hawk knew of, and was currently pursuing her third. She moved and spoke with a brisk, no-nonsense efficiency, and by all accounts could be charming or overwhelming as the mood took her. She was dressed in a simple shirt and trousers, topped with a chain-mail vest that had been polished within an inch of its life, and wore a sword on her hip in a plain, regulation issue scabbard. She'd been with the SWAT team for seven years, two of them as leader and tactician. She had a good if somewhat spotty record, and preferred to dismiss her failures as learning experiences. Given that her team usually wasn't called in until things had got totally out of hand, Winter had built up a good reputation for finding solutions to problems at the last possible moment. She also had a reputation for convoluted and devious strategies, which Hawk felt might come in very handy just at the moment. He had a strong feeling there was a lot more to this situation than met the eye.

He glanced across at Stuart Barber, the weaponmaster, and felt a little reassured. Even walking down an empty corridor in the midst of friends and allies, Barber exuded an air of danger and menace. He was a tall, powerfully-built man in his mid-twenties, with arms so tightly muscled the veins bulged fiercely even when his arms were apparently relaxed. He had a broad, brutal-looking sword on his hip, in a battered leather scabbard, and wore a long chain-mail vest that had been repaired many times, not always neatly. He had a long, angular head, with pale, pinched features accentuated by dark hair cropped short in a military cut. He had a constant slight scowl that made him look more thoughtful than bad-tempered.

John MacReady, the negotiator, looked like everyone's favourite uncle. It was his job to talk people out of things before Winter let Barber loose on them. MacReady was average height and well-padded, in a friendly, non-threatening way. He smiled a lot, and had the charming gift of convincing people he was giving them his entire attention while they were talking. He was in his mid-forties, going bald, and trying to hide it with a somewhat desperate hairstyle. He had an easy, companiable way about him that made him hard to distrust, but Hawk decided to try anyway. He didn't put much faith in people who smiled too much. It wasn't natural.

The sorcerer called Storm was a large, awkward-looking man in his late twenties. He was easily six foot six inches, and his broad frame made him look even taller. His robe of sorcerer's black looked as if it hadn't been cleaned in months, and the state of his long black hair and beard suggested they'd never even been threatened with a comb. He scowled fiercely at nothing and everything, and just grunted whenever Winter addressed him. His hands curled and uncurled into fists at his side, and he strode along with his beard jutting out before him, as though just waiting for some fool to pick a quarrel with him. All in all, he looked rather like some mystical hermit who'd spent years in a cave meditating on the nature of man and the universe, and come up with some very unsatisfactory answers. The sorcerer looked round suddenly, and caught Hawk's eye.

"What are you staring at?"

"I was just wondering about your name," said Hawk easily.

"My name? What about it?"

"Well, Storm's not exactly a usual name for a sorcerer. A weather wizard, maybe, but . . ."

"It suits me," said the sorcerer flatly. "Want to make something of it?"

Hawk thought about it for a moment, and then shook his head. "Not right now. I was just curious."

Storm sniffed dismissively, and looked away. Jessica Winter fell back a few steps to walk alongside Hawk. She smiled at him briefly. "Don't mind Storm," she said briskly, not bothering to lower her voice. "He's a gloomy bugger, but he knows his job."

"Just what kind of a setup are we walking into?" asked Fisher, moving up on Hawk's other side. "As I understand it, you've had a full briefing. We just got the edited highlights."

Winter nodded quickly. "Not surprisingly, the situation isn't as simple and straightforward as it appears. The riot broke out far too suddenly and too efficiently for it to have been entirely spontaneous. Somebody had to be behind it, pulling the strings and pointing people in the right direction. But the Governor's attempts to negotiate got nowhere, because the rioters couldn't agree on a leader to represent them. Which suggests that whoever is behind the riot is keeping his head down. Which in turn suggests that person had his own reasons for starting it."

"Like breaking someone out, under cover of the chaos?" said Fisher.

"Got it in one," said Winter. "But so far no one's got out over the walls or through the gates; the prison guards have seen to that. The Governor's insistence on regular panic drills seems to have paid off. The real problem lies with Hell Wing, which is where we come in. If someone's managed to get in there and bust any of those creatures loose, we could be in real trouble. You could break out any number of people in the chaos that would cause. And if that someone's let them all loose . . . we might as well evacuate the entire city."

"That bad?" said Hawk.

"Worse."

Hawk thought about it. "Might this be a good time to suggest a strategic retreat, so we can wait for the God Squad to back us up?"

Storm sniffed loudly. "The word retreat isn't in our vocabulary."

"It's in mine," said Hawk.

"Just how well-confined are these supernatural prisoners?" asked Fisher hurriedly.

"Very," said Winter. "Hell Wing is a separate pocket dimension linked to Damnation Row by a single doorway, protected by armed guards and a number of powerful magical wards. Each inmate is confined separately behind bars of cold iron, backed up by an individually tailored geas, a magical compulsion that prevents them from escaping. There's never been an escape from Hell Wing. The system's supposed to be foolproof."

"Unless it's been sabotaged from inside," said Hawk.

"Exactly."

Fisher frowned. "All of this suggests the riot was planned well in advance. But the prison didn't become dangerously overcrowded until just recently."

"It was a fairly predictable situation," said Winter. "Once it was known the Kings were coming here. Especially if our mysterious planners knew of that in advance."

From up ahead came the sound of ragged cheering, interspersed with occasional screams and catcalls.

"We'll have to take it carefully from here on in," said MacReady quietly. "We're getting close to the occupied Wings. We have to pass right by them to get to Hell Wing. The Governor's going to try and distract them with new attempts at negotiating, but there's no telling how long that will last. It's bedlam in there."

A scream rose suddenly in the distance, drowned out quickly by stamping feet and baying voices. Fisher shivered despite herself.

"What the hell are they doing?"

"They'll have got to the sex offenders by now," said MacReady. "There's a social status among criminals, even in Damnation Row, and sex offenders and child molesters are right at the bottom of the list. The other prisoners loathe and despise them. They call them beasts, and assault them every chance they get. Mostly they're held in solitary confinement, for their own protection. But right now the prisoners are holding mock trials and killing the rapists and child abusers, one by one.

"Of course, when they've finished with that, there are various political and religious factions, all eager to settle old grudges. When the dust's settled from that, and the prisoners have demolished as much of the prison building as they can, they'll turn on the seventeen prison staff they were able to get their hands on, and try and use them as a lever for an escape. When that doesn't work, they'll kill them too."

"We can't let that happen," said Fisher. "We have to put a stop to this."

"We will," said Winter. "Once we've made sure Hell Wing is secure. I know, Fisher, you want to rush in there and rescue them, but we can't. Part of this job, perhaps the hardest part, is learning to turn your back on one evil so you can concentrate on a greater one."

It was ominously quiet in the distance. Hawk scowled. "Should have put a geas on the lot of them. Then there wouldn't have been all this trouble in the first place."

"It's been suggested many times," said Winter, "but it would cost like hell, and the Council won't go for it. Cells and bars come a lot cheaper than magic."

"Hold it," said Storm suddenly, his voice so sharp and commanding that everyone stopped dead where they were. The sorcerer stared silently at the empty corridor ahead of them, his scowl gradually deepening. "We're almost there," he said finally, his voice now low and thoughtful. "The next bend leads into Sorcerers' Row, where the magic-users are confined. They're held in separate cells, backed up by an individual geas. After that, there's nothing between us and Hell Wing."

"Why have we stopped?" said Winter quietly. "What's wrong, Storm?"

"I don't know. My inner Sight's not much use here. Too many security spells. But I ought to be picking up some trace of the magic-users on Sorcerers' Row, and I'm not getting anything. Just traces of stray magic, scattered all over the place, as though something very powerful happened here not long ago. I don't like the feel of it, Jessica."

"Draw your weapons," said Winter, glancing back at the others, and there was a quick rasp of steel on leather as the team's swords left their scabbards. Hawk hefted his axe thoughtfully, and then frowned as he realised MacReady was unarmed.

"Where's your sword?" he said quietly.

"I don't need one," said the negotiator calmly. "I lead a charmed life."

Hawk decided he wasn't going to ask, if only because MacReady was obviously waiting for him to do so. He nodded calmly to the negotiator, and moved forward to join Winter and Storm.

"I don't like standing around here, Winter. It makes us too good a target. If there's a problem with Sorcerers' Row, let's check it out."

Winter looked at him coolly. "I lead the team, Captain Hawk, and that means I make the decisions. We're going to take this slow and easy, one step at a time. I don't believe in rushing into things."

Hawk shrugged. "You're in charge, Winter. What's the plan?"

Winter frowned. "It's possible the rioters could have broken the magic-users out of their cells, but not very likely; the geas should still hold them. Captain Hawk, you and your partner check out the situation. Barber, back them up. Everyone else stays put. And Hawk, no heroics, please. Just take a quick look around, and then come back and tell me what you saw. Got it?"

"Got it," said Hawk.

He moved slowly forward, axe held at the ready before him. Fisher moved silently at his side, and Barber brought up the rear. Hawk would rather not have had him there, on the grounds that he didn't want to be worrying about what Barber was doing when he should be concentrating on getting the job done, but he couldn't say no. He didn't want to upset Winter this early in their professional relationship. Or Barber, for that matter. He looked like he knew how to use that sword. Hawk sighed inaudibly and concentrated on the darkening corridor ahead. Some of the lamps had gone out, and Hawk's gaze darted from shadow to shadow as he approached the bend in the corridor. The continuing silence seemed to grow thicker and more menacing, and Hawk had a growing conviction that someone, or something, was waiting for him just out of sight round the corner.

He eased to a halt, his shoulder pressed against the wall just before the bend, then glanced back at Fisher and Barber. He

gestured for them to stay put, took a firm grip on his axe,
and then jumped forward to stare down the side corridor
into Sorcerers' Row. It stretched away before him, all gloom
and shadow, lit only by half a dozen wall lamps at irregular
intervals. The place was deserted, but all the cell doors had
been torn out of their frames and lay scattered across the
floor. The open cells were dark and silent, and reminded Hawk
unpleasantly of the gap left after a tooth has been pulled. He
stayed where he was, and gestured for Fisher and Barber to
join him. They did so quickly, and Fisher whistled softly.

"We got here too late, Hawk. Whatever happened here
is over."

"We don't know that yet," said Hawk. "We've still got to
check the cells. Fisher, watch my back. Barber, stay put and
watch the corridor. Both ends. And let's all be very careful.
I don't like the feel of this."

"Blood has been spilled here," said Barber quietly. "A lot
of it. Some of it's still pretty fresh."

"I don't see any blood," said Fisher.

"I can smell it," said Barber.

Hawk and Fisher looked at each other briefly, and then
moved cautiously towards the first cell. Fisher took one of
the lamps from its niche in the wall and held it up to give
Hawk more light. He grunted acknowledgement, and glanced
down at the solid steel door lying warped and twisted on the
floor before him. At first he thought it must have been buckled
by some form of intense heat, but there was no trace of any
melting or scorching on the metal. The door was a good two
inches thick. Hawk didn't want to think about the kind of
strength that could warp that thickness of steel.

There were a few small splashes of blood in the cell doorway, dry and almost black. Hawk eased forward a step at a
time, ready for any attack, and then swore softly as the light
from Fisher's lamp filled the cell. The cell's occupant had been
nailed to the far wall with a dozen daggers and left to bleed to
death. Given the amount of blood soaking the floor below him,
he'd taken a long time to die.

Hawk moved quickly from cell to cell, with Fisher close
behind him. Every cell held a dead man. They'd all been killed
in different ways, and none of them had died easily. They all
wore sorcerer's black, but their magic hadn't protected them.

Hawk sent Barber back to fetch the rest of the team while he and Fisher dutifully searched the bodies for any sign of life. It didn't take long. Winter walked slowly down Sorcerers' Row, frowning, with MacReady at her side. Storm darted from cell to cell, muttering under his breath. Barber sheathed his sword and leaned against the corridor wall with his arms folded. He looked completely relaxed, but Hawk noted that he was still keeping a careful watch on both ends of the corridor. Storm finally finished his inspection and stalked back to report to Winter. Hawk and Fisher joined them.

"What happened here?" said Hawk. "I thought they were supposed to be magic-users. Why didn't they defend themselves?"

"Their geas wouldn't let them," said Storm, bitterly. "They were helpless in their cells when the killers came."

"Why kill them at all?" said Fisher. "Why should the rioters hate magic-users enough to do something like this to them?"

"There was no hate in this," said Storm. "This was cold and calculated, every bloody bit of it. It's a mass sacrifice, a ritual designed to increase magical power. If one sorcerer sacrifices another, he can add the dead man's magic to his own. And if a sorcerer were to sacrifice all these magic-users, one after another . . . he'd have more than enough magic to smash through into Hell Wing, and make a new doorway."

"Wait a minute," said Hawk. "All the sorcerers in this prison were held here, on Sorcerers' Row, and none of them are missing. There's a dead body in every cell."

"Someone must have smuggled a sorcerer in, disguised as a prisoner," said Winter. "Probably bribed a guard to look the other way. This riot was carefully planned, people, right down to the last detail."

Fisher frowned. "So someone could have already entered Hell Wing and let the creatures out?"

"I don't know," said Storm. "Maybe. I can tell there's a new dimensional doorway close at hand, now I know what I'm looking for, but I can't tell if anyone's been through it recently."

"Great," said Fisher. "Just what this case needed, more complications." She looked at Winter. "All right, leader, what are we going to do?"

"Go into Hell Wing, and see what's happened," said Winter evenly. "Our orders were to do whatever is necessary to prevent the inmates of Hell Wing from breaking out. Nothing has happened to change that."

"Except we now face a rogue sorcerer and an unknown number of rioters as well as whatever's locked up in there," said Hawk. "I didn't like the odds when we started, and I like them even less now. I don't do suicide missions."

"Right," said Fisher.

Winter looked at them both steadily. "As long as you're a part of the SWAT team, you'll do whatever I require you to do. If that isn't acceptable, you can leave any time."

Hawk smiled coldly. "We'll stay. For now."

"That isn't good enough, Captain."

"It's all you're going to get."

Fisher pushed in between Hawk and Winter, and glared at them both impartially. "If you two have quite finished flexing your muscles at each other, may I remind you we've still got a job to do? You can butt heads later, on your own time."

Winter nodded stiffly. "Your partner is right, Captain Hawk; we can continue this later. I take it I can rely on your co-operation for the remainder of this mission?"

"Sure," said Hawk. "I can be professional when I have to be."

"Good." Winter took a deep, steadying breath and let it out slowly. "The situation isn't necessarily as bad as it sounds. I think we have to assume some of the rioters have entered Hell Wing, presumably to release the inmates in the hope that they'd add to the general chaos. But if the fools have managed to break any of the geases and some of the creatures are loose, I think we can also safely assume that those rioters are now dead. Which means we're free to concentrate on recapturing those creatures that have broken loose."

"Just how powerful are these . . . creatures?" asked Fisher.

"Very," said Storm shortly. "Personally, I think we should just seal off the entire Wing, and forget how to find it."

"Those are not our orders," said Winter. "They have a right to a fair trial."

Storm sniffed. "That's not why our Lords and masters want these things kept alive. Creatures of Power like these could prove very useful as weapons, just in case the Peace Treaty doesn't work out after all. . . ."

"That's none of our business, Storm!"

"Wait a minute," said Hawk. "Are you saying we're supposed to take these things alive?"

"If at all possible, yes," said Winter. "Do you have a problem with that?"

"This case gets better by the minute," growled Hawk. "Look, before we go any further, I want a full briefing on these Creatures of Power. What exactly are we going to be facing in Hell Wing?"

"To start with, there's the Pale Men," said Winter steadily. "They're not real, but that just makes them more dangerous. They can take on the aspect of people you used to be but no longer are. The longer they hold the contact, the more real they become, while you fade into a ghost, a fancy, a might-have-been. Sorcerers create Pale Men from old love letters, blood spilled in anger, an engagement ring from a marriage that failed, or a baby's shoes bought for a child that was never born. Any unfinished emotion that can still be tapped. Be wary of them. They're very good at finding chinks in your emotional armour that you never knew you had."

"How many of them are there?" said Fisher.

"We don't know. It tends to vary. We don't know why. Then there's Johnny Nobody. We think he used to be human, perhaps a sorcerer who lost a duel. Now he's just a human shape, consisting of guts and muscle and blood held together by surface tension. He has no skin and no bones, but he still stands upright. He screams a lot, but he never speaks. When we caught him, he was killing people for their skin and bones. Apparently he can use them to replace what he lost, for a time, but his body keeps rejecting them, so he has to keep searching for more."

"I'm surprised he hasn't killed himself," said Fisher.

"He's tried, several times," said Winter. "His curse won't let him die. Now, if I may continue . . . Messerschmann's Portrait is a magical booby trap left behind by the sorcerer Void when he had to leave Haven in a hurry earlier this year, pursued by half the sorcerers in Magus Court. We still don't know what he did to upset them, but it must have been pretty extreme. They're a hard-boiled bunch in Magus Court. Anyway, the

Portrait was brought here for safekeeping, and it's been in Hell Wing ever since. The creature in the Portrait may have been human once, but it sure as hell isn't now. According to the experts who examined the Portrait, the creature is actually alive, trapped in the Portrait by some powerful magic they don't fully understand. And it wants out. Apparently, if it locks eyes with you long enough, it can walk out into the world, and you would be trapped in the Portrait, in its place. So don't get careless around it."

"You should be safe enough, Hawk," said Fisher. "It'd have a hard job locking eyes with you."

Hawk winked his single eye. Winter coughed loudly to get their attention.

"Crawling Jenny is something of an enigma. It's a living mixture of moss, fungi, and cobwebs, with staring eyes and snapping mouths. It was only five or six feet in diameter when it was first removed from the Street of Gods because it was menacing the tourists. Now it fills most of its cell. If some fool's let Crawling Jenny loose and it's been feeding all this time, there's no telling how big it might be by now.

"The Brimstone Boys are human constructs, neither living nor dead. They smell of dust and sulphur, and their eyes bleed. Their presence distorts reality, and they bring entropy wherever they go. There are only two of them, thank all the Gods, but watch yourselves; they're dangerous. We lost five Constables and two sorcerers taking them. I don't want to add to that number.

"And finally, we come to Who Knows. We don't know what that is. It's big, very nasty, and completely invisible. And judging by the state of its victims' bodies, it's got a hell of a lot of teeth. They caught it with nets, pushed it into its cell on the end of several long poles, and nobody's gone near it since. It hasn't been fed for over a month, but it's still alive—as far as anyone can tell."

"I've just had a great idea," said Fisher, when Winter finally paused for breath. "Let's turn around, go back, and swear blind we couldn't find Hell Wing."

"I'll go along with that," said Barber.

Winter's mouth twitched. "It's tempting, I'll admit, but no. We're SWAT, and we can handle anything. It says so in our contract. Listen up, people. This is how we're going to do it. Storm, you open up the gateway and then stand back. Barber, Hawk, and Fisher—you'll go through first. If you see something and it moves, hit it. Hard. Storm will be right behind you, to provide whatever magical support you need. I'll bring up the rear. Mac, you stay back here and guard the entrance. I don't want anyone sneaking up on us from behind."

"You never let me in on the exciting stuff," said MacReady.

"Yes," said Winter. "And aren't you grateful?"

"Very."

Winter smiled, and turned back to the others. "Take your places, people. Storm, open the gateway."

The sorcerer walked a few steps down the corridor and began muttering to himself under his breath. Barber stepped forward to take the point, and Hawk and Fisher moved in on either side of him. Barber glanced at them briefly, and frowned.

"Don't you people believe in armour? This isn't some bar brawl we're walking into."

"Armour just slows you down," said Hawk. "The Guard experiments with it from time to time, but it's never caught on. With the kind of work we do, it's more important for us to be able to move freely and react quickly. You can't chase a pickpocket down a crowded street while wearing chain mail. Our cloaks have steel mesh built into them, but that's it."

"And you don't even wear that, most of the time, unless I nag you," said Fisher.

Hawk shrugged. "Don't like cloaks. They get in the way while I'm fighting."

"I've always believed in armour," said Barber, swinging his sword loosely before him. He seemed perfectly relaxed, but his gaze never left Storm. "It doesn't matter how good you are with a blade, there's always someone better, or luckier, and that's when a good set of chain mail comes into its own."

He broke off as the sorcerer's voice rose suddenly, and then cut off sharply. The floor lurched and dropped away beneath their feet for a heart-stopping moment before becoming firm again. A huge metal door hung unsupported on the air right in front of them, floating two or three inches off the ground. An eight-foot-tall slab of roughly beaten steel, it gleamed dully in the lamplight, and then, as they watched, it swung slowly open to reveal a featureless, impenetrable darkness. A cold breeze blew steadily from the doorway, carrying vague, blurred sounds from off in the distance. Hawk thought he heard something that might have been screaming, or laughter, but it was gone too quickly for him to identify it.

"Move it," said Storm tightly. "I don't know how long I can keep the gateway open. There's so much stray magic around, it's distorting my spells."

"You heard the man," said Winter. "Go go go!"

Barber stepped through the doorway, and the darkness swallowed him up. Hawk and Fisher followed him in, blades at the ready. The darkness quickly gave way to a vague, sourceless silver glow. Barber, Hawk, and Fisher moved immediately to take up a defensive pattern, looking quickly about them for possible threats. They were standing in a narrow corridor that seemed to stretch away forever. The walls and the low ceiling were both covered with a thick mass of dirty grey cobwebs. The floor was a pale, pockmarked stone, splashed here and there with dark spots of dried blood. There was a brief disturbance in the air behind them as first Storm and then Winter appeared out of nowhere to join them.

"All clear here, Jessica," said Barber quietly. "No sign of anyone, or anything."

"If this is Hell Wing, I don't think much of it," said Fisher. "Don't they ever clean up in here?"

"I'm not sure where or what this is," said Storm. "It doesn't feel like Hell Wing. The air is charged with magic, but there's no trace of the standard security spells that ought to be here. Everything . . . feels wrong."

"Are you saying you've brought us to the wrong place?" asked Hawk dangerously.

"Of course not!" snapped the sorcerer. "This is where Hell Wing used to be. This is what has . . . replaced Hell Wing. I think we have to assume the creatures have broken loose. All of them."

Barber cursed softly, and hefted his sword. "I don't like this, Jessica. They must have known somebody would be coming. Odds are this place is one big trap, set and primed just for us."

"Could be," said Winter. "But let's not panic just yet, all right? Nothing's actually threatened us so far. Storm, where does this corridor lead?"

Storm shook his head angrily. "I can't tell. My Sight's all but useless here. But there's something up ahead; I can feel it. I think it's watching us."

"Then let's go find it," said Winter briskly. "Barber, you have the point. Let's take this one step at a time, people. And remember, we're not just looking for the creatures. The rioters who opened the gateway have got to be here somewhere. And, people, when we find them, I don't want any heroics. If any of the rioters want to surrender, that's fine, but no one's to take any chances with them. All right; move out. Let's get the job done."

They moved off down the corridor, and the darkness retreated before them so that they moved always in the same sourceless silver glow. The thick matted cobwebs that furred the walls and ceiling hung down here and there in grimy streamers that swayed gently on the air, stirred by an unfelt breeze. Noises came and went in the distance, lingering just long enough to chill the blood and disturb the mind. Hawk held his axe before him, his hands clutching the haft so tightly that his knuckles showed white. His instincts were screaming at him to get out while he still could, but he couldn't just turn tail and run. Not in front of Winter. Besides, she was right; even if this place was a trap, they still had a job to do. He glared at the darkness ahead of them, and then glanced back over his shoulder. The darkness was there too, following the pool of light the team moved in. More and more it seemed to Hawk that they were moving through the body of some immense unnatural beast, as though they'd been swallowed alive and were soon to be digested.

Barber stopped suddenly, and they all piled up behind him, somehow just managing to avoid toppling each other. Barber silently indicated the right-hand wall, and they crowded round to examine it. There was a ragged break in the thick matting of dirty grey cobwebs, revealing a plain wooden door, standing slightly ajar. The wood was scarred and gouged as though by claws, and splashed with dried blood. The heavy iron lock had been smashed, and was half hanging away from the door. Winter gestured for them all to move back, and they did so.

"It seems my first guess was wrong," said Storm quietly. "This is Hell Wing, after all, merely hidden and disguised by this . . . transformation. The lock quite clearly bears the prison's official mark. Presumably the door leads to what was originally one of the cells."

"Any idea what's in there?" asked Winter softly.

"Something magical, but that's all I can tell. Might be alive, might not. Again, there's so much stray magic floating around, my Sight can't see through it."

"Then why not just open the door and take a look?" said Hawk bluntly. "I've had it up to here with sneaking around, and I'm just in the mood to hit something. All we have to do is kick the door in, and then fill the gap so that whatever's in there can't escape."

"Sounds good to me," said Fisher. "Who gets to kick the door in?"

"I do," said Barber. "I'm still the point man."

He looked at Winter, and she nodded. Barber moved silently back to the door and the others formed up behind him, weapons at the ready. Barber took a firm grip on his sword, lifted his left boot, and slammed it hard against the door. The heavy door swung inward on groaning hinges, revealing half of the small, gloomy cell. Barber hit the door again and it swung all the way open. Everybody tensed, ready for any sudden sound or movement, but nothing happened. The cell wasn't much bigger than a privy, and it smelled much the same. The only illumination was the silver glow falling in from the corridor outside, but it was more than enough to show that the cell was completely empty. There was no bed or other furnishings— only some filthy straw on the floor.

Some of the tension went out of Hawk, and he lowered his axe. "Looks like you got it wrong this time, Storm; no one's home. Whoever or whatever used to be locked up in here is long gone now."

"With a trusting nature like yours, Captain, I'm astonished you've lasted as long as you have," the sorcerer said acidly. "The cell's occupant is quite likely still here, held by its geas, even though the lock has been broken. You just can't see it, that's all."

Anyone else would have blushed. As it was, Hawk spent a moment looking down at his boots before nodding briefly to the sorcerer and then staring into the cell with renewed interest. "Right. I'd forgotten about Who Knows, the invisible creature. You're sure the geas is still controlling it?"

"Of course!" snapped Storm. "If it wasn't, the creature would have attacked us by now."

"Not necessarily," said Winter slowly. "It might just be waiting for us to lower our guard. Which presents us with something of a problem. If it isn't still held by its geas, we can't afford to just turn our backs and walk away. It might come after us. The reports I saw described it as immensely strong and entirely malevolent."

"Which means," said Barber, "someone's going to have to go into that cell and check the thing's actually there."

"Good idea," said Fisher. "Hawk, just pop in and check it out, would you?"

Hawk looked at her. "*You* pop in and check it out. Do I look crazy?"

"Good point."

"I'll do it," said Barber.

"No you won't," said Winter quickly. "No one's going into that cell. I can't afford to lose any of you. Barber, hand me an incendiary."

Barber smiled briefly, and reached into a leather pouch at his belt. He brought out a small smooth stone that glowed a dull, sullen red in the gloom, like a coal that had been left too long in the fire, and handed it carefully to Winter. She hefted it briefly, and then tossed it casually from hand to hand while staring into the apparently empty cell. Barber winced. Winter turned to Hawk and Fisher, and gestured with the glowing stone.

"I don't suppose you've seen one of these before. It's something new the Guard sorcerers came up with. We're field-testing them. Each incendiary is a moment taken out of time from an exploding volcano; an instant of appalling heat and violence fixed in time like an insect trapped in amber. All I have to do is say the right Word, throw the damn thing as far as I can, and a few seconds later the spell collapses, releasing all that heat and violence. Which is pretty unfortunate for anything that happens to be in the vicinity at the time. If Who Knows is in that cell, it's about to get a very nasty surprise. Stand ready, people. As soon as I throw this thing, I want that door slammed shut fast and everyone out of the way of the blast."

"What kind of range does it cover?" said Hawk.

"That's one of the things we're testing."

"I had a suspicion you were going to say something like that."

Winter lifted the stone to her mouth, whispered something, and then tossed the incendiary into the cell. She stepped quickly back and to one side. Hawk and Barber slammed the cell door shut and put their backs to the wall on either side of it. A moment later, the door was blown clean off its hinges by a blast of superheated air and hurled into the corridor. Hawk put up an arm to protect his face from the sudden, intense heat, and a glaring crimson light filled the corridor. The wooden door frame burst into flames, and the cobwebs on the corridor wall opposite scorched and blackened in an instant. In the heart of the leaping flames that filled the cell something dark and shapeless thrashed and screamed and was finally still. The temperature in the corridor grew intolerably hot, and Hawk backed away down the corridor, mopping at the sweat that ran down his face. The others moved with him, and he was about to suggest they all run like hell for the gateway, when the flames suddenly died away. The crimson glare disappeared, and the temperature dropped as quickly as it had risen. There was a vile smell on the smoky air, but the only sound was the quiet crackling of the flames as they consumed the door frame. Hawk moved slowly forward and peered cautiously into the cell. The walls were blackened with soot, and smoke hung heavily on the still air, but there was no sign of the cell's occupant, dead or alive.

"Think we got it?" asked Fisher, just behind him.

Hawk shrugged. "Who knows? But we'd better hope so. If the incendiary didn't kill it, I'd hate to think of the mood it must be in."

"It's dead," said Storm shortly. "I felt it die."

"Handy things, those incendiaries," said Hawk casually as he and Fisher turned back to face the others. "How long do you think it'll be before they're released to the rest of the Guard?"

"Hopefully never, in your case," said Storm. "Given your reputation for death and destruction."

"You don't want to believe everything you hear," said Hawk.

"Just the bad bits," said Fisher.

Hawk looked at her reproachfully. Winter coughed behind a raised hand. "Let's move it, people. We've got a lot more ground to cover yet. Barber, take the point again. Everyone else as before. Let's go."

They moved on down the corridor, and the sourceless silver glow moved with them. Hawk glanced back over his shoulder, expecting to see the burning door frame glowing in the gloom, but there was only the darkness, deep and impenetrable. Hawk turned away, and didn't look back again. The corridor seemed to go on forever, and without any way of judging how far they'd come, Hawk began to lose his sense of time. It seemed like they'd been walking for hours, but still the corridor stretched away before them, the only sound the quiet slapping of their boots on the stone floor. The dense growth of filthy matted cobwebs on the walls and ceiling grew steadily thicker, making the corridor seem increasingly narrow. Storm had to bend forward to avoid brushing the cobwebs with his head. All of them were careful to avoid touching the stuff. It looked diseased.

They finally came to another cell, with the door standing slightly open, as before. Storm stared at it for a long time, but was finally forced to admit he couldn't See anything anymore. Magic was running loose in Hell Wing, and he had become as blind as the rest of them. In the end, Barber kicked the door in, and he and Hawk charged in with weapons at the ready. The cell looked much like the last one, save for a canvas on an easel standing in the middle of the room, facing the back wall. Averting their eyes from the painting, Hawk and Barber checked the cell thoroughly, but there was nothing else there. Winter directed the others to stay out in the corridor and told Hawk to inspect the canvas. If it was what they thought it was, his single eye should help protect him from the painting's curse. Barber stood by, carefully watching Hawk rather than the painting, so that if anything went wrong he could pull Hawk away before the curse could affect him. That was the theory, anyway.

Hawk glanced out the cell door, and nodded reassuringly to Fisher. She wasn't fooled, but gave him a smile anyway. Hawk stepped in front of the easel, and looked for the first time at Messerschmann's Portrait. The scene was a bleak and open plain, arid and fractured, with no trace of life anywhere, save for the single figure of a man in the foreground. The man stared wildly out of the Portrait, so close it seemed Hawk could

almost reach out and touch him. He was wearing a torn and
ragged prison uniform, and his face was twisted with terror
and madness.

"Damn," said Hawk, hardly aware he'd spoken aloud. "It's
got out."

The background scene had been painted with staggering
realism. Hawk could almost feel the oppressive heat wafting
out of the painting at him. The figure in the foreground was so
alive he seemed almost to be moving, drawing closer. . . . Suddenly Hawk was falling, and he put out his hands instinctively
to break his fall. His palms slapped hard against the cold stone
floor of the cell, and he was suddenly shocked into awareness
again. His gaze fell on the Portrait, and he scrabbled backwards
across the floor away from it, his gaze averted, until his back
was pressed against the far cell wall.

"Take it easy," said Fisher, kneeling down beside him.
"Barber spotted something was wrong, and pulled you away
from the Portrait when you wouldn't answer him. You feeling
all right now?"

"Sure," said Hawk quickly. "Fine. Help me up, would you?"

Fisher and Barber got him on his feet again, and he smiled
his thanks and waved them away. He was careful not even to
glance in the Portrait's direction as he left the cell to make his
report to Winter.

"Whatever was in the Portrait originally has got out and is
running loose somewhere in Hell Wing. One of the rioters has
taken its place. Is there any way we can get him out?"

"Only by replacing him with someone else," said Storm.
"That's the way the curse works."

"Then there's nothing more we can do here," said Winter. "If you've fully recovered, Captain, I think we should
move on."

Hawk nodded quickly, and the SWAT team set off down
the corridor again.

"At least we've got one less rioter to worry about," said
Hawk after a while. The others looked at him. "Just trying to
look on the bright side," he explained.

"Nice try," said Winter. "Hang on to that cheerfulness.
You're going to need it. From what I've heard, we'd be better
off facing a dozen rioters with the plague than the Portrait's
original occupant. It might have been human once, but its time

in the Portrait changed it. Now it's a nightmare in flesh and blood, every evil thought you ever had given shape and form, and it's running loose in Hell Wing with us. So, along with all our other problems, we're going to have to track it down and kill it before we leave. Assuming it can be killed."

"Are you always this optimistic?" asked Fisher.

Winter snorted. "If there was any room for optimism, they wouldn't have called us in."

"Something's coming," said Storm suddenly. "I can't See it, but I can feel it. Something powerful . . ."

Winter barked orders, and the SWAT team fell quickly into a defensive formation, with Barber, Hawk, and Fisher at the point, weapons at the ready. Hawk glanced thoughtfully at Barber. Now that there was finally a chance at some action, the weaponmaster had come fully alive. His dark eyes were fixed eagerly on the gloom ahead, and his grin was disturbingly wolfish. A sudden conviction rooted itself in Hawk that Barber would look just the same if the order ever came down for the weaponmaster to go after him or Fisher. Barber didn't give a damn for the law or for justice. He was just a man born to kill, a butcher waiting to be unleashed, and to him one target was as good as any other. There was no room in a man like Barber for conscience or ethics.

A sudden sound caught Hawk's attention, and his thoughts snapped back to the situation at hand. Something was coming towards them out of the darkness. Hawk's grip tightened on his axe. Footsteps sounded distinctly in the gloom, drawing steadily closer. There were two separate sets of footsteps, and Hawk smiled and relaxed a little. It was only a couple of rioters. But the more he listened, the more it seemed to him there was something wrong with the footsteps. They were too slow, too steady, and they seemed to echo unnaturally long on the quiet. The air was tense, and Hawk could feel his hackles rising. There was something bad hidden in the darkness, something he didn't want to see. A slight breeze blew out of the gloom towards him. It smelt of dust and sulphur.

"They're coming," said Storm softly. "The chaos bringers, the lords of entropy. The dust and ruins of reality. The Brimstone Boys."

Hawk glared at the sorcerer, and then back at the darkness. Storm had sounded shaken, almost unnerved. If just the approach of the Brimstone Boys was enough to rattle a hardened SWAT man, Hawk had a strong feeling he didn't want to face them with nothing but his axe. He fell back a step and glanced across at Winter.

"Might I suggest this would be a good time to try out another of those incendiary things?"

Winter nodded sharply and gestured to Barber. He took another of the glowing stones from his pouch, whispered the activating Word, and threw the stone into the darkness. They all tensed, waiting for the explosion, but nothing happened. Storm laughed brusquely, a bleak, unpleasant sound.

"That won't stop them. They control reality, run rings round the warp and weft of space itself. Cause and effect run backwards where they look. They're the Brimstone Boys; they undo natural laws, turn certainties into whims and maybes."

"Then do something!" snapped Winter. "Use your magic. You're supposed to be a top-level sorcerer, dammit! You didn't sound this worried when you first told us about them."

"I didn't know," whispered Storm, staring unseeingly at the gloom. "I couldn't know. They're too big. Too powerful. There's nothing we can do."

Winter grabbed him by the shoulder and hauled him back out of the way. "His nerve's gone," she said shortly to the others. "The Brimstone Boys must have got to him somehow. I'm not taking any chances with these bastards. The minute you see them, kill them."

"We're supposed to take these creatures alive, remember?" said Barber mildly.

"To hell with that," Winter snapped. "Anything that can take out an experienced sorcerer like Storm so easily is too dangerous to mess about with."

Hawk nodded, and he and Fisher moved forward to stand on either side of Barber. The weaponmaster was quivering slightly, like a hound straining at the leash, or a horse readying for a charge, but his sword hand was perfectly steady. Hawk glared into the darkness, and then looked down suddenly. The corridor floor seemed to be shifting subtly under his feet, stretching and contracting. His boots were sinking into the solid stone floor as though it had turned to mud. He looked across at Barber and Fisher to see if they'd noticed it too, and was shocked to discover that they were now yards away, as though the corridor had somehow expanded vastly while he wasn't looking. He jerked his boots free from the sticky stone, and backed away. The ceiling was impossibly far above him, and the wall was running with boiling water that steamed and spat at him. Birds were singing, harsh and raucous, and somewhere children screamed in agony. The light changed to golden summer sunlight, suffusing the air like bitter honey. Hawk smelled dust and sulphur, so strong he could hardly breathe. And out of the darkness, stepping slow and sombre, came the Brimstone Boys.

They might have been human once, but now they were impossibly, obscenely old. Their bodies were twisted and withered, turned in upon themselves by time, and there were gaping holes in their anatomy where skin and bone had rotted away to dust and nothingness. Their wrinkled skin was grey and colorless, and tore when movement stretched it. Their faces were the worst. Their lips were gone, and their impossibly wide smiles were crammed with huge blocky teeth like bony chisels. Blood ran constantly from their dirty yellow eyes and dripped from their awful smiles, spattering their ancient tattered skin.

Barber shouted something incoherent, and launched himself at the nearest figure. His sword flew in a deadly pattern, but the blade didn't even come close to touching the creature. Barber strained and struggled, but it was as though he and the ancient figures, only a few feet apart, lived in separate worlds, where they could see each other but not touch. Fisher drew a knife from her boot and threw it at the other figure. The knife tumbled end over end, shrinking slowly as though crossing some impossible distance but still not reaching its target. The withered creature looked at Fisher with its bleeding eyes, and she cried out as she began to sink into the floor. Despite all her struggles to resist, the flagstones sucked her down into themselves like a treacherous marsh. She struck at the floor with her sword, and sparks flew as the steel blade hit solid stone.

Hawk ran towards her, but she seemed to recede into the distance as he ran. He pushed himself harder, but the faster he ran, the further away she seemed to be. Somewhere between the two of them, Barber sobbed with helpless rage as he struggled futilely to touch the Brimstone Boys with his sword. Hawk could vaguely hear Winter shouting something, but all he could think of was Fisher. The stone floor was lapping up around her shoulders. The light was growing dimmer. Sounds echoed strangely. And then something gold and shining flew slowly past him, gleaming richly in the fading light, and landed on the floor between the Brimstone Boys. They looked down at it, and despite himself, Hawk's gaze was drawn to it too. It was a pocket watch.

He could hear it ticking in the endless quiet. Ticktocking away the seconds, turning past into present into future. The Brimstone Boys raised their awful heads, their grinning mouths stretched wide in soundless screams. Dust fell endlessly through golden light. The floor grew solid again, spitting out Fisher, and the walls rushed in on either side. The ceiling fell back to its previous height. And the Brimstone Boys crumbled into dust and blew away.

Hawk looked around him, and the corridor was just as it had always been. The silver light pushed back the darkness, and the floor was solid and reliable under his feet. Fisher picked up the throwing knife from the floor before her, looked at it for a moment, and then slipped it back into her boot. Barber put away his sword and shook his head slowly, breathing heavily. Hawk turned and looked back at Winter and the sorcerer Storm, who seemed to have completely recovered from his daze. In fact, he was actually smiling quite smugly.

"All right," said Hawk. "What happened?"

Storm's smile widened. "It's all very simple and straight-forward, really," he said airily. "The Brimstone Boys distorted reality wherever they went, but they weren't very stable. They could play all kinds of tricks with space and probabilities and the laws of reality, but they were still vulnerable to time. The ordered sequence of events was anathema to their existence. It was already eroding away at them; that's why they looked so ancient. I just speeded the process up a bit, with an augmented timepiece whose reality was a little bit stronger than theirs."

"What was all that nonsense you were spouting before?" demanded Fisher. "I thought you'd gone off your head."

"That was the idea," said Storm smugly. "They didn't see me as a threat, so they ignored me. Which gave me time to work my magic on the watch. I could have been an actor, you know."

He stretched out his hand, and the watch flew through the air to nestle snugly in his hand. Storm checked the time, and put the watch back into his pocket.

"Heads up," said Barber suddenly. "We've got company again."

"Now what?" demanded Hawk, spinning round to face the darkness, and then freezing on the spot as he saw what was watching them from the edge of the silver glow. A human shape, formed of bloody organs and viscera, but no skin, stood trembling on legs of muscle and tendons but no bones. Its naked eyes stared wetly from a flat crimson mess that might once have been its face. It breathed noisily, and they could see its lungs rising and falling in what had once been its chest.

"Johnny Nobody," said Hawk. "Poor bastard. Are we going to have to kill him too?"

"Hopefully not," said Winter. "We're going to be in enough trouble over Who Knows and the Brimstone Boys. With a little luck, we might be able to herd this thing back into its cell. It's supposed to be strong and quick, but not very bright."

And then something pounced on Johnny Nobody from behind and smashed it to the floor. Blood spurted through the air as its attacker tore it apart and stuffed the gory chunks into its mouth. The newcomer looked up at the SWAT team, its mouth stretched in a bloody grin as it ate and swallowed chunks of Johnny Nobody's unnatural flesh. What upset Hawk the most was how ordinary the creature looked. It was a man, dressed in tatters, with wide, staring eyes you only had to meet for a moment to know their owner was utterly insane. Just looking at him made Hawk's skin crawl. What was left of Johnny Nobody kicked and struggled, unable to die despite its awful wounds, but incapable of breaking its attacker's hold. The crazy man squatted over the body, ripping out strings of viscera and giggling to himself in between bloody mouthfuls.

"Who the hell is that?" asked Fisher softly. "One of the rioters?"

"I don't think so," said Winter. "I think we're looking at the original occupant of Messerschmann's Portrait."

"I thought he was supposed to be some kind of monster," said Hawk.

"Well, isn't he?" said Winter, and Hawk had no answer. The SWAT leader looked at Barber. "Knock him out, Barber.

Maybe our sorcerers can do something to bring his mind back."

Barber shrugged. "I'll do what I can, but bringing them in alive isn't what I do best."

He advanced slowly on the madman, who looked up sharply and growled at him like an animal. Barber stopped where he was and sheathed his sword. Moving slowly and carefully, he reached inside one of his pockets and brought out a small steel ball, no more than an inch or so in diameter. He hefted it once in his hand, glanced at the madman, and then snapped his arm forward. The steel ball sped through the air and struck the madman right between the eyes. He fell backwards and lay still, without making a sound. Barber walked over to him, checked his pulse, and then bent down beside him to retrieve his steel ball. Johnny Nobody twitched and shuddered, leaking blood and other fluids, and Barber's lips thinned back from his teeth as he saw the raw wounds slowly knitting themselves together. He moved quickly back to the others, dragging the unconscious madman with him.

"About time we had a little luck," said Winter. "Johnny Nobody's in no shape to give us any trouble, and we've got ourselves a nice little bonus in the form of our unconscious friend here. At least now we'll have something to show for our trouble."

"Winter," said Fisher slowly, "I think we've got another problem."

There was something in the way she said it that made everyone's head snap round to see what she was talking about. Thick tendrils of the dirty grey cobwebs had dropped from the ceiling and were wriggling towards Johnny Nobody. The bloody shape struggled feebly, but the grey strands whipped around it and dragged the body slowly away along the floor into the darkness, leaving a trail of blood and other things on the stone floor. Hawk looked at the thick mass of cobwebs covering the walls and ceiling, and made a connection he should have made some time back. He looked at Winter.

"It's Crawling Jenny, isn't it? All of it."

"Took you long enough to work it out," said Winter. "The rioters must have opened its cell and let it out. Which is probably why we haven't seen any of them since. According to the reports I saw, Crawling Jenny is carnivorous, and always ravenously hungry."

"Are you saying this stuff ate all the rioters?" said Fisher, glaring distrustfully at the nearest wall.

"It seems likely. Where else could it have got enough mass to grow like this? I hate to think how big the creature must be in total."

"Why didn't you tell us what this stuff was before?" said Hawk. "We've been walking through it all unknowing, totally at its mercy. It could have attacked us at any time."

"No it couldn't," said Storm. "I've been shielding us. It doesn't even know we're here."

"There wasn't any point in attacking its outer reaches," said Winter. "It'd just grow some more. No, I've been waiting for something like this to happen. Since Johnny Nobody is undoubtedly heading for the creature's stomach, all we have to do is follow it. I'm not sure if Crawling Jenny has any vulnerable organs, but if it has, that's where they'll be."

She sat set off down the corridor without looking back, hurrying to catch up with the dragging sounds ahead. The others exchanged glances and moved quickly after her. Barber carried the unconscious madman over his shoulder in a fireman's lift. It didn't seem to slow him down any. Hawk glared suspiciously at the thick mass of cobwebs lining the corridor, but it seemed quiet enough at the moment. Which was just as well, because Hawk had a strong feeling his axe wasn't going to be much use against a bunch of cobwebs.

They soon caught up with the tendrils dragging the body, and followed at a respectful distance. Storm's magic kept them unseen and unheard as far as Crawling Jenny was concerned, but no one felt like pushing their luck. Hawk in particular was careful to keep to the centre of the corridor, well away from both walls. He found it only too easy to visualize hundreds of tentacles suddenly lashing out from the walls and ceiling, wrapping up victims in helpless bundles and dragging them off to the waiting stomach.

Eventually, the tendrils dragged the body into a dark opening in the wall. Winter gestured quickly for everyone to stay where they were. Barber lowered the unconscious madman to the floor, and stretched easily. He wasn't even breathing hard.

Winter moved slowly forward to peer into the opening, and
the others moved quietly in behind her, careful not to crowd
each other so that they could still retreat in a hurry if they
had to. The silver light from the corridor shone brightly behind
them, and Hawk's lip curled in disgust at the sight ahead. The
narrow stone cell was filled with a soft, pulsating mass of
mould and fungi studded with lidless, staring eyes that burned
with a horrid awareness. Sheets of gauzy cobwebs anchored
the mass to the walls and ceiling, and frayed away in questing
tendrils. As the team watched, two of the tendrils dropped
Johnny Nobody's writhing body onto the central mass, and a
dozen snapping mouths opened, crammed with grinding yellow
teeth. They tore the body apart and consumed it in a matter of
seconds.

"Damn," said Winter. "We've lost another one."

"So much for Johnny Nobody," said Barber quietly. "Poor
Johnny, we hardly knew you."

"I don't know about you," said Hawk quietly to Winter, "but
it seems to me that swords and axes aren't going to be much
use against something like that. You could hack at it for hours
and still not know if you'd hit anything vital."

"Agreed," said Winter. "Luckily, we should still have one
incendiary left." She looked at Barber, who nodded quickly,
and produced another of the glowing stones from his pouch.
Winter nodded, and looked back at the slowly pulsating mass
before her. "When you're ready, Barber, throw the incendiary
into one of those mouths. As soon as the damned thing's
swallowed it, everyone turn and run like fury. I'm not sure
what effect an incendiary will have on a creature like that, but
I don't think we should hang around to find out. And Barber—
don't miss. Or you're fired."

He grinned, murmured the activating Word, and tossed the
glowing stone into one of the snapping mouths. It went in
easily, and Crawling Jenny swallowed the incendiary reflex-
ively. The SWAT team turned as one and bolted back down the
corridor, Barber pausing just long enough to sling the unconscious madman over his shoulder again. A muffled explosion
went off behind them, like a roll of faraway thunder, quickly
drowned out by a deafening keening that filled the narrow
corridor as the creature screamed with all its many mouths.
A blast of intense heat caught up with the running figures

and passed them by. Hawk flinched instinctively, but Storm's magic protected them.

Rivulets of flame ran along the walls and ceiling, hungrily consuming the thick cobwebs. Burning tendrils thrust out of the furry mass and lashed blindly at the running SWAT team. Hawk and Fisher cut fiercely at the tendrils, slicing through them easily. Burning lengths of cobwebs fell to the corridor floor, writhing and twisting as the flames consumed them. Charred and darkened masses of cobwebs fell limply from the walls and ceiling as a thick choking smoke filled the corridor. Storm suddenly stumbled to a halt, and the others piled up around him.

"What is it?" yelled Hawk, struggling to be heard over the screaming creature and the roaring of the flames.

"The exit's just ahead," yelled Storm, "but something's got there before us."

"What do you mean, 'something'?" Hawk hefted his axe and peered through the thickening smoke but couldn't see anything. The flames pressed closer.

Storm's hands clenched into fists. Stray magic sputtered on the air before him. "Them. They've found us. The Pale Men."

They came out of the darkness and into the light, shifting forms that hovered on the edge of meaning and recognition. Smoke drifted around and through them, like ghostly ectoplasm. Hawk slowly lowered his axe as it grew too heavy for him. His vision greyed in and out, and the roar and heat of the fire seemed far away and unimportant. The world rolled back upon itself, back into yesterday and beyond.

Memories surged through him, of all the people he'd been, some so strange to him now he hardly recognised them. Some smiled sadly at what he'd become, while others pointed accusing fingers or turned their heads away. His mind began to drift apart, fragmenting into forgotten dreams and hopes and might-have-beens. He screamed soundlessly, a long, wordless howl of denial, and his thoughts slowly began to clear. He was who he was because of all the people he'd been, and even if he didn't always like that person very much, he knew he couldn't go back. He'd paid too high a price for the lessons he'd learned to turn his back on them now. He concentrated on his memories, hugging them to him jealously, and the ghosts of his past faded away and were gone. He was Hawk, and no one was going to take that away from him. Not even himself.

The world lurched and he was back in the narrow stone corridor again, choking on the thick smoke and flinching away from the roaring flames as they closed in around him. The rest of the team were standing still as statues, eyes vague and far away. Some of them were already beginning to look frayed and uncertain, their features growing indistinct as the Pale Men leeched the pasts out of them. Hawk glared briefly at the shifting figures shining brightly through the smoke and grabbed Storm's shoulder. For a moment his fingers seemed to sink into the sorcerer's flesh, and then it suddenly hardened and became solid, as though Hawk's touch had reaffirmed its reality. Shape and meaning flooded back into Storm's face, and he shook his head sharply, as though waking from a nagging dream. He looked at Hawk, and then at the Pale Men, and his face darkened.

"Get out of the way, you bastards!"

He thrust one outstretched hand at the drifting figures, and a blast of raw magic exploded in the corridor. It beat on the air like a captured wild bird, and the Pale Men were suddenly gone, as though they'd never been there at all. Hawk looked questioningly at Storm.

"Is that it? Wave your hand and they disappear?"

"Of course," said Storm. "They're only as real as you allow them to be. Now help me get the others out of here."

Hawk nodded quickly, and started pushing the others down the corridor. Their faces were already clearing as they shook off their yesterdays. Smoke filled the corridor, and a wave of roaring flame came rushing towards them. Storm howled a Word of Power, and gestured sharply with his hand, and a solid steel door was suddenly floating on the air before them. It swung open, and the SWAT team plunged through. They fell into the corridor beyond, and the door slammed shut behind them.

For a while, they all lay where they were on the cool stone floor, coughing the smoke out of their lungs and gasping at the blessedly fresh air. Eventually, they sat up and looked around them, sharing shaken but triumphant smiles. Hawk knew he was grinning like a fool, and didn't give a damn. There was nothing like almost dying to make you feel glad to be alive.

"Excuse me," said a polite, unfamiliar voice, "but can anyone tell me what I'm doing here?"

They all looked round sharply, and found that the madman Barber had brought out with them was now sitting up and looking at them, his eyes clear and sane and more than a little puzzled. Storm chuckled suddenly.

"Well, it would appear the Pale Men did some good, in spite of themselves. By calling back his memories, they made him sane again."

The ex-madman looked around him. "I have a strong feeling I'm going to regret asking this, but by any chance are we in prison?"

Hawk chuckled. "Don't worry about it. It's only temporary. Who are you?"

"Wulf Saxon. I think."

Winter rose painfully to her feet and nodded to MacReady, who had been standing patiently to one side, waiting for them to notice him. As far as Hawk could tell, the negotiator hadn't moved an inch from where they'd left him.

"Mission over," said Winter, just a little breathlessly. "Any trouble on your end, Mac?"

"Not really."

He glanced back down the corridor. Hawk followed his gaze and for the first time took in the seven dead men, dressed in prisoner's uniforms, lying crumpled on the corridor floor. Hawk gave the unarmed negotiator a hard look, and he smiled back enigmatically.

"Like I said: I have a charmed life."

I'm not going to ask, thought Hawk firmly. "Well," he said, in the tone of someone determined to change the subject. "Another successful mission accomplished."

Winter looked at him. "You have got to be joking. All the creatures we were supposed to capture are dead, and Hell Wing is a blazing inferno! It'll cost a fortune to rebuild. How the hell can it be a success?"

Fisher grinned. "We're alive, aren't we?"

Back in the Governor's office, the SWAT team stood more or less at attention, and waited patiently for the Governor to calm down. The riots had finally been crushed, and peace restored to Damnation Row, but only after a number of fatalities among both inmates and prison staff. The damage to parts of the prison was extensive, but that wasn't too important; it would just give the inmates something to do to keep them out of mischief. Nothing like a good building project to keep prisoners busy. Not to mention too exhausted to think about rioting again.

Even so, it probably hadn't been the best time to inform the Governor that all his potentially valuable Hell Wing inmates were unfortunately deceased, and the Wing itself was a burnt-out ruin.

The Governor finally stopped shouting, partly because he was beginning to lose his voice, and threw himself into the chair behind his desk. He glared impartially at the SWAT team, and drummed his fingers on his desk. Hawk cleared his throat cautiously, and the Governor's glare fell on him like a hungry predator just waiting for its prey to provide an opening.

"Yes, Captain Hawk? You have something to say, perhaps? Something that will excuse your pitiable performance on this mission, and give some indication as to why I shouldn't lock you all up in the dirtiest, foulest dungeon I can find and then throw the key down the nearest sewer?"

"Well," said Hawk, "things could have turned out worse." The Governor's face went an interesting shade of puce, but Hawk pressed on anyway. "Our main objective, according to your orders, was to prevent the inmates of Hell Wing from escaping and wreaking havoc in the city. I think we can safely assume the city is no longer in any danger from those inmates. Hell Wing itself is somewhat scorched and blackened, I'll admit, but solid stone walls are pretty fire-resistant, as a rule. A lot of scrubbing and a lick of paint, and the place'll be as good as new. And on top of all that, we managed to rescue Wulf Saxon from Messerschmann's Portrait, and restore his sanity. I don't think we did too badly, all things considered."

He waited with interest to see what the Governor's response would be. The odds favoured a coronary, but he wouldn't rule out a stroke. The Governor took several deep breaths to calm himself down, and fixed Hawk with a withering stare.

"Wulf Saxon has disappeared. But we were able to learn a few things of interest about him, by consulting our prison records. In his time, some twenty-three years ago, Saxon was a well-known figure in this city. He was a thief, a forger, and a confidence trickster. He was also an ex-Guard, ex-city Councillor, and the founder of three separate religions, two of which are still doing very well for themselves on the Street of Gods. He's a confirmed troublemaker, a revolutionary, and a major pain in the arse, and you've let him loose in the city again!"

Hawk smiled, and shook his head. "We had him captured. Your people let him loose."

"He's still an extremely dangerous individual that this city was well rid of, until you became involved!"

Fisher leaned forward suddenly. "If he's that dangerous, does that mean there's a reward for his capture?"

"Good point, Isobel," said Hawk, and they both looked expectantly at the Governor.

The Governor decided to ignore both Hawk and Fisher, for the sake of his blood pressure, and turned to Winter. "Regretfully, I have no choice but to commend you and your SWAT team for your actions. Officially, at least. The city Council has chosen to disregard my objections, and has ordered me to congratulate you on your handling of the situation." He scowled at Winter. "Well done."

"Thank you," said Winter graciously. "We were just doing our job. Have you discovered any more about the forces behind the riot?"

The Governor sniffed, and shuffled through the papers on his desk. "Unlikely as it seems, the whole thing may have been engineered to cover a single prisoner's escape. A man named Ritenour. He disappeared early on in the riot, and there's a growing body of evidence that he received help in doing so from both inside and outside the prison."

Winter frowned. "A riot this big, and this bloody, just to free one man? Who is this Ritenour? I've never heard of him."

"No reason why you should have," said the Governor, running his eyes quickly down the file before him. "Ritenour is a sorcerer shaman, specialising in animal magic, of all things. I wouldn't have thought there was much work for him in a city like Haven, unless he likes working with rats, but he's been here three years to our certain knowledge. He's worked with a few big names in his time, but he's never amounted to anything himself. He was in here awaiting trial for nonpayment of taxes, which is why he wasn't guarded as closely as he might have been."

"If he worked for big names in the past," said Hawk slowly, "maybe one of them arranged for him to be sprung, on the grounds he knew something important, something they couldn't risk coming out at his trial. Prisoners tend to become very talkative when faced with the possibility of a long sentence in Damnation Row."

"My people are busy checking that connection at this moment, Captain," said the Governor sharply. "They know their job. Now then, I have one last piece of business with you all, and then with any luck I can get you out of my life forever. It seems the security forces protecting the two Kings and the signing of the Peace Treaty have decided there might just be some connection between Ritenour's escape and a plot against the two Kings. I can't see it as very likely myself, but, as usual, no one's interested in my opinions. The SWAT team, including Captains Hawk and Fisher, are to report to the head of the security forces at Champion House, to discuss the situation. That's it. Now get out of my office, and let me get back to clearing up the mess you people have made of my prison."

Everyone bowed formally, except for the Governor, who ostentatiously busied himself with the files before him. Hawk and Fisher looked at each other, nodded firmly, and advanced on the Governor. They each took one end of his desk, lifted it up, and overturned it. Papers fluttered on the air like startled butterflies. The Governor started to rise spluttering from his chair, and then dropped quickly back into it as Hawk and Fisher leaned over him, their eyes cold and menacing.

"Don't shout at us," said Hawk. "We've had a hard day."

"Right," said Fisher.

The Governor looked at them both. At that moment, all the awful stories he'd heard about Hawk and Fisher seemed a lot more believable.

"If you've quite finished intimidating a superior officer, can we get out of here?" said Winter. "Those security types don't like to be kept waiting. Besides, if we're lucky, we might get to meet the Kings themselves."

"That'll make a change," said Hawk as he and Fisher headed unhurriedly for the door.

"Yeah," said Fisher. "If we're really lucky, maybe we'll get to intimidate them too."

"I wish I thought you were joking," said Winter.

2

Something To Believe In

When it rains in Haven, it really rains. The rain hammered down without mercy, beating with spiteful persistence at every exposed surface. Ritenour—sorcerer, shaman, and now ex-convict—looked around him with interest as he strode along behind the taciturn man-at-arms called Horn. They were both protected by Ritenour's rain-avoidance spell, but everyone else in the crowded street looked like so many half-drowned sewer rats. The rains had barely begun when Ritenour had been thrown into Damnation Row, but they were in full force now, as blindly unstoppable as death or taxes. A continuous wave of water three inches deep washed down the cobbled street, past the overflowing gutters. Ritenour stamped enthusiastically through the water, smiling merrily at those people he splashed. He ignored the furious looks and muttered curses, secure in the knowledge that Horn wouldn't allow him to come to any harm.

Ritenour's smile widened as they made their way through the Northside. He didn't know where he was going, but he didn't give a damn. He was back in the open air again, and even the stinking streets of the Northside seemed light and fresh after the filthy rat-hole he'd shared with three other magic-users on Sorcerers' Row. In fact, he felt so good about things in general, he didn't even think about killing the insensitive men and women who crowded around him in the packed street. There'd be time for such things later.

He studied the back of the man in front of him thoughtfully. Horn hadn't said much to him since collecting him from the professionally anonymous men who'd smuggled him out of Damnation Row under cover of the riot. Apparently Horn fancied himself as the strong, silent type. Deeds, not words—that sort of thing. Ritenour sighed happily. Such types were delightfully easy to manipulate. Not that he had any such thing in mind at the moment, of course. Horn was taking him to Daniel Madigan, and you don't kill the goose that may produce golden eggs. Not until you've got your hands on the golden eggs, anyway.

Ritenour wondered, not for the first time, what a terrorist's terrorist like Madigan wanted with a lowly sorcerer shaman like him. Arranging the prison riot must have cost Madigan a pretty penny; he had to be expecting Ritenour to provide something of more than equal value in return. Ritenour shrugged. Whatever it was, he was in no position to argue. He'd only been in gaol for tax evasion, but all too soon he'd have ended up in Court under a truthspell, and then they'd have found out all about his experiments in human as well as animal vivisection. They'd have hanged him for that, even though his experiments had been pursued strictly in the interests of sorcerous research. Madigan had rescued him in the very nick of time, whether the terrorist knew it or not.

He let his mind drift on to other matters. Horn had promised him, on Madigan's behalf, a great deal of money if he would agree to work with the terrorist on a project of mutual interest. Ritenour was always interested in large amounts of money. People had no idea how expensive sorcerous research was these days, particularly when your subjects insisted on dying. But it had to be said that Madigan was not the sort of person Ritenour would have chosen to work with. The man was an idealist, and fanatically devoted to his Cause: the overthrowing and destruction of Outremer. He was very intelligent, inhumanly devious and determined, and had raised violence and murder to a fine art. Ritenour frowned slightly. Whatever Madigan wanted him for, it was bound to be unpleasant and not a little dangerous. In the event he decided to go through with this project, he'd better be careful to get most of his money up front. Just in case he had to disappear in a hurry.

Horn stopped suddenly before a pleasantly anonymous little tavern tucked away in a side court. Ritenour looked automatically for a sign, to see what the place was called, but there didn't seem to be one. Which implied the tavern was both expensive and exclusive (you either knew about it already or you didn't matter), and therefore very security conscious. Just the sort of place he'd expect to find Madigan. The best place to lie low was out in the open, hidden behind a cloud of money and privilege.

Horn held open the door for him, and then followed him into the dimly lit tavern. People sat around tables in small, intimate groups, talking animatedly in lowered voices. No one looked up as Horn led the way through the tables to a hidden stairway at the back of the room. The stairs led up to a narrow hallway, and Horn stopped before the second door. It had no number on it, but there was an inconspicuous peephole. Horn knocked three times, paused, and then knocked twice. Ritenour smiled. Secret knocks, no less. Terrorists did so love their little rituals. He wondered hopefully if there'd be a secret password as well, but the door swung open almost immediately, suggesting someone had already studied Horn through the peephole. Ritenour assumed a carefully amiable expression and followed Horn in. The door shut firmly behind him, and he heard four separate bolts sliding into place. He didn't look back, and instead put on his best open smile and looked casually about him.

The room was surprisingly large for tavern lodgings, and very comfortably furnished. Apparently, Madigan was one of those people who believed the mind works best when the body is well cared for. Ritenour was glad they had something in common. Most of the fanatics he'd had dealings with in the past had firmly believed in the virtues of poverty and making do with the barest essentials. Luxuries were only for the rich and the decadent. They also believed in compulsory hair shirts and cold baths, and had shown no trace whatsoever of a sense of humour. Ritenour wouldn't have dealt with such killjoys at all if his experiments hadn't required so many human subjects. His main problem had always been obtaining them discreetly. After all, he couldn't just go out into the streets and drag passersby into his laboratory. People would talk.

A young man and attractive woman, seated at a table at the far end of the room, were keeping a watchful eye on him. Ritenour gave them his best charming smile. Another man was standing guard by the door, arms folded across his massive chest. He had to be the largest man Ritenour had ever seen, and he was watching Ritenour closely. The sorcerer nodded to him politely, uncomfortably aware that Horn hadn't moved from his side since they'd entered the room. Ritenour didn't need to be told what would happen if Madigan decided he couldn't use him after all. Or, to be more exact, what might happen. Ritenour might be unarmed, but he was never helpless. He always kept a few nasty surprises up his metaphorical sleeves, just in case of situations like this. You met all sorts, as a working sorcerer.

One man was standing on his own before the open fireplace, his face cold and calm, and Ritenour knew at once that this had to be Daniel Madigan. Even standing still and silent, he radiated power and authority, as though there was nothing he couldn't do if he but put his mind to it. He stepped forward suddenly, and Ritenour's heart jumped painfully. Although Madigan wore no sword, Ritenour knew the man was dangerous, that violence and murder were as natural to him as breathing. The threat of sudden death hung about him like a bloodied shroud. Ritenour felt an almost overwhelming urge to back away, but somehow made himself hold his ground. Out of the corner of his eye, he could see the other terrorists looking at Madigan with respect, and something that might have been awe or fear. Or both. Madigan held out a hand for Ritenour to shake, and the sorcerer did so, finding a small satisfaction in the knowledge that his hand wasn't shaking. Madigan's hand was cold and hard, like a store mannequin's. There was no warmth or emotion in the handshake, and Ritenour let go as soon as he politely could. Madigan gestured at the two chairs before the open fire.

"Good of you to come and see me, sir sorcerer. Please; take a seat. Make yourself comfortable. And then we can have a little talk, you and I."

"Of course," said Ritenour, bowing formally. His mind was racing. When in doubt, take the initiative away from your opponent. "I wonder if I could prevail on you for a bite of something, and perhaps a glass of wine? Prison fare tends to be infrequent, and bordering on inedible."

There was a moment of silence as Madigan stared at him impassively, and Ritenour wondered if he'd pushed it too far, too early. Everyone else in the room seemed to have gone very still. And then Madigan bowed slightly, and everyone relaxed a little. He nodded to the young man sitting at the table, and he rose quickly to his feet and left the room, fumbling at the door's bolts in his haste. Ritenour followed Madigan to the two chairs by the fire, and was careful to let Madigan sit down first. Horn moved in to stand beside Madigan's chair.

"Allow me to introduce my associates in this glorious venture," said Madigan mildly. "You've already met Horn, though I doubt he's told you much about himself. He is the warrior of our little group, a most excellent fighter and an experienced killer. His family were deported from Outremer some generations ago, stripped of title and land and property. Horn has vowed to avenge that ancient insult.

"The young lady watching you so intently from that table is Eleanour Todd, my second-in-command. When I am not available, she is my voice and my authority. Her parents died in an Outremer cell. She fought as a mercenary for the Low Kingdoms for several years, but now they have betrayed her by seeking peace with Outremer she has joined me to exact a more personal revenge.

"The large gentleman at the door is Bailey. If he has another name, I've been unable to discover it. Bailey is a long-time mercenary and a seasoned campaigner. And yet despite his many years of loyal service to both Outremer and the Low Kingdoms, he has nothing to show for it, while those he served have grown fat and rich at his expense. I have promised him a chance to make them pay in blood and terror."

Someone outside the door gave the secret knock. Bailey looked through the peephole, and then pulled back the bolts and opened the door. The young man who'd left only a few moments before bustled in carrying a tray of cold meats and a glass of wine. He set down the tray before Ritenour, who smiled and nodded his thanks. The young man grinned cheerfully, and bobbed his head like a puppy that's just got a trick right, then looked quickly at Madigan to check he'd done the right thing.

"And this young gentleman is Ellis Glen," said Madigan dryly. "One of the most savage and vicious killers it has ever been my good fortune to encounter. You must let him show you his necklace of human teeth some time. It's really quite impressive. I have given his life shape and meaning, and he has vowed to obey me in everything. I expect great things of Ellis."

He tilted his head slightly, dismissing Glen, and the young man scurried over to sit at the table, blushing like a girl who'd been complimented on her beauty. Madigan settled back in his chair and waved for Ritenour to begin his meal. The sorcerer did so, carefully not hurrying. More and more it seemed to him he couldn't afford to seem weak in front of these people. Madigan watched him patiently, his face calm and serene. Ritenour could feel the pressure of the others' watching eyes, and took the opportunity his meal provided to study them unobtrusively.

Horn looked to be standard hired muscle, big as an ox and nearly as smart. You could find a dozen like him in most taverns in the Northside, ready for any kind of trouble as long as it paid well. He had a square, meaty face that had taken a few too many knocks in its time. He wore a constant scowl, aimed for the moment at Ritenour, but its unvarying depth suggested it was probably his usual expression anyway. And yet there was something about the man that disturbed the sorcerer on some deep, basic level. He had the strong feeling that Horn was the kind of warrior who would just keep coming towards you, no matter how badly you injured him, until either you were dead or he was.

Ritenour suppressed a shudder and switched his gaze to Eleanour Todd. She was altogether easier on the eye, and Ritenour flashed her his most winning smile. She looked coldly back, her gaze fixed unwaveringly on him as he ate. Judging by the length of her splendid legs, she would be easily his height when standing, and her large frame was lithely muscular. She wore a standard mercenary's outfit, hard-wearing and braced with leather in strategic places for protection, but cut tightly here and there to emphasise her femininity. With her thick mane of long black hair and calm dark eyes, she reminded Ritenour of nothing so much as a trained fighting cat, awaiting only her master's instruction to leap upon her prey and rend it with slow, malicious glee. She held his gaze for a moment, and then smiled slowly. Ritenour's stomach muscles tightened. Her front teeth had been filed to sharp points. Ritenour nodded politely and looked away, making a firm mental note never to turn his back on her.

The huge warrior, Bailey, could well be a problem. He had to be in his late forties, maybe even early fifties, but he was still in magnificent shape, with a broad muscular chest and shoulders so wide he probably had to turn sideways when he walked through a doorway. Even standing still on the other side of the room, he seemed to be looming over everyone else. He made Horn look almost petite. And yet his face was painfully gaunt, and there were dark shadows under his eyes, as though he'd been having trouble sleeping. Ritenour shrugged inwardly. Any mercenary Bailey's age was bound to have more than a few ghosts haunting his memories. Ritenour studied the man's face thoughtfully, searching for clues. Bailey's hair was iron-grey, cropped short in a military cut. His eyes were icy blue, and his mouth was a thin line like a knife-cut. Ritenour could see control in the face, and strength, but his cold mask hid everything else. Ritenour decided he wouldn't turn his back on this one either.

Despite Madigan's unsettling praises of the young man, Ritenour didn't see Ellis Glen as much of a problem. He was barely out of his teens, tall and gangling and not yet into his full growth. His face was bright and open, and he was so full of energy it was all he could do to sit still at his table while Ritenour ate. He was probably only there to run errands and take care of the scutwork no one else wanted to be bothered with. Useful battle fodder too; someone expendable Madigan could send into dangerous situations to check for traps and ambushes.

And finally, of course, there was Daniel Madigan himself. You only had to look at him for a moment to know he was the leader. He was darkly handsome and effortlessly charismatic, and even sitting still and silent, he radiated strength and authority and presence. He was the first person everyone's eyes went to on entering a room, drawing attention in much the same way a wolf would, or any other predator. Looked at coolly, he wasn't physically all that outstanding. He was slightly less than average height, and certainly not muscular, but still he was the most dangerous man in the room, and everyone knew it. Ritenour felt increasingly unsettled by Madigan's gaze, but forced himself to continue his meal and his appraisal of the terrorist leader.

The more he studied Madigan, the clearer it became that violence of thought and deed was always simmering just below a calm surface. And yet there was nothing special you could put your finger on about his face or bearing. Ritenour had heard it said that Madigan, when he felt like it, could turn off his personality in a moment, and become just another anonymous face in the crowd. It was an attribute that had enabled him to escape from many traps and tight corners in his time. Ritenour studied the man's features carefully. Just now, Madigan was showing him a cool, unemotional politician's face, half hidden behind a neatly trimmed beard. His eyes were dark and unwavering, and his occasional smile came and went so quickly you couldn't be sure whether you'd seen it or not. He looked to be in his early thirties, but had to be at least ten years older, unless he'd started his career of death and terror as a child. Not that Ritenour would put that past him. If ever a man had been born to violence and intrigue and sudden death, it was Daniel Madigan. No one knew how many people he'd killed down the years, how many towns and villages he'd destroyed in blood and fire, how many outrages he'd committed in the name of his Cause.

He had vowed to overthrow and destroy Outremer. No one knew why. There were many stories, mostly concerning the fate of his unknown family, but they were only stories. The Low Kingdoms had long since disowned him and his actions. He was too extreme, too ruthless . . . too dangerous to be associated with, even at a distance. Madigan didn't care. He went his own way, following his own Cause, ready to kill or destroy anyone or anything that got in his way.

And now he was sitting opposite Ritenour, studying him coolly and waiting to talk to him. With a start, Ritenour realised he'd finished his meal and was staring openly at Madigan. He buried his face in his wineglass and fought his way back to some kind of composure. He finally lowered his glass and put it carefully down on the arm of his chair, aware that the other terrorists were watching him with varying shades of impatience.

"Did the vintage meet with your approval?" asked Madigan.

"An excellent choice," said Ritenour, smiling calmly back. In fact, he'd been so preoccupied he hadn't a clue as to what he'd just drunk. It could have been dishwater for all he knew. He braced himself, and met Madigan's unnerving gaze as firmly as he could. "What do you want with me, Madigan? I'm no one special, and we both know it. I'm just another mid-level sorcerer, in a city infested with them. What makes me so important to you that you were ready to start a riot to break me out of Damnation Row?"

"You're not just a sorcerer," said Madigan easily. "You're also a shaman, a man with intimate knowledge of the life and death of animals and men. I have a use for a shaman. Particularly one who's followed the path of your recent experiments. Oh yes, my friend, I know all the secrets of your laboratory. I make it my business to know such things. Relax; no one else need ever know. Providing you do this little job for me."

"What job?" said Ritenour. "What do you want me to do?"

Madigan leaned forward, smiling slightly. "Together, you and I are going to rewrite history. We're going to kill the Kings of Outremer and the Low Kingdoms."

Ritenour looked at him blankly, too stunned even to register the shock that he felt. He'd known the Kings had arrived in Haven. That news had penetrated even Damnation Row's thick walls. But the sheer enormity of the plan took his breath away. He realized his mouth was hanging open, and shut it with a snap.

"Let me get this right," he said finally, too thrown even to care about sounding respectful. "You're planning to kill *both* Kings? Why both? I thought your quarrel was just with Outremer?"

"It is. I have dedicated my life to that country's destruction."

"Then why the hell . . . ?" Horn stirred suddenly at Madigan's side, reacting to the baffled anger in Ritenour's voice, and he shut up quickly to give his mind a chance to catch up with his mouth. There had to be a reason. Madigan did nothing without a reason. "Why do you want to kill your own King?"

"Because the Low Kingdoms' Parliament has betrayed us all by agreeing to this new Peace Treaty. Once this worthless scrap of paper has been signed, land that is rightfully ours and has been for generations will be given away to our hereditary enemies. I will not allow that to happen. There can be no peace with Outremer. As long as that country exists, it is an abomination in the sight of the Gods. That land was ours, and will be again. Outremer must be brought down, no matter what the price. So, both their King and ours must die, and in such a fashion that no one knows who is responsible. Both Parliaments will blame the other, both will deny any knowledge of any plot, and in the end there will be war. The people of both countries will demand it. And Outremer will be wiped from the face of the earth."

"We're going to do all this?" said Ritenour. "Just the six of us?"

"I have a hundred armed men at my command, hand-picked and assembled just for this project. But if all goes well, we shouldn't even need them much, except to ensure our security once we've taken control of Champion House. You must learn to trust me, sir sorcerer. Everyone in this room has committed their lives to carrying out this plan."

"You're committed to your Cause," said Ritenour bluntly. "I'm not. I'm here because I was promised a great deal of money. And all this talk of dying for a Cause makes me nervous. Dead men are notorious for not paying their bills."

Madigan chuckled briefly. It wasn't a pleasant sound. "Don't worry, my friend. You'll get your money. It's being held in a safe place until after this mission is over. And to answer the question you didn't ask; no, you will not be required to die for our Cause. Once you have performed the task I require of you, you are free to leave."

There was a knock at the door, an ordinary, everyday knock, and Madigan's people tensed, their hands moving quickly to their weapons. Bailey stared through the peephole, grunted once and relaxed. "It's all right. It's just the traitor." He unbolted the door and pulled it open, and a young nobleman strode in as if he owned the place.

He was tall and very slender, with a skin so pale it all but boasted that its owner never voluntarily put a foot outdoors. His long, narrow face bore two beauty spots and a look of utter disdain. He was dressed in the latest fashion, with tightly cut trousers and a padded jerkin with a chin-high collar. He had the kind of natural poise and arrogance that comes only

with regular practice since childhood, and his formal bow to
Madigan bordered on insolence. He swept off his wet cloak
and handed it to Bailey without looking at him. The old warrior
held the dripping garment between thumb and forefinger, and
for a moment Ritenour thought Bailey might tell the young
nobleman what he could do with it. But Madigan glanced
briefly at him, and Bailey hung the cloak carefully on the rack
by the door. The young noble strutted forward, ostentatiously
ignoring everyone, and warmed his hands by the fire.

"Beastly weather out. Damned if I know why your city
weather wizards allow it. My new boots are positively ruined."
He glared at Ritenour as though it was his fault. The sorcerer
smiled in response, and made a mental note of the young
man's face for future attention. The nobleman sniffed loudly
and turned his glare on Madigan. "This is the sorcerer fellow,
is it? Are you sure he's up to the job? I've seen better dressed
scarecrows."

"I don't need him for his fashion sense," said Madigan calmly. "Have you brought the information I require, Sir Roland?"

"Of course. You don't think I'd venture out in this bloody
downpour unless it was absolutely necessary, do you?"

He pulled a roll of papers from inside his jerkin, and moved
over to spread them out on the table, scowling at Glen and
Eleanour Todd until they stood up and got out of the way.
Ritenour and Madigan got up and went over to join him at
the table. The sorcerer studied Sir Roland with interest. Either
the man had nerves of steel, or he was totally insensitive to
the fact that he was making enemies of some very dangerous
people. Sir Roland secured his papers at the corners with the
terrorists' wineglasses, and gestured impatiently for Madigan
to move in beside him. He did so, and everyone else crowded
in behind them.

"These are the floor plans for Champion House," said Sir
Roland brusquely. "All the details you'll need are here, including the location and nature of all the security spells. I've also
marked the routes of the various security patrols, and how
many men-at-arms you can expect to encounter at each point.
You'll find details of their movements, a timetable for each
patrol and so on, in the other papers. I don't have time to go
through those with you now. I've also got you the plans you
requested for the cellar, though what good that's going to do

you is beyond me. No one's been down there for simply ages, and the whole place is a mess. It's full of rubbish and probably crawling with rats. And if you're thinking of breaking in that way, you can forget it. The cellar was built on solid concrete, and there are unbreakable security wards to prevent anyone from teleporting into the House.

"Now then, this sheet gives you both Kings' separate schedules, inside and outside the building, complete with details of how much protection they'll have. With these schedules, you'll be able to tell exactly where each King should be at any given moment. There are bound to be alterations from time to time, to accommodate any whims or fears of the Kings' security people, but I'll see you're kept up to date as much as possible. For the moment, everyone's so afraid of offending somebody that they're all following their schedules to the letter, but you know how paranoid security people can get. You'd almost think they had something to worry about. Finally, this sheet gives you the names of those people who can be trusted to support you, once the operation is underway. You'll notice the list includes names from the parties of both countries." The young noble smiled slightly. "Though of course they won't reveal themselves unless it becomes absolutely necessary. Still, I think you can rely on them to keep their fellow hostages in line, prevent any heroics, that sort of thing.

"I think you'll find everything you need is here. I must say I'm rather looking forward to seeing Their Majesties' faces when they discover they're being held for ransom. Glorious fun. Now then, I must be off. I have to get back before I'm missed. I don't see any need for us to meet again, Madigan, but if you must contact me, do be terribly discreet. We don't want anything to go wrong at this late stage, now do we?"

He turned away from the table, and gestured imperiously for Bailey to fetch him his cloak. Bailey did so, after a look at Madigan, and Sir Roland swung the cloak around his shoulders with a practised dramatic gesture. Ritenour almost felt like applauding. Sir Roland bowed briefly to Madigan, ignored everyone else, and left. Bailey closed and bolted the door behind him. Ritenour looked at Madigan.

"Dear Roland doesn't know what's really going on, does he?"

Madigan's smile flickered briefly. "He and his fellow conspirators believe they're part of a plot to disrupt the Peace
Signing with a kidnapping. They believe this will delay the
Signing, buy them time to sow seeds of doubt in their precious
Parliaments, and generally stir up bad feeling on both sides.
They also expect a large share of the ransom money to find
its way into their hands. I fear they're going to be somewhat
disappointed. I'm rather looking forward to seeing their faces
when we execute the two Kings right before their eyes."

"Glorious fun," said Eleanour Todd, and everyone laughed.

"About these conspirators," said Ritenour diffidently, indi-
cating the relevant page. "You do realise that all of them, and
most particularly including Sir Roland, will have to die? Along
with everyone who could identify us."

Madigan nodded. "Believe me, sir sorcerer, no one will
be left alive to point the finger, and no one will pursue us.
Haven . . . will have its own problems."

Ritenour looked around him, taking in the mocking smiles
on the terrorists' faces, and a sudden chill clutched at his heart.
"What exactly are you planning, Madigan? What do you want
from me?"

Madigan told him.

Wulf Saxon strode through the old familiar district he used to
live in, and no one knew him. The last time he'd walked these
streets, twenty-three years ago, people had waved and smiled
and some had even cheered. Everyone wanted to know him
then—the local lad who'd made good. The city Councillor
who'd started out in the same mean streets as them. But
now no one recognised his face, and in a way he was glad.
The Northside had always been rough and ready, shaped by
poverty and need, but it had never seemed this bad. There
was no pride or spirit left in the quiet, defeated people who
scurried through the pouring rain with their heads bowed. The
once brightly painted buildings were grey and faceless with
accumulated soot and filth. Garbage blocked the gutters, and
sullen-eyed bravos shouldered their way through the crowds
without anyone so much as raising a murmur of protest.

Saxon had expected some changes after his long absence,
but nothing like this. The Northside he remembered had been
vile, corrupt, and dangerous, but the people had a spark then,

a vitality that enabled them to rise above all that and claim their own little victories against an uncaring world. Whatever spark these people might once have possessed had been beaten out of them. Saxon trudged on down the street, letting his feet guide him where they would. He should have felt angry or depressed, but mostly he just felt tired. He'd spent the last few hours tracking down names and memories, only to find that most of the people he'd once known were now either missing or dead. Some names only produced blank faces. It seemed many things could change in twenty-three years.

He found himself standing in front of a tavern with a famili-ar name, the Monkey's Drum, and decided he could use a drink. He pushed the door open and stepped inside, his eyes narrowing against the sudden gloom. He took off his cloak and flapped it briskly out the open door a few times to lose the worst of the rain, and then hung it on a nearby peg. He shut the door and turned to study the tavern's interior with a critical eye.

It was fairly clean, in an absent-minded sort of way, and half-full of patrons sitting quietly at their tables, talking in lowered voices. None of them looked at Saxon for more than the briefest of moments, to make sure he wasn't the Guard. He smiled sourly, and headed for the bar. It seemed some things never changed. The Monkey's Drum had always been a place where you could buy and sell and make a deal. He made his way through the closely packed tables and ordered a brandy at the bar. The price made him wince, but he paid it with as much good grace as he could muster. Inflation could do a lot to prices in twenty-three years. The money he'd set aside in his secret lock-up all those years ago wasn't going to last nearly as long as he'd hoped. Twenty-three years . . . He kept repeating the number of years to himself, as though he could make himself believe it through sheer repetition, but it didn't get any easier. It was as though he'd gone to sleep in one world and awakened in another that bore only a nightmarish resemblance to the one he remembered.

That would teach him to try and steal a sorcerer's painting.

He smiled, and shrugged resignedly. Being a city Councillor had proved surprisingly expensive, and the pittance the city paid wasn't nearly enough to keep him in the style to which he intended to become accustomed. So he'd gone back to his previous occupation as a gentleman crook, a burglar with style and panache, and had broken into the house of a sorcerer he'd known was currently out of town. He'd been doing quite well, sidestepping all the sorcerer's protective wards with his usual skill, only to end up being eaten by Messerschmann's bloody Portrait. Sometimes there's no justice in this world.

Saxon put his back against the bar and looked round the room, sipping at his brandy while he wondered what to do next. He couldn't stay here, but he didn't know where else to go. Or even if there was any point in going anywhere. His ex-wife was probably still around somewhere, but there was nothing he wanted to say to her. She was the only woman he'd ever wanted, but it had only taken her a few years of marriage to decide that she didn't want him. No, he didn't want to see her. Besides, he owned her twenty-three years of back alimony payments. And then his gaze stumbled across a familiar face, and he straightened up. The years had not been kind to the face, but he recognized it anyway. He strode through the tables, a smile tugging at his lips, and loomed over the figure drinking alone at a table half hidden in the shadows.

"William Doyle. I represent the city auditor. Taxes division. I want to see all your receipts for the last four years."

The man choked on his drink and went bright red. He coughed quickly to get his breath back, and tried on an ingratiating smile. It didn't suit him. "Listen, I can explain everything. . . ."

"Relax, Billy," said Saxon, dropping into the chair opposite him. "You always were easy to get a rise out of. It's your own fault, for having such a guilty conscience. Well, no words of cheer and greeting for an old friend?"

Billy Doyle looked at him blankly for a long moment, and then slow recognition crept into his flushed face. "Wulf . . . Wulf Saxon. I'll be damned. I never thought to see you again. How many years has it been?"

"Too many," said Saxon.

"You're looking good, Wulf. You haven't changed a bit."

"Wish I could say the same for you. The years have not been kind to you, Billy boy."

Doyle shrugged, and drank his wine. Saxon looked at him wonderingly. The Billy Doyle he remembered had been a scrawny, intense young man in his early twenties. Not much

in the way of muscle, but more than enough energy to keep
him going long after most men gave up and dropped out. Billy
never gave up. And now here he was, a man in his late forties,
weighing twice what he used to and none of it muscle. The
thinning hair was still jet-black, but had a flat, shiny look that
suggested it was probably helped along with a little dye. The
face that had once been so sharp and fierce was now coarse
and almost piggy, the familiar features blurred with fat like
a cheap caricature. He looked like his own father. Or like
his father might have looked after too many good meals and
too many nights on booze. His clothes might once have been
stylish, but showed signs of having been washed and mended
too many times. Without having to be told, Saxon knew that
Billy Doyle was no longer one of life's successes.

Doyle looked at him, frowning. "You haven't changed at all,
Wulf. It's uncanny. What happened. You raise enough money
for a rejuvenation spell?"

"In a way. So, what's been happening in your life, Billy?
What are you doing these days?"

"Oh, this and that. Wheeling and dealing. You know how
it is."

"I used to," said Saxon, slumping unhappily in his chair.
"But things have changed while I was away. I went to where
my old house used to be, and they'd torn it down and replaced
it with some mock-Gothic monstrosity. The people who lived
there had never even heard of me. I went to the old neighbourhood and there was no trace of my family anywhere.
Everyone I ever knew is either dead or moved on. You're
the first friendly face I've seen all day."

Doyle looked at the clock on the wall, and gulped at his
drink. "Listen," he said, trying hard to sound casual, "I'd love
to sit and chat about the old days, but I'm waiting for someone.
Business; you know how it is."

"You're nervous, Billy," said Saxon thoughtfully. "Now,
what have you got to be nervous about? After all, this is me,
your old friend Wulf. We never used to have secrets from each
other. Or can it be that this particular piece of business you're
involved in is something you know I wouldn't approve of?"

"Listen, Wulf . . ."

"Now, there aren't many things I don't approve of. I've tried
most things once, and twice if I enjoyed it. And I was, after all,

a gentleman thief, who robbed from the rich and kept it. But there was one thing I never would look the other way for, and that hasn't changed. Tell me, Billy boy, have you got yourself involved in childnapping?"

"Where do you get off, coming on so self-righteous?" said Doyle hotly. "You've been away; you don't know what it's like here these days. Things have changed. It's always been hard to make a living here, but these days there's even less money around than there used to be. You've got to fight for every penny and watch your back every minute of the day. If you won't take on a job, there are a dozen men waiting to take your place. There's a market for kids—brothels, fighting pits, sorcerers, you name it. And who's going to miss a few brats from the streets, anyway? Their parents are probably glad they've got one less mouth to feed. I can't afford to be proud anymore. The money's good, and that's all I care about."

"You used to care," said Saxon.

"That was a long time ago. Don't try and interfere, Wulf. You'll get hurt."

"Are you threatening me, Billy?"

"If that's what it takes."

"You wouldn't hurt me, Billy boy. Not after everything we've been through together."

"That was someone else. Get out of here, Wulf. You don't belong here anymore. Times have changed, and you haven't changed with them. You've got soft."

He looked past Saxon's shoulder, and rose quickly to his feet. Saxon got up too, and looked around, carefully moving away from the table so that his sword arm wouldn't be crowded. Two bravos were standing by the table, staring at him suspiciously. One of them was holding a young boy by the arm, as much to hold him up as prevent him escaping. He couldn't have been more than nine or ten years old, and his blank face and empty eyes showed he'd been drugged. Saxon looked at the bravos thoughtfully. They were nothing special; just off-the-shelf muscle. He looked at Doyle.

"Can't let you do this, Billy. Not this."

"It's what I do now, Wulf. Stay out of it."

"We used to be friends."

"And now you're just a witness." Doyle looked at the two bravos and gestured jerkily at Saxon. "Kill him, and dispose of the body. I'll take care of the merchandise."

The bravos grinned, and the one holding the boy let go of his arm. The child stood still, staring at nothing as the bravos advanced on Saxon. They went to draw their swords, and Saxon stepped forward to meet them with empty hands. He smiled once, and then his fist lashed out with supernatural speed. The first bravo's head whipped round as the force of the blow smashed his jaw and broke his neck, and he crumpled lifelessly to the floor. The other bravo cried out with shock and rage, and Saxon turned to face him.

The bravo cut at him with his sword, and Saxon's hand snapped out and closed on the man's wrist, bringing the sword to a sudden halt. The bravo strained against the hold, but couldn't move his arm an inch. Saxon twisted his hand, and there was a sickening crunching sound as the man's wrist bones shattered. All the color went out of his face, and the sword fell from his limp fingers. Saxon let go of him. The bravo snatched a knife from his belt with his other hand, and Saxon slammed a punch into his gut. His hand sank in deeply, and blood burst from the man's mouth. Saxon pulled back his hand, and the bravo fell to the floor and lay still. Saxon heard a footstep behind him, and turned round to see Billy Doyle backing slowly away, a sword in his hand. Saxon looked at him, and Doyle dropped the sword. His eyes were wide and frightened, and his hands were trembling.

"You're not even breathing hard," he said numbly. "Who are you?"

"I'm Wulf Saxon, and I'm back. My time away has . . . changed me somewhat. I'm faster, stronger. And I don't have a lot of patience anymore. But some things about me haven't changed at all. You're out of the childnapping business, Billy. As of now. I'll hand the boy over to the Guard. You'd better start running."

Doyle stood where he was, deathly pale. He licked his lips, and shifted his feet uncertainly. "You wouldn't set the Guard on me, Wulf. You wouldn't do that to me. We're old friends, remember? You were never the sort to betray a friend."

"That was someone else," said Saxon. "One question, and then you can go. The correct answer buys you a half-hour start. If you lie to me, I'll hunt you down and kill you. Where's my sister, Billy? Where's Annathea?"

Doyle smiled. "Yeah, figures you'd have a job tracking her down. She doesn't use that name anymore. Hasn't for a long time. Ask for Jenny Grove, down on Cheape Street. Grove used to be her old man. Ran off years ago. He never was worth much."

"Where on Cheape Street?"

"Just ask. They all know Jenny Grove round there. But you aren't going to like what you'll find, Wulf. I'm not the only one that's changed. Your precious sister's been through a lot since you abandoned her."

"Start running, Billy. Your half hour starts now. And pass the word around. Wulf Saxon is back, and he's in a real bad mood."

Billy Doyle took in Saxon's icy blue eyes and the flat menace in his voice, and nodded stiffly, the smile gone from his mouth as though it had never been there. He was very close to death, and he knew it. He turned and headed for the door at a fast walk that was almost a run. He grabbed a drab-looking cloak from the rack, pulled open the door, and looked back at Saxon. "I'll see you regret this, Wulf. I have friends, important people, with connections. They aren't going to like this at all. Haven's changed since your day. There are people out there now who'll eat you alive."

"Send them," said Saxon. "Send them all. Twenty-eight minutes left, Billy boy."

Doyle turned and left, slamming the door behind him. Saxon looked around him unhurriedly, but no one moved at their tables. The tavern's patrons watched in silence as Saxon took the drugged boy by the arm and headed for the door. He collected his cloak, slung it round his shoulders, and pulled open the door. It was still raining. He looked back into the tavern, and the patrons met his gaze like so many wild dogs, cowed for the moment but still dangerous. Saxon bowed to them politely.

"You've got five minutes to get out of here by the back door. Then I'm setting fire to the tavern."

He handed the boy over to a Guard Constable who came to watch the fire brigade as they tried to put out the blazing tavern. The driving rain kept the fire from spreading, but the Monkey's Drum was already beyond saving. There were occasional explosions inside as the flames reached new caches of booze. Saxon watched for a while, enjoying the spectacle, and then got directions to Cheape Street from the Constable and set off deeper into the Northside.

He didn't know this particular area very well, except by reputation, and undoubtedly that had also changed in the past twenty-three years, along with everything else. Certainly the streets he passed through seemed increasingly dingy and squalid, and he grew thankful for the heavy rain that hid the worst details from him. A slow, sick feeling squirmed in his gut as he wondered what Doyle had meant in his comments about Annathea. And why should she have changed her first name, just because she got married? It didn't make sense. Anyone would think she was hiding from someone.

It didn't occur to him until some time later that she might have been hiding from him.

Cheape Street turned out to be right on the edge of the Devil's Hook, a square mile of slums and alleyways bordering the Docks. The Hook was where you ended up when you'd fallen so far there was nowhere else to go but the cemetery. Poverty and suffering were as much a part of the Devil's Hook as the filthy air and fouled streets. Death and sudden violence were a part of everyday life. Saxon kept his hand conspicuously near his sword, and turned a hard glare on anyone who even looked like they were getting too close. He had no trouble in finding the address he'd been given, and stared in disbelief at the sagging tenements huddled together in the rain. This was the kind of place where absentee landlords crammed whole families into one room, and no one could afford to complain. What the hell was Annathea doing here? He stopped a few people at random, using the Jenny Grove name, and got directions to a second-floor flat right at the end of the tenement building.

Saxon found the right entrance and strode into the narrow hallway. Four men were sitting on the stairs, blocking his way. They were pretty much what he expected. Young, over-muscled, and out of work, with too much time on their hands and nothing to do but make trouble to relieve the endless boredom. Probably saw this filthy old fleatrap as their territory, and were glad of a chance to manhandle an outsider. Unfortunately for them, Saxon wasn't in the mood to play along. He strode towards them, smiling calmly, and they moved to block off the stairs completely. The oldest, who couldn't have been more than twenty, grinned insolently up at Saxon. He wore battered leathers pierced with cheap brass rings in rough patterns, and made a big play out of pretending to clean his filthy nails with the point of a vicious-looking knife.

"Where do you think you're going?"

"I'm visiting my sister," said Saxon. "Is there a problem?"

"Yeah. You could say that. You're not from around here, not with fancy clothes like those. You don't belong here. This is Serpent territory. We're the Serpents. You want to walk around where we live, that's going to cost you. Think of it as an informal community tax."

The others laughed at that, a soft dangerous sound, and watched Saxon with dark, unblinking eyes. Saxon just nodded, unmoved.

"And how much would this tax be?"

"Everything you've got, friend, everything you've got."

The young tough rose lithely to his feet, holding his knife out before him. Saxon stepped forward, took him by the throat with one hand, and lifted him off his feet. The Serpent's eyes bulged and his grin vanished. His feet kicked helplessly inches above the floor. He started to lift his knife, and Saxon turned and threw him the length of the hall. He slammed into the end wall by the door, and slid unconscious to the floor. Saxon looked at the Serpents still blocking the stairs, and they scrambled to get out of his way.

He started up the stairs, and one of them produced a length of steel chain from somewhere and whipped it viciously at Saxon's face, aiming for the eyes. The other two produced knives and moved forward, their eyes eager for blood. Saxon swayed easily to one side and the chain missed, though he felt the breath of its passing on his face. His attacker stumbled forward, caught off balance, and Saxon took the Serpent's throat in his hand and crushed it. Blood flew from the man's mouth, and he fell dying to the floor. Saxon kicked him out of the way. That left two.

He slapped the knife out of one Serpent's hand, and kicked the other in the leg. He felt, as well as heard, the bone break beneath his boot. The man fell back, screaming and clutching at his leg. The other was down on one knee, scrabbling frantically for his knife. Saxon kicked him in the face. The Serpent's

neck snapped under the impact, and he flew backwards to lie
unmoving on the hall floor. Saxon turned and looked at the last
Serpent, who cringed from him, his back pressed against the
stairway banisters. Saxon reached down, grabbed a handful of
the man's leathers, and lifted him up effortlessly, so that they
were face to face. Sweat ran down the Serpent's face, and his
eyes were wide with shock and fear.

"*Who are you?*"

"I'm Saxon. Wulf Saxon. I've been away, but now I'm
back. I'm going up to visit my sister now. If anyone feels
like coming up after me and disturbing my visit, I'm relying
on you to convince them that it's a bad idea. Because if anyone
else annoys me, I'm going to get really unpleasant."

He dropped the Serpent, and continued on up the stairs
without looking back. The second floor was dark and gloomy.
The windows had been boarded up, and there were no lamps.
The doors all looked much the same, old and hard-used and
covered with an ancient coat of peeling paint. The numbers
had been crudely carved into the wood, probably because
any attached number would have been prised off and stol-
en in the hope someone would pay a few pennies for it.
In this kind of neighbourhood, anything that wasn't actually
nailed down and guarded with a drawn sword was considered
fair game.

He found the right door, raised a hand to knock, and then
hesitated. He wondered suddenly if he wanted to meet the
person his sister had become. Billy Doyle had been a good
sort once; brave, reliable, honourable. Saxon slowly lowered
his hand. His sister was Annathea, not this Jenny Grove;
whoever she was. Perhaps the best thing would be to just turn
around and leave. That way he'd at least have his memories
of Annathea. He pushed the temptation aside. He had to know.
Whatever she'd done, whoever she'd become, she was still
family, and there might be something he could do to help. He
knocked briskly at the door. There was a pause, and then he
heard the muffled sound of footsteps from inside.

"Who is it?"

Something clutched at Saxon's heart like a fist. The voice
had been that of an old woman. He had to cough and clear his
throat before he could answer.

"It's me, Anna. It's your long-lost brother, Wulf."

There was a long pause, and then he heard the sound of bolts being drawn, and the door opened to reveal a faded, middle-aged woman in a shapeless grey robe. Her thin grey hair had been pulled back into a tight bun, and he didn't know her face at all. Saxon relaxed a little, and some of the weight lifted from his heart. He had come to the wrong place after all. He'd make his excuses, apologise for disturbing the old lady, and leave. And then she leaned forward, and raised a veined hand to touch his arm, her face full of wonder.

"Wulf? Is it really you, Wulf?"

"Annathea?"

The woman smiled sadly. "No one's called me that in years. Come in, Wulf. Come in and tell me why you abandoned your family all those years ago."

She stepped back while he was still searching for an answer, and gestured for him to enter. He did so, and she shut the door, carefully pushing home the two heavy bolts. Saxon stood uncertainly in his sister's single room and looked around him, as much to give him an excuse for not speaking as anything else. It was clean, if not particularly tidy, with a few pieces of battered old furniture that wouldn't have looked out of place in the city dump. Which was probably where they'd come from. A narrow bed was pushed up against the far wall, the bedclothes held together by patches and rough stitching.

The woman gestured for him to sit down on one of the uncomfortable-looking chairs pulled up to the fire. He did so, and she slowly lowered herself into the facing chair. Her bones cracked loudly in the quiet, sounding almost like the damp logs spitting in the fire. For a while Saxon and the woman just sat there, looking at each other. He still couldn't see his sister in the drawn, wrinkled face before him.

"I hear you used to be married," he said finally.

"Ah yes. Dear Robbie. He was so alive, always joking and smiling and full of big plans. Sometimes I think I married him because he reminded me so much of you. That should have warned me, but I was lonely and he was insistent. He ran through what was left of the family fortune in twelve months, and then I woke up one morning and he was gone. He left me a nice little note, thanking me for all the good times. I never saw him again. Things were hard for a while after that. I had no money, and Robbie left a lot of debts behind him. But I coped. I had to."

"Wait a minute," said Saxon, confused. "What about the rest of the family? Why didn't they help you?"

Jenny Grove looked at him. "I thought you'd know by now. They're all dead, Wulf. It broke mother's heart when you ran off and left us without even a word or a note. Father spent a lot of money hiring private agents to try and track you down, but it was all money wasted. Your friends were convinced something must have happened to you, but they couldn't find out anything either. Mother died not long after you left. She was never very strong. Father faded away once she was gone, and followed her a year later. George and Curt both became soldiers. George joined the army, and Curt became a mercenary. You know they never could agree on anything. They died fighting on opposite sides of the same battle, over fifteen years ago. That just left me. For a long time I clung to the hope that you might come back to help me, but you never did. After a while, after a long while, I stopped hoping. It hurt too much. How could you do it, Wulf? You meant so much to us; we were all so proud of you. How could you just run off and leave us?"

"I didn't," said Saxon. "I got caught in a sorcerer's trap. I was only released today. That's why I haven't aged. For me, twenty-three years ago was yesterday."

"Stealing," said Jenny Grove. "You were out stealing again, weren't you? Everything you had, wealth and power and position; that wasn't enough for you, was it? You had to have your stupid little thrills as well, didn't you?"

"Yes. I'm sorry."

She looked at him, too tired and beaten down even to be bitter, and he had to look away. There was a long, awkward silence as he searched for something to say.

"Why . . . Jenny Grove?" he said finally.

She shrugged. "Your money took us out of the Northside, and let us live the good life, for a while. I wish it hadn't. It made it so much harder to go back to being nothing again. Annathea and her life became just a dream, a dream I wanted to forget, because it drove me mad. So I became Jenny Grove, who'd never been anything but poor, and had no memories to forget."

"But what about our friends? Did none of them help you?"

"Friends . . . you'd be surprised how quickly friends disappear once the money's run out. And you made a lot of enemies when you disappeared so suddenly. Friends who'd been as close as family wouldn't even speak to us, because of the way you left them in the lurch. They were convinced we must have known about it, you see. Not everyone turned their back on me. Billy Doyle—you remember Billy—he helped sort out the debts Robbie left me, and helped me start a new life. I drove him away in the end. He was part of the old days, and I just wanted to forget. Dear Billy; he had such a crush on me when we were younger. I don't suppose you remember that."

"I remember," said Saxon. "He told me where to find you."

"That was good of him."

"Yes, it was. He said . . . everyone around here knew you. What do you do, these days?"

"I read the cards, tell fortunes, that sort of thing. Father would never have approved, but it's harmless enough. Mostly I just tell them what they want to hear, and they go away happy. I have my regular customers, and they bring me enough to get by on."

Saxon smiled for the first time. "That's a relief, at least. From the way Billy said it, I was afraid you might have been a . . . well, a lady of the evening."

"You mean a whore. I was, dear. What else was there for me, then? But I got too old for that. I decided I'd spent enough time staring at my bedroom ceiling, and took up the cards instead. Dear me, Wulf, you look shocked. You shouldn't. There are worse ways to make money, and you'll find most of them here in the Hook. Why did you come here, Wulf? What do you want from me?"

Saxon looked at her. "You're my sister."

"No," said Jenny Grove flatly. "That was someone else. Annathea Saxon died years ago—of a broken heart, like her parents. Go away, Wulf. We've nothing to say to each other. All you can do is stir up memories best forgotten by both of us. Go away, Wulf. Please."

Saxon rose slowly to his feet. He felt so helpless it hurt. "I'll get some money together, and then I'll come back and see you again."

"Goodbye, Wulf."

"Goodbye, Anna."

He left without saying any more, and without looking back. Jenny Grove stared into the crackling fire, and wouldn't let herself cry until she was sure he'd gone.

Saxon stomped down the stairs, scowling angrily. There had to be someone left from his past who'd be glad to see him. Someone he'd started on the road to success . . . He smiled suddenly. Richard Anderson. Young Richard had been just starting out in Reform politics twenty-three years ago, and Saxon had provided both financial and personal backing when no one else believed in Anderson at all. Saxon had believed in him. Richard Anderson had shown drive and ambition and an almost savage grasp of how to play the political game. If anyone had succeeded and prospered in Saxon's absence, it would be Anderson. And someone with his genius for keeping a high profile shouldn't be that difficult to track down.

He started down the stairs that led to the ground floor, and then stopped suddenly, his hand dropping to his sword. The entry hall was crammed with a dozen young toughs and bravos, all wearing the same leathers as the four Serpents he'd encountered earlier. Apparently the survivor had gone running for his friends. Well, crawling anyway. They carried knives and clubs and lengths of steel chain, and they looked at Saxon with mocking grins and hungry eyes. Saxon looked calmly out at them.

"I've had a bad day, my friends. You're about to have a worse one."

He ran down the last few stairs and launched himself into their midst. He landed heavily on two Serpents, and his weight threw them all to the floor. He lashed out with his fist, and one Serpent's face disappeared in a mess of blood and broken bone. Stamping down hard as he rose to his feet, Saxon felt the other Serpent's ribs break and splinter under his boot. Knives and bludgeons flailed around him, but he was too fast for them. He moved among the Serpents like a deadly ghost, his fists lashing out with supernatural strength and fury. He picked up one of his assailants and used him as a living flail with which to batter his fellows. The Serpent screamed at first, but not for long. Bones broke and splintered, blood flew on the air, and Serpents fell to the floor and did not rise again. Saxon soon tired of that, and threw the limp body away. He needed it to be more personal. He needed to get his hands on them.

But the few remaining Serpents turned and ran rather than face him, and he was left alone in the hallway, surrounded by the dead and the dying. Blood pooled on the floor and ran down the walls, the stink of it heavy on the air. Saxon looked slowly around him, almost disappointed there was no one left on whom he could take out his frustration, and realised suddenly that he wasn't even breathing hard. Something strange had happened to him during his time in the Portrait. He'd lost his mind, and recovered it in some fashion he didn't really understand, but he'd gained something too. Not only had he not aged, but when he fought it was as though all the lost years burned in him at once. He was stronger and faster than anyone he'd ever known. The Serpents hadn't been able to lay a finger on him. His gaze moved slowly over the broken and bloodied bodies that lay scattered across the hallway, and he grinned suddenly. He'd been away, but now he was back, and he wasn't in the mood to take any shit from anyone. Haven might have gone to hell while he was away, but he was going to drag it back to civilisation, kicking and screaming all the way if necessary.

He left the tenement building and strode off into the Northside, in search of Richard Anderson.

"Councillor Anderson," said Saxon. "I'm impressed, Richard; really. You've come up in the world."

Saxon leaned back in his chair and puffed happily at the long cigar he'd taken from the box on Anderson's desk. The rich smell of cigar smoke filled the office, obliterating the damp smell from Saxon's clothes. There were fresh bloodstains on his clothes too, but so far, Anderson had carefully refrained from mentioning them. Saxon looked around the office, taking his time. He liked the office. It had been his once, back when he'd been a Reform Councillor. One of the first Reform Councillors, in fact. The office had been extensively renovated and refurnished since then, of course, and it looked a hundred times better. Everything was top quality now, including the paintings on the walls. Saxon could remember when the only painting had been a portrait of their main Conservative rival. They'd used it for knife-throwing practice. Saxon sighed, and looked down at the floor. There was even a fitted carpet now, with an intimidatingly deep pile. He looked back at the man sitting on the opposite side of the desk, and tried hard to keep the frown off his face.

Councillor Richard Anderson was a stocky, tolerably handsome man in his middle forties, dressed in sober but acceptably fashionable clothes. Saxon thought he looked ridiculous, but then fashions had changed a lot in the past twenty-three years. Anderson looked impassively back at Saxon, wearing a standard politician's face—polite but uninvolved. There was nothing in his expression or posture to show how he felt about seeing the man who had once been his closest friend and colleague, back from the dead after all the long years. Nothing except the slow anger in his eyes.

"What the hell happened to you, Richard?" said Saxon finally. "How did you of all people end up as a Conservative Councillor? You used to be even more of a Reformer than I was; a hotheaded rebel who couldn't wait to get into politics and start making changes. What happened?"

"I grew up," said Anderson. "What happened to you?"

"Long story. Tell me about the others. I assume they haven't all become Conservatives. What's Dave Carrera doing these days?"

"He's an old man now. Sixty-one, I think. Left politics after he lost two elections in a row. Runs a catering business in the Eastside."

"And Howard Kilronan?"

"Runs a tavern, the Inn of the Black Freighter."

"Aaron Cooney, Padraig Moran?"

"Aaron was killed in a tavern brawl, twenty years ago. I don't know what happened to Padraig. I lost touch over the years."

Saxon shook his head disgustedly. "And we were going to change the world. We had such hopes and such plans. . . . I take it there is still a Reform movement in Haven?"

"Of course. It's even had a few successes of late. But it won't last. Idealists don't last long in Haven as a rule. What are you doing here, Wulf?"

"I came to see a friend," said Saxon. "I don't seem to have many left."

"What did you expect, after running out on us like that? All our plans fell apart without you there to lead us. You were a Councillor, Wulf; you had responsibilities, not just to us but to all the people who worked and campaigned on your behalf. When you just up and vanished, a lot of people lost heart, and we lost the Seat on the Council back to the Conservatives. All of us who'd put money into the Cause lost everything. Billy Doyle spent a year in a debtors' prison. You know how he felt about you, and your sister. Have you seen her yet?"

"Yes. Why didn't you do something to help her?"

"I tried. She didn't want to know."

They sat in silence for a while, both of them holding back angry words. Saxon stubbed out his cigar. The taste had gone flat. He rose to his feet and nodded briskly to Anderson. "Time to go. I'll see you again, Richard; at the next election. This is my office, and I'm going to get it back."

"No, wait; don't go." Anderson rose quickly to his feet and gestured uncertainly. "Stay and talk for a while. You still haven't told me how you've stayed so young. What have you been doing all these years?"

Saxon looked at him. Anderson's voice had been carefully casual, and yet there had been a definite wrong note; a hint of something that might have been alarm, or even desperation. Why should it suddenly matter so much to Anderson whether he left or not? A sudden intuition flared within him, and he moved over to look out the window. In the street below, Guard Constables were gathering outside the house. Saxon cursed dispassionately, and turned back to look at Anderson.

"You son of a bitch. You set me up."

Anderson's face paled, but he stood his ground. "You're a wanted criminal, Wulf. A common murderer and arsonist. I know my duty."

Saxon stepped forward, his face set and grim. Anderson backed quickly away, until his back slammed up against the wall. Saxon picked up the heavy wooden desk between them and threw it effortlessly to one side, and then stood still, staring coldly at Anderson.

"I ought to tear your head right off your shoulders. After all the things I did for you . . . But it seems I'm a bit pressed for time at the moment. I'll see you again, Richard; and then we'll continue this conversation."

He turned away and headed for the door. Anderson struggled to regain his composure.

"They'll find you, Saxon! There's nowhere you can hide. They'll hunt you down and kill you like a rabid dog!"

Saxon smiled at him, and Anderson flinched. Saxon laughed softly. "Anyone who finds me will regret it. I've got nothing left to lose, Richard; and that makes me dangerous. Very dangerous."

He left the office, not even bothering to slam the door behind him. He ran down the stairs to meet the Guard, feeling his new strength mount within him like a fever. He wasn't going to let the Guard stop him. He had things to do. He wasn't sure what they were yet, but he was sure of one thing: someone was going to pay for all the years he'd lost, for all the friends and hopes that had been taken from him. The first of the Guard Constables appeared at the bottom of the stairs, and Saxon smiled down at him.

"You know something? I've had a really bad day. You're about to have a worse one."

The other Guards arrived, and he threw himself at them.

The cemetery wasn't much to look at, just a plot of open land covered with earth mounds and headstones. Incense sticks burned at regular intervals, but the smell was still pretty bad. Saxon stood looking down at the single modest stone bearing both his parents' names, and felt more numb than anything. He'd never meant for them to be buried here. He'd always intended they should be laid to rest in one of the more discreet, upmarket cemeteries on the outskirts of the city. But by the time they died, most of the money he'd brought to the family was gone, and so they were buried here. At least they were together, as they'd wanted.

The rain had died away to a miserable drizzle, though the sky was still dark and overcast. Saxon stood with his head bare, and let the rain run down his face like tears. He felt cold, inside and out. He knelt down beside the headstone, and set about methodically clearing the weeds away from the stone and the grave. He'd known his parents would probably be dead, as soon as he was told how many years he'd been away, but he hadn't really believed it. Then Anna told him they'd died, but he still didn't believe it, not really. For him it was only yesterday that they'd both been alive and well, and proud of him. Their son, the city Councillor. And now they were gone, and they'd died believing he deserted them, and all the people who depended on him. He stopped weeding and sat still, and the tears burst from him with a violence that shook him.

They finally passed, leaving him feeling weak and drained. He'd never felt so alone. In the past, there had always been family and friends to look out for him, to pick him up when he fell over his own feet from trying to run too fast. They'd always been there when he needed them, family and friends, and Mum and Dad. Now they were gone, and there was no one left but him. So that would have to be enough.

He'd drifted into Reform politics because he thought people needed him, to protect them from the scum who preyed on them, both inside and outside the law. That seemed more true than ever now. Except that things had got so bad he couldn't tell the guilty from the innocent anymore. Something had to be done, but he no longer had any faith in politics; he needed to take a more personal stand. To get his hands on the bad guys and make them hurt, the way he was hurting. He could do that. He was different now; stronger, faster, maybe even unbeatable. He could find the people responsible for making Haven what it had become, and exact vengeance for himself and everyone else who'd lost all hope and faith in the future. He smiled slowly, his eyes cold and savage. He would have his vengeance, and the Gods help anyone who got in his way.

He rose to his feet, and took one last look at the headstone. Whatever happened, he didn't think he'd be coming back.

"Goodbye; Mum, Dad. I'll make you proud of me again. I'll put things right. I promise."

He turned and left the cemetery, and walked back into the unsuspecting city.

3

Hostages

The rain was still hammering down, and Hawk was getting distinctly tired of it. He pulled his hood well forward and ran after Jessica Winter as she led the SWAT team down the wide, empty road that led into Mulberry Crescent. They'd been running flat out for the last five streets, ever since Winter got the emergency call from the Guard communications sorcerer. She was still running well and strongly, but Hawk was starting to find it hard going. Personally, he thought she was just showing off. Whatever the emergency was, it couldn't be so important they had to sprint all the way there. Hawk had never been much of a one for running, mainly because he'd always tended towards stamina rather than speed. But he couldn't afford to look bad before the rest of the team, so he gritted his teeth and pounded along in Winter's wake, glaring at her unresponsive back.

He still found the time to keep a wary eye on his surroundings, and was surprised to find the street was totally empty. Even allowing for the foul weather, there should have been some kind of crowd out on the street, celebrating the Peace Treaty. But though strings of brightly colored bunting hung damply above them, and flags flapped limply in the gusting wind, the SWAT team were alone in the middle of the fashionable Westside street. And that was strange in itself. Guards weren't usually welcome in the Westside. The well-to-do and high-placed families who lived there tended to prefer their own

private guards when it came to keeping the peace; men who
knew where their loyalties lay, and could be relied on to look
the other way at the proper moments. Hawk smiled sourly. It
would appear the private guards had run into something they
couldn't handle, and had been forced to call in the SWAT
team. Hawk's grin widened at the thought. He bet that had
rankled. Hawk didn't have much use for private guards. In
his experience, they tended to be overpaid, overdressed, and
about as much use as a chocolate teapot.

Winter finally slowed to a halt at the end of the street,
and looked out over Mulberry Crescent. The rest of the
team formed up around her. Hawk did his best to hide
his lack of breath, and squinted through the rain at the
killing ground before him. Bodies lay scattered the length
of the Crescent. Men, women, and children lay twisted and
broken, like discarded toys a destructive child had tired of.
Water pooled around the bodies, tinted pink with blood. Hawk
counted twenty-nine in plain sight, and had a sick feeling there
were probably more he couldn't see yet. No one moved in the
Crescent, and no one stared from the windows. If there was
anybody left alive, they were keeping their heads well down.
Which suggested that whatever had happened here, it wasn't
over yet.

There was still no sign anywhere of the private guards,
which didn't surprise Hawk one bit. They were all very well
when it came to moving on undesirables and manhandling the
occasional troublemaker, but show them a real problem and
they tended to be suddenly scarce on the ground. He looked at
the pathetic contorted bodies lying abandoned in the rain, and
his hands curled into fists. Someone was going to pay for this.
One way or another. He looked at Winter, who was standing
silently beside him.

"I think it's time you filled us in on why we're here, Winter.
The Crescent looks like it was ambushed. What exactly are we
dealing with here?"

"A sniper," said Winter, not taking her eyes off the scene
before her. "He's been active for less than forty minutes,
but there are already thirty-two dead that we know of. No
wounded. He kills every time. And just to complicate things,
he's a magic-user, and a pretty powerful one at that. He's holed
up in an upper storey of one of these houses, somewhere down

the far end. He's been using his magic to blast everything that moves, irrespective of who or what it might be. Local guards have cleared the streets, but it's up to us to do something about the sniper." She glanced briefly at Storm. "Well, do you See anything useful?"

"Not really," said Storm, scowling unhappily. "He's in the third house from the end, down on the left, but he's protected himself very thoroughly against any form of magical attack. I can break through his wards, given enough time, but he could do a hell of a lot of damage to the surrounding area before I took him out."

"Be specific. How much damage?"

"He could demolish every building for at least four blocks in every direction, and kill hundreds of people. That specific enough for you?"

Winter scowled, and rubbed her chin thoughtfully with a thumb knuckle. "What kind of magic has he been using?"

"All sorts. For a psychotic killer, he's very versatile. The air's heavy with unexpended magic. I can still See his victims dying as they ran for safety. Some had all the life drained out of them, so they could feel themselves dying. Others were transformed into things that didn't live long. Luckily. And some were just blown apart, for the fun of it. We've got a bad one here, Jessica. He's powerful, versatile, and ready to do anything to get what he wants."

Winter nodded. "Question is, what does he want? Attention, revenge; what?"

Hawk spun round suddenly, his axe flashing out to stop a finger's breadth from the throat of a private guard behind him. All the color drained from the man's face, and Hawk grinned at him nastily. "I don't like people sneaking up on me, particularly when they do it so badly. Takes all the challenge out of it. I could hear you coming even through the pouring rain." He lowered his axe but didn't put it away. "All right; who are you, and what do you want?"

The private guard swallowed hard. Color was slowly seeping back into his face, but it was still pale enough to clash interestingly with the vivid vermilion and green of his uniform. He cleared his throat and looked pleadingly at Winter. "Corporal Guthrie, of Lord Dunford's guards, ma'am. I'm your local liason officer."

"About time you got here," said Winter. "Fill us in. What's the background on this case?"

Corporal Guthrie moved over to join her, giving Hawk and his axe a wide berth.

"The sorcerer Domain has been a resident of Mulberry Crescent for years. Always quiet and polite. Never any trouble. But about three-quarters of an hour ago, he suddenly appeared at a window on the upper floor of his house and started screaming at people down in the street. We don't know about what. Everybody who was in the street at that time is dead. According to one eyewitness who watched from his window, Domain just lashed out with his magic for no reason, killing everyone in sight. No one's dared leave their houses since. We've sealed off the Crescent at both ends, and evacuated the houses farthest from Domain, but we daren't get too close for fear of starting him off again. A doctor went in a while ago under a white flag to check the bodies, just in case there was anyone alive. There wasn't, so he approached Domain's house, to try and reason with him. The sorcerer told the doctor he wanted to be left alone, and that he'd kill anyone who tried to interfere with him."

"I'd like to talk to this doctor," said Winter. "He might be able to tell us all kinds of useful things."

"I don't think so," said Guthrie. "Domain destroyed his mind. All he does is repeat the sorcerer's message, over and over again."

Fisher swore harshly. "Let's just take the bastard out. Storm can protect us with his magic, and Hawk and I will go in and carve him up. It'll be a pleasure."

"It's not as simple as that," said Guthrie.

"I had a feeling he was going to say that," said Hawk.

"Domain has a hostage," said Guthrie. "Susan Wallinger, twenty-one years old. She was Domain's lady friend. We have reason to believe she wished to end the relationship, and had gone to his home to tell him so. It would appear Domain took this rather badly. He's threatened to kill her if she tries to leave, or if we send anyone in after her."

"You know the city's policy on hostages," said Winter. "They're expendable."

"Yes, ma'am. But Susan Wallinger is Councillor Wallinger's daughter."

"That is going to complicate things," said Fisher.

Hawk nodded grimly. Councillor Wallinger was one of the leading lights of the Conservatives, and his many businesses helped to provide a large part of the Party's funds. No wonder the Council had called in the SWAT team so quickly. They were expected to save the hostage as well as take out the sniper. Which, as Fisher pointed out, complicated the hell out of things. Hawk looked out over the corpse-strewn street, and his mouth tightened. As long as Domain was running loose, he was a menace. From the sound of his mental state, anything might set him off again, and next time he might not limit himself to the people in plain sight. He might decide to blow up every house in the Crescent, along with everyone in them. He might do something even worse. He was a sorcerer, after all, and they had no idea as to the limits of his power. One way or another, Domain had to be stopped. Hawk hefted his axe and studied the sorcerer's house. He'd get the girl out alive if he could, but if push came to shove, she was expendable— and to hell with who her father was.

Poor lass.

"We have a standard routine for handling hostage situations," said Winter, looking hard at Hawk and Fisher. "And we're going to follow it here, by the numbers. I don't want either of you doing anything without a direct order from me first. Is that clear?"

"Oh sure," said Hawk. Fisher nodded innocently. Winter glared at them both, unimpressed.

"I'm not unfamiliar with your reputations, Captains. Common belief has it that you're as dangerous as the black death, and about as subtle. You'll find we do things differently on the SWAT team. Whenever possible, our job is to resolve a crisis situation without resorting to violence. Nine times out of ten we get better results by talking and listening than we would if we used force. MacReady is our negotiator, and a damned good one. Until he's tried everything he can think of, and they've all failed, no one else does squat. Is that clear?"

"And if he does fail?" said Fisher.

"Then I'll unleash you and Hawk and Barber, and you'll go in after Domain, under Storm's protection. But that's as a last resort only." She looked at Corporal Guthrie. "You'd better get back to your people and tell them what's happening. I'll be sending Mac down to talk to Domain in a few moments. Tell everyone to get their heads down and keep them down. Just in case."

The Corporal nodded jerkily, and hurried off into the rain. Hawk stared after him.

"Nice uniform," he said solemnly. "Vermilion and green. Cute."

Winter's mouth twitched. "Maybe he just wants to be sure he can be seen at night. All right, Mac; let's do this by the numbers, nice and easy. Your first job is to persuade him to let the girl go. Promise him whatever it takes. Councillor Wallinger will make good on practically anything, if it will get him his daughter back safe and sound. Once she's safely out of the way, then you can concentrate on trying to talk him down."

MacReady looked at her steadily. "Assuming he won't give up the girl, which has priority: getting her out or getting him down?"

"If it comes to that, the girl is expendable," said Winter. "Why do you think I sent Guthrie away before I briefed you? Now get going. We're wasting time."

MacReady nodded, and headed unhurriedly down the street towards Domain's house. Hawk looked sharply at Storm. "Aren't you going to give him any protection?"

"He doesn't need any," said Storm. "He's protected by a Family charm; magic can't touch him, swords can't cut him, and drugs won't poison him. You could drop him off a ten-storey building, and he'd probably just bounce. At the same time, the charm doesn't allow him to use any offensive weapons, which is just as well, or he'd have taken over the whole damn country by now. As it is, he makes a damned good negotiator."

He fell silent as a low, rumbling sound trembled in the ground under their feet. Hawk looked quickly about him, but the street was still empty. The rumbling grew louder and more ominous, and then the street next to MacReady exploded. Solid stone tore like paper, and cobbles flew through the air like shrapnel. Hawk held up his cloak as a shield, and cobblestones pattered against it like hailstones in a sudden storm. It was all over in a few seconds, and Hawk slowly lowered his cloak and looked around him. None of the others were hurt. Fisher had her sword in her hand, and was glaring about her for someone to use it on. She looked down the street, and her eyes widened. Hawk followed her gaze.

MacReady was standing unharmed amid vicious-looking fragments of broken stone and concrete, staring calmly into a jagged rent in the ground. The explosion didn't seem to have harmed him at all, even though it must have gone off practically in his ear. His clothing wasn't even mussed. He shook his head, turned his back on the gaping fissure, and walked on down the street. The outer wall of a nearby house bulged suddenly outwards and collapsed over him. When the dust cloud settled, washed quickly out of the air by the driving rain, MacReady was still standing there, entirely unhurt, surrounded by rubble. He clambered awkwardly over some of the larger pieces, and continued on his way. Lightning stabbed down from the overcast sky, again and again, but didn't even come close to touching him. Magic spat and sparkled around him, scraping across the air like fingernails on a blackboard, but MacReady walked steadily on. He looked almost bored. Eventually he came to the third house from the end on the left, and looked up at the top floor. A dark shape showed briefly at one of the windows, and then was gone. MacReady pushed open the front door and walked inside.

Winter stirred at Hawk's side. "Well, if nothing else, I think we can be fairly sure that Domain knows he's coming."

It was very quiet inside the house, out of the driving rain, and MacReady paused in the gloomy hallway to take off his cloak and hang it neatly on the wall rack. A woman's cloak was already hanging there, barely damp to his touch. Presumably Susan Wallinger's. He looked around him. All was still except for the loud ticking of a clock somewhere close at hand, and an occasional quiet creaking as the old house settled itself. MacReady moved over to the nearest door. It was standing slightly ajar, and he pushed it open. A headless body lay sprawled before the open fireplace. Blood and gore had soaked into the rich pile carpet where his head should have been. There was no sign of the head itself. Judging by the ragged state of the neck, the head hadn't been neatly severed with a blade. It had been torn off by brute force. MacReady stepped back into the hall and headed for the stairs. The body might have been a failed negotiator, or someone who lived in the house. It might even have been a friend of Domain's.

Hello, Domain. Guess what? I'm going to be your friend. I'm going to win your trust and then abuse it. I'm going to persuade you to give up your hostage and come down peacefully, so that we can put you on trial, find you guilty, and execute you. I won't tell you that, of course. I'll tell you comforting lies and make you think they're true. Why? Because it's my job, and I'm good at it.

And because I get so horribly bored waiting to die, and outwitting kill-crazy lunatics like you is the only fun I have left.

He made his way up the stairs, making no attempt to be quiet. He wanted Domain to know he was coming. If the sorcerer thought he was sneaking up on him, he might panic and harm the girl. MacReady shook his head in mock disapproval. He couldn't allow that. Getting the girl out alive was part of the game, and he didn't like to lose. He stepped onto the dimly lit landing, bracing himself mentally against any further sorcerous attacks, but nothing happened. There was a door at the end of the hall with a light showing round its edges. He started towards the door, and it flew open suddenly as Domain lurched out into the hall.

His robe of sorcerer's black was torn and ragged, and there was dried blood on his sleeves and hands. He was tall and painfully thin, and barely into his early twenties. His face was deathly pale, split almost in two by a wide death's-head grin. His eyes were wide and staring, and they didn't blink often enough. He was shaking with suppressed emotion, ready to lash out at anyone or anything that seemed to threaten him. MacReady stayed where he was, and smiled calmly at the sorcerer.

"Stay where you are!" snapped Domain, his voice harsh and tinged with hysteria. "One step closer and I'll kill her! I will!"

"I believe you," said MacReady earnestly. "I'll do whatever you say, sir sorcerer. You're in charge here. My name is John MacReady. I've come to talk to you and Susan."

"You've come to take her away from me!"

"No, I'm just here to talk to you, that's all. You've got yourself in a bit of a mess, Domain. I'm here to help you find a way out of it. The authorities have promised not to interfere. You just tell me what you want, and I'll tell them. There must be something you want. You don't want to stay here, do you?"

"No. Something bad happened here." Domain's gaze turned inward for a moment, and then the crazy glare was back in his eyes, as though he couldn't bear to think about what he'd seen in that moment. "I'm getting out of here, and Susan's coming with me. I'll kill anyone who tries to stop us!"

"Yes, Domain. We understand that. That's why I'm here. We don't want any more deaths. Could I speak to Susan? Perhaps between the three of us we can come up with a plan that will get you both out of the city without anyone else having to be hurt."

The sorcerer studied him suspiciously for a dangerously long moment, and then jerked his head at the open door behind him. "She's in here. But no tricks. I may not be able to hurt you, but I can still hurt her. I'll kill her if I have to, to keep her with me!"

"I'll do exactly as you say, Domain. Just tell me what to do. You're in charge here."

MacReady kept up a low, soothing monologue as he slowly approached Domain. It didn't really matter what he said. The man had clearly gone beyond the point where he could be reached with logic, but he could still be soothed, charmed, manipulated. The important thing now was to keep pressing home the idea that Domain was in charge of the situation, and MacReady was only there to carry out his wishes. As long as Domain was feeling confident and in control, he shouldn't feel the need to lash out with his magic. And then MacReady entered the room, and his words stuck in his throat.

Blood had spattered the walls and pooled on the floor. Dark footprints showed where Domain had walked unheedingly through the blood. The corpse of a young woman stood unsupported in the middle of the room, her head hanging limply to show a broken neck. Her eyes were open, but they saw nothing at all. Blood had run thickly from her nose and mouth, and dried blackly on her neck and chest. Flies buzzed around her. MacReady wondered briefly if she'd died before or after Domain lost his mind.

I'll kill her if I have to, to keep her with me.

"It's all right, darling," said Domain to the dead woman. "Don't be frightened. This is John MacReady. He's just come to talk to us. I won't let him take you away. You're safe here, with me."

The corpse walked slowly towards him, her head lolling limply from side to side. The corpse stood beside the sorcerer, and he put a comforting arm round its shoulders, and hugged it to him. MacReady smiled at them both, his face open and guileless.

"Hello, Susan; it's nice to meet you. Well, the first thing I have to do is report back to my superiors that you're alive and well, and with Domain of your own free will."

"Of course she is," said Domain. "We love each other. We're going to be married. And nothing will ever part us. Nothing . . ." His voice trailed away, and his gaze became troubled for a moment, as though reality was nudging at his mind, but the moment passed and he smiled fondly at the dead woman, animated only by his magic. "Don't worry, darling. I won't let them hurt you."

"Is there anything you want me to tell the authorities?" said MacReady carefully. The response would tell him a lot about what was going on in the madman's mind.

"Yes," said Domain flatly. "Tell them to go away and leave us alone. Susan and I will be leaving here soon. If anyone gets in our way, I'll kill them. Tell them that, John MacReady."

"Of course." MacReady bowed formally. "May I go now, sir sorcerer?"

Domain dismissed him with a wave of his hand, all his attention fixed on the dead woman at his side. Quiet music rang out on the air from nowhere, some pleasant, forgettable melody that had been popular recently. Domain took the dead woman in his arms and they danced together to music that had been their song, once.

The SWAT team had found a columned porch to shelter under, and stood huddled together in the narrow space, staring out into the rain. Hawk scowled, and shifted impatiently from foot to foot. He hated standing around doing nothing. A thought struck him, and he looked suddenly at Winter.

"If MacReady's immune to any kind of attack, why doesn't he just grab the girl and punch out Domain?"

"The charm won't let him," said Winter sharply. "If he behaves aggressively, the charm stops working. If he tried anything with Domain, he'd be dead in a second. His job is to talk to Domain, and that's all. Don't worry about it, Captain; he's very good at his job. He'll get the girl out alive if anyone can."

"Something's happening," said Fisher. "There's movement down the street."

They all turned to look. A stream of people were pouring out of a house halfway down the street and running towards the SWAT team. Some of them glanced back at Domain's house, or at the bodies lying sprawled in the rain, but for the most part the only thing in their minds was flight. Their eyes were fixed and staring, and they ran with the awkward, determined speed of desperation and sheer terror.

"They must have been caught in the street when people started dying," said Winter. "Dammit, why couldn't they have stayed in the house? Do they think it's all over, just because it's been quiet for a while?"

"You have to stop them," said Storm. "If Domain should see them . . ."

"There's nothing I can do," said Winter. "Nothing anyone can do now."

They stood together, watching the group run, hoping they'd make it to safety and knowing the odds were they wouldn't. They were close enough now for the SWAT team to hear their pounding footsteps on the broken ground, even through the rain.

"Run," said Storm quietly. "Run your hearts out, damn you."

There were seven men in the group, and three women. Hawk could just make out their faces through the rain. His breathing speeded up as he silently urged the runners on. They were closer now, only a few seconds from safety. The man in the lead faltered suddenly, frowning as though confused, and his head exploded in a flurry of blood and gore. His body stumbled on for a few more steps, and then fell twitching to the blood-slick cobbles. The woman behind him screamed shrilly, but ran on through his blood and brains. Her screams were cut off suddenly as she was jerked up off the ground and high up into the air. She clawed desperately at her throat, as though pulling at some invisible noose. Her eyes bulged, and her tongue protruded from her mouth. She fell back towards the ground, gathering speed with every second until she was falling impossibly fast. She hit the street with a sickening sound, her body crushed by the impact into something no longer human. The others kept running.

One woman just disappeared. For a moment the rain outlined an empty silhouette, and then there was a flat, popping sound as air rushed in to fill the space where she'd been. Two men collapsed and fell screaming to the cobbles. Their bodies melted and ran away in the rain, leaving nothing behind. Their screams seemed to echo on the air long after they'd gone. The five surviving runners suddenly stumbled to a halt, four men and a woman soaked to the skin by the pouring rain. They looked at each other, and started laughing. They stood together in the rain, their faces blank and their eyes empty, and laughed their minds away.

Hawk beat at one of the portico's columns with his fist. Fisher was cursing in a flat, angry whisper. Storm had looked away, but Winter watched the scene before her with a cold, detached professionalism. Barber was still watching Domain's house at the end of the street. The front door opened, and MacReady stepped out into the rain. He pulled the hood of his cloak well forward and walked unhurriedly back up the street, stepping carefully to avoid the pools of blood. He gave the laughing group a wide berth, but they didn't even know he was there. Hawk looked at Storm.

"Wasn't there anything you could have done to protect them?"

"No," said Winter. "There wasn't. Domain mustn't know about Storm yet. He's our ace in the hole, in case we have to end this siege the hard way. How many times do I have to say it, Captain Hawk? Our responsibility is to the city, not individuals. Compared to the hundreds Domain could kill if we don't stop him, those few people were expendable. They should have stayed where they were. There's no room in a SWAT team for sentiment, Captain; we have to take the long view."

"Is it all right if I feel sorry for the poor bastards?" said Fisher tightly.

"Of course. As long as it doesn't get in the way of the job."

The SWAT team watched in silence as MacReady made his way through the rain to join them. He stepped into the porticoed shelter, shook himself briskly, then looked at Winter and shook his head.

"How bad is it?" said Winter.

"About as bad as it could be. Susan Wallinger is dead. Domain has animated her corpse, and talks to it as if it were alive. He's quite mad. There's no way I can reach him with logic or promises. I hate it when they're mad. Takes all the fun out of it. I was really looking forward to rescuing the girl." He looked back at Domain's house. "Bastard."

"What's the present situation?" said Winter, ignoring his bad temper.

MacReady sniffed and shrugged. "At the moment I'm supposed to be negotiating a safe passage for Domain and Susan to leave the city. But you can forget that. In his present condition he's too dangerous to be allowed to run loose, even if we were leading him into a trap. He could lash out at anyone or anything, for any reason. In his madness he's tapping into levels of power that would normally be far beyond him. As long as we've got him bottled up here, there's a limit to the damage he can do."

"So we're going to take him out," said Barber, showing an interest in the proceedings for the first time. "Good. I haven't killed a sorcerer in ages."

Storm gave him a sideways look but said nothing. Hawk coughed loudly, to get everyone's attention.

"I think we can safely assume that the time for negotiations has passed. From the sound of it, Domain very definitely doesn't have both his oars in the water anymore. So what's the procedure, Winter? Do we just burst in under Storm's protection and kill Domain?"

"Not exactly," said Winter. "You and Fisher will go in first, making as much noise as possible, and hold Domain's attention while Barber sneaks in the back and cuts him down from behind. Not very sporting, I'll admit, but I'm not taking any chances with this one. He could do a lot of damage before we take him down. So please; no heroics, from anyone. If you screw up on this, you won't be the only ones to suffer."

"Wait a minute," said Fisher, frowning. "What can go wrong? I thought Storm was going to protect us against Domain's magic?"

"I can protect you from any direct magical attack," said Storm quickly, "but Domain's a very versatile sorcerer. He'll almost certainly animate the bodies of those he killed and use them to defend himself. He might even animate the physical structure of the house itself. I can't protect you from things like that without dropping the wards that protect you from his magic."

"Relax," said Fisher. "We can look after ourselves."

"I'm sure you can," said Winter. "After all, you're the infamous Hawk and Fisher, aren't you? If you're as good as your reputation, this should be a walk in the park for you."

Hawk smiled coldly. "We're not as good as our reputation. We're better."

"Then this is your chance to prove it."

Fisher glared at Winter, her hand resting on her sword hilt. Hawk drew his axe. Barber stirred, and moved a little closer to Winter. The atmosphere on the crowded porch was suddenly uncomfortably tense. Hawk smiled coldly at Winter, and looked across at Barber.

"I don't suppose you've any of those incendiaries left?"

"Sorry. They were only experimental prototypes, and I used them all in Hell Wing."

"Got anything else we could use?"

Barber shrugged. "Nothing you could learn to use quickly, and like Winter said, we're pushed for time. You just go in there and do what you're good at; hit anything that moves. I'll be around, even if you can't see me. Now let's go, before Domain figures out he's not going to get what he's waiting for."

Hawk nodded, pulled his hood up over his head and stepped out into the rain. Fisher gave Winter one last glare, and hurried after him. She sniffed loudly.

"Walk in the park," she growled to Hawk. "Has she seen the park lately?"

They strode down the middle of the street, not bothering to hide themselves. Domain would know they were coming. They avoided the laughing victims, staring sightlessly ahead as the rain ran down their contorted faces like tears. They stepped carefully over and around the dead bodies, and Hawk gripped his axe tightly. He looked constantly around him, but there was no sign of movement anywhere in the street, and the roar of the rain cut off every other sound. The first he and Isobel would know about any attack was when it hit them.

Hawk and Fisher were almost halfway down the street when the sky opened up. Lightning stabbed down, dazzling them both with its glare. The cobbled street split open under the bolt's impact, sending Hawk and Fisher staggering sideways as the ground heaved beneath them, but the lightning didn't even come close to touching them. Hawk broke into a run, with Fisher right beside him. Storm's magic might be able to protect them as thoroughly as MacReady's charm had protected him, but Hawk didn't feel like putting it to the test. Domain's house loomed up before them, strange lights glowing at its windows. Hawk kicked in the front door, and they darted into the hallway while lightning flared impotently in the street outside. Hawk slammed the door shut behind them, and put his back against it.

They stood together a moment, getting their breath back and staring round the gloomy hall. Hawk pointed at the stairs, and Fisher nodded. They moved forward silently and took the steps one at a time, checking for booby traps and keeping a careful watch on the dark shadows around them. They'd barely reached the halfway mark when the front door slammed open behind them. Hawk and Fisher looked back, blades at the ready. A dead man stood in the doorway, rain running down its face and trickling across its unblinking eyes.

Hawk ran back down the stairs and threw himself at the lich. His axe flashed briefly as he buried it in the lich's chest. The dead man staggered back under the impact, but didn't fall. It reached for Hawk with clutching hands, its colorless lips stretching slowly in another man's smile. Domain's smile. Hawk wrenched his axe free and struck at the lich again, this time aiming for the hip. The impact drove the lich to the ground this time, and Hawk bent over it. He pressed a boot on its chest to hold it down, and jerked the axehead free. The lich grabbed his ankle with a pale hand, the dead fingers closing like a vise. Hawk grimaced as pain shot up his leg, and swung his axe with both hands. The heavy axehead tore through the lich's throat and sank into the cobbles beneath. The dead hand's hold tightened, and Hawk had to grit his teeth to keep from crying out. He used the axe as a lever and tore the lich's head from its body. The head rolled away into the rain, its mouth working soundlessly. The grip on Hawk's ankle didn't loosen, and the body heaved beneath his foot as it tried to rise again.

Fisher was suddenly at his side, and her sword sliced through the lich's wrist, severing the gripping hand. Hawk staggered back, and between them, he and Fisher pried the hand from his ankle. It fell away into the street, its fingers still flexing angrily, like a huge fleshy spider. The headless body heaved itself up onto its knees. Fisher moved in behind it, and cut through its leg muscles. More dark shadows appeared in the rain, heading towards Hawk and Fisher with fixed eyes and reaching hands.

Hawk cursed quickly and darted back through the open front door. Fisher glared at the approaching liches, and then hurried into the house after him. The dead moved purposefully forward. Hawk pushed the door shut and slammed the bolts home. There were only two, and neither of them looked particularly sturdy. Hawk looked quickly about him.

"I wonder if there's a back door to this place?"

Fisher raised an eyebrow. "Are you suggesting we make a run for it?"

"The thought had occurred to me. I don't like the situation, and I definitely don't like the odds."

"It's going to make a bad impression on the SWAT team if we run away."

"It'd make an even worse impression if we got killed." Hawk scowled. "But you're right. We can't leave. We've got to hold Domain's attention until Barber can get to him. Or there's no telling how many more Domain might kill."

"So what's the plan?" said Fisher. "Make a stand here, and hope we can hold off the liches until Barber makes his move?"

"To hell with that," said Hawk. "There's too many of the damn things, and if they're all as determined as that first one, they're going to take a lot of stopping. All it needs is for one of them to get in a lucky blow, and we could be in real trouble. We can't even keep them out of the house. That door won't last five minutes against a determined assault. I've got a better idea. Let's head up those stairs, find Domain, and cut him into little pieces. That should hold his attention."

"Sounds good to me," said Fisher. "Assuming Storm's protection holds up under attack at such close quarters."

"Would you rather face the liches?" asked Hawk.

"Good point," said Fisher. "Let's go."

A headless body lurched out of the room to their left, reaching for them with blindly grasping hands. Hawk and Fisher separated, and hit it from different sides. Hawk slammed his axe into the lich's ribs, throwing the dead thing back against the wall. Fisher's sword licked out and sliced through the back of the lich's left leg, and the creature sank to one knee. Hawk pulled his axe free, and swung it with both hands. The heavy blade all but severed the lich's right leg below the knee, and the dead man sprawled helplessly on the floor. Hawk indicated the stairs with a jerk of his head, and Fisher nodded quickly. Hawk kicked the headless body aside, and ran for the stairs with Fisher right beside him. Behind them, the lich scrabbled furiously on the floor, trying to pull itself after them with its arms. The front door shuddered suddenly in its frame as dead fists hammered on it. A window shattered somewhere close at hand. Hawk and Fisher pounded up the stairs, and didn't look back.

Barber made his way unhurriedly down the rain-swept street, and neither the living nor the dead saw him pass. He carried his sword at the ready, but he didn't expect to have to use it yet. No one knew he was there, and no one would, until he'd thrust his sword into Domain's back and put an end to all this nonsense. In the end, as in so many SWAT operations, it all came down to him and his sword. Storm could cast his spells, and MacReady could talk, and Winter could plot her strategies, but in the end they always turned to him and his sword. Which was why he stayed with them. He needed to kill just as much as they needed him to put an end to killers.

Not that he enjoyed the killing; he took no pleasure in death or suffering. It was simply that he was so very good at what he did, and he took a real satisfaction in doing a difficult job that no-one else could do, and doing it superbly. He didn't care who he killed; he barely remembered their faces, let alone their names. He didn't even care what they'd done; their various crimes or outrages were of no interest to him. All that mattered was the opportunity to kill; to kill with a style and expertise that no one else could match.

And the Council actually paid him to do it.

He drifted down the street, unseen and unheard, and made his way round to the rear of Domain's house, searching for the back door. The door stuck when he tried it, but it swung open easily enough when he put his shoulder to it. He stepped into the gloom, wary but unconcerned, and pushed the door shut behind him. He wasn't expecting any trouble. When he was working, no one could see or hear him, unless he wanted them to. A useful talent for an assassin.

Domain would never even know what hit him.

Hawk and Fisher were only halfway up the stairs when the front door burst open, and dead things spilled into the hall. Hawk pressed on, heading for the narrow landing with Fisher only a step or so behind him. The stairs suddenly lurched and heaved beneath them like a ship at sea, and they had to fight to keep their balance. Jagged mouths and staring eyes formed in the wall beside them. The wooden panelling steamed and bubbled. Hawk moved to the middle of the stairs, away from the manifestations, and glanced back over his shoulder. The first of the dead had reached the stairs. The hall was full of liches, soaked and dripping with rainwater that couldn't entirely wash away the blood from their wounds, their empty eyes fixed unwaveringly on the two Guards.

The stairs lurched again, and Hawk grabbed at the banister to steady himself. It writhed under his hand like a huge worm; all cold and slimy and raised segments. Hawk snarled and snatched his hand away, and plunged forward, heading for the landing. Fisher called out behind him, and he looked back to see her struggling to pull her foot free from a step that had turned to bottomless mud. She cut at the step with her sword, but the blade swept through the thick mud and out again without even slowing. Hawk grabbed her arm and pulled hard, and her foot came free with a slow, sucking sound. They threw themselves forward and out onto the landing, and ran towards the door MacReady had described in his briefing.

Blood ran down the wall in thick streams, and a dirty yellow mist curled and twisted on the air, hot and acrid. Jagged holes appeared in the floor beneath their feet, falling away forever. Hawk and Fisher jumped over them without slowing. Behind them, something large and awful began to form out of the shadows. The air was suddenly full of the stench of decaying meat and freshly spilled blood, and something giggled softly in anticipation. Hawk and Fisher reached Domain's door and Fisher kicked it open. They ran into the room, and Hawk slammed the door shut behind them.

Everything seemed still and calm and quiet in the comfortable, cosy little room. For a moment it seemed almost a sanctuary from the madness running loose in the house, until Hawk took in the blood splashed across the wall and floor, and the dead woman standing beside the seated sorcerer, one hand resting on his shoulder. Hawk met Domain's gaze, and knew the real madness was right there in the room with him, held at bay only by Storm's protection. Outside in the hallway, heavy footsteps moved slowly closer, the floor trembling slightly with each impact. Fisher glanced back at the door.

"Call it off, Domain," she said harshly.

"Or what? Do you really think you can do anything to threaten me?" Domain smiled, the same smile Hawk had seen on the faces of the dead men. "This is my house, and I don't want you here. You've come to take Susan away from me."

"That's why you have to stop whatever's out there," said Hawk quickly. "If it comes in here after us, Susan could get hurt. Couldn't she?"

Domain nodded reluctantly, and there was a sudden silence as the heavy footsteps stopped, followed by a small clap of thunder as air rushed in to fill a gap where something large had been only a moment before. The sorcerer leaned back in his chair as though it were a throne, and looked crossly at Hawk and Fisher.

"I thought I'd made it clear I didn't want to be disturbed. How many people do I have to kill to make you leave us alone?"

"We don't want you to kill anyone," said Hawk. "That's why we're here."

Domain made a dismissive gesture, as though he'd caught them in an obvious lie. "I know why you're here. Perhaps if I changed you into something amusing, and sent you back that way, then they'd understand not to play games with me."

"You can't hurt us," said Fisher. "We're protected."

Domain looked at her narrowly, and then at Hawk. "So you are. A very sophisticated defence, too. I could break it, but that would take too much out of me. I have to keep something back to protect Susan. So unless you're stupid enough to attack me, I'll just wait, and let the things I've called up come and take you." He scowled suddenly. "I should have known I couldn't depend on the city to bargain in good faith. I'll punish them for this. I'll turn their precious city into a nightmare they'll never forget."

In the corners of the room, the shadows grew darker. A presence was gathering in the room, something huge and awful pressing against the walls of reality. And beyond that, Hawk could hear dead feet ascending the stairs and making their way onto the landing. The dead woman standing beside Domain's chair smiled emptily at nothing, like a hostess waiting to greet expected guests. Hawk and Fisher looked desperately at each other, but saw no answer in each other's faces. The presence growing in the shadows was almost overpowering, and the dead were almost outside the door.

"Don't worry, Susan," said Domain comfortingly to the dead woman. "It'll all be over soon, and then we'll be together, forever. No one's ever going to take you away from me."

The door swung silently open, and Barber eased into the room, his sword at the ready. Hawk and Fisher looked quickly away, to avoid drawing Domain's attention to him. They'd been briefed on Barber's special talent, but it was still hard to believe Domain couldn't see him. Barber moved slowly forward across the room, making no more noise than a breath of air. Hawk found he was holding his breath. The sorcerer smiled at his dead love, unconcerned. Barber moved in behind Domain and raised his sword. And then Domain raised his left hand. Light flared briefly around the upraised fingers, and Barber froze where he was, unable to move. Domain turned unhurriedly in his chair to look at him.

"Did you really think you could break into my house, and I wouldn't know? There's a power in me, assassin, a power beyond your worst nightmares, and it's more than enough to see through your simple glamour. I knew the city would send someone like you. They want to take my love away from me. I won't let them. I'll destroy this whole stinking city first!"

He gestured sharply, and Barber flew across the room to crash into the opposite wall. He slid to the floor, only half conscious but still somehow hanging onto his sword. Footsteps clumped heavily in the hallway outside, and Domain smiled broadly as the dead spilled into the room. Fisher raised her sword and went to meet them. Hawk lifted his axe and threw it in one swift motion, with all his strength behind it. The axe flew through the air and buried itself to the haft in Susan's skull. The impact slammed the dead woman backwards, and she staggered clumsily in a circle. Domain screamed, and jumped out of his chair to grab her by the arms. He howled wordlessly in horror and despair, and the dead woman crumpled limply to the floor, no longer sustained by the sorcerer's will. Domain sank to his knees beside her, and started to cry. The dead men in the doorway fell to the floor and lay still, and the invading presence was suddenly gone. The room seemed somehow lighter, and the shadows were only shadows. The only sound in the small, unexceptional room were the anguished sobs of a heartbroken young man crying for his lost love.

Fisher lowered her sword, and nodded to Hawk. "Nice thinking. Even he couldn't believe she was still alive with an axe buried between her eyes."

"Right. He's no danger anymore. Poor bastard. Though I think we'd better get Storm in here as soon as possible, just in case." He shook his head slowly. "What a mess. So many dead, and all for love."

"I'm fine, thank you," said Barber, getting slowly and painfully to his feet.

Hawk turned and grinned at him. "Next time, try not to make so much noise."

Barber just looked at him.

The beggars sat clustered together outside the main gate of Champion House, lined up ten or twelve deep in places. They were of all ages, from babes to ancients, and wore only the barest rags and scraps of clothing, the better to show off their various diseases and deformities. Some were clearly on the edge of starvation, little more than skin stretched over bone, while others lacked legs or hands or eyes. The rain poured down upon their bare heads, but they paid it no attention. It was the least of their troubles. Some wore the vestiges of army uniforms, complete with faded campaign ribbons. They stood out from the others, in that they seemed to have a little pride left. If they were lucky, they'd soon lose it. It just made being a beggar that much harder.

The beggars huddled together, as much for company as comfort, their eyes fixed on the main gate, waiting patiently for someone to go in or out. The honour guards supplied by the Brotherhood of Steel for the two Kings' protection stared out over the beggars, ignoring them completely. They posed no threat to the House's security, as long as they continued to keep a respectable distance, and were therefore of no interest. The beggars sat together in the rain, heads bowed, and among them sat Wulf Saxon.

He watched the main gate carefully, from beneath lowered brows. He'd been there almost two hours, shivering in the damp and the cold, and had put together a pretty good picture of the House's outer security system. The honour guards were everywhere, watching all the entrances and checking everyone's credentials carefully before allowing them to enter. They took their time and didn't allow anyone to hurry them, no matter how important-seeming or obviously aristocratic the applicant might be. The Brotherhood of Steel trained its people well. Saxon frowned, thinking his way unhurriedly through the problem. There had to be magical protections around the House as well, which suggested that the successful applicants had been issued charms of some kind which allowed them to enter the grounds without setting off the alarms. He'd have to acquire one. After he found a way in.

He hugged his knees to his chest, and ignored the rain trickling down his face with proper beggarlike indifference. He'd suffered worse discomfort in his early career as a confidence trickster, before he discovered politics. Though there were those who'd claimed he'd just graduated from the smaller arena to the large. He smiled to himself, and his fingers drifted casually over his left trouser leg, pressing against the long leather canister strapped to his shin. The baggy trousers hid it from view, but he liked to remind himself of its presence now and again. It helped fuel his anger. The contents of the canister would be his revenge against the two Kings. The first of many blows against the heartless and corrupt authorities who'd made Haven the hellhole it was and kept it that way because it suited their interests to do so. He was going to hurt them, hurt them all in the ways that would hurt them the most, until finally his vengeance forced them to make reforms, for fear of what he'd do next.

He made himself concentrate on the problem at hand, and reluctantly decided against a frontal assault. No matter how good his disguise, or how persuasive his arguments, there were just too many guards at the main gate and too many ways for things to go wrong. Not to mention too many witnesses. Fouling up in public would destroy his reputation before he even had a chance to re-establish it. And there was still the problem of the House's protective wards. He wasn't going to get anywhere without the right charms. Saxon shrugged. Fate would provide, or she wouldn't. He tended to prefer simple plans, whenever possible, mainly because they allowed more room for improvisation if circumstances suddenly changed. Though he could be as obscure and devious as the next man, when he felt like it. The more intricate schemes appealed to his creative nature, if not his better judgement.

He rose to his feet and stumbled off through the crowd of beggars, his head carefully bowed, his whole attitude one of utter dejection. No one looked at him. Beggars tended to be invisible, except when they got under people's feet. Saxon made his way into a nearby dark alley, listened for a long moment to be sure he was alone, and then straightened up with a low sigh of relief. All that bowing his head and hunching over was doing his back no good at all. He stepped briskly over to the nearest drainpipe, took a firm grip, and climbed up onto the roof. The pipe creaked threateningly under his weight, but he knew it would hold. He'd checked it out earlier, just to be on the safe side. He pulled himself up over the guttering and onto the sloping roof in one easy motion, so quietly he didn't even disturb a dozing pigeon in the eaves. He padded softly over the rain-slick slates to the far edge of the roof, and jumped easily onto the adjoining roof. The gap was only a few feet, and he didn't look down. The length of the drop would only have worried him; he was better off not knowing. He crossed two more roofs in the same fashion, and crouched down on the edge of the final roof, a ragged gargoyle in the driving rain. A narrow alley was all that separated him from Champion House.

The wall surrounding the grounds stared aggressively back at him: ten feet of featureless stone topped with iron spikes and a generous scattering of broken glass. A single narrow gate looked out onto the alley, a tradesman's entrance manned by two large, professional-looking men-at-arms. They both wore chain mail, and had long, businesslike swords on their hips. Saxon had spotted the gate on his first reconnoitre, and had marked it down in his memory as a definite possibility. Tradesmen had been in and out of Champion House all morning, bringing extra supplies for the new guests and their entourages. At the moment, a large confectioner's cart was parked at the end of the alley, and a stream of white-coated staff were carrying covered trays past the men-at-arms. Saxon grinned. Perfect. The confectioner hadn't even questioned the unexpected order when Saxon delivered it to him, clad in his most impressive-looking footman's outfit. Of course, it had helped that the order had been written on engraved notepaper bearing the Champion House crest. Saxon believed in getting all the details right.

He was just grateful he'd had the foresight to store all his con man's props in his secret lock-up all those years ago. Actually, it hadn't really been foresight. He just hadn't wanted to take a chance on any of them turning up unexpectedly to embarrass him after he'd become an eminently respectable Councillor. . . .

And he never could bear to throw anything away.

He slid silently over the edge of the roof, and padded quickly down the fire escape, the few unavoidable sounds drowned out by the pounding rain. He stood very still in the shadows, under the fire escape, and waited patiently for just the right moment. A white-coated confectioner's assistant came out of the side gate with his hands in his pockets, and headed unhurriedly for the cart at the end of the alley. He passed by the fire escape, whistling tunelessly, and two strong hands shot out of nowhere and dragged him into the shadows.

Saxon emerged from the shadows a few moments later wearing a white coat, and headed for the confectioner's cart. The coat fit like a tent, but you couldn't have everything. More's the pity. At the cart, a harried-looking supervisor handed him down a covered tray, and Saxon balanced it on his shoulder as he'd seen the others do. He kept his face carefully averted, but the supervisor was too busy to notice anyway.

"Get a move on," he growled to Saxon, without looking up from the list he was checking. "We're way behind schedule, and if the boss chews on my arse because we got back late, you can bet I'm going to chew on yours. And don't think I didn't spot you sloping off to lounge about behind the fire escape. You pull that again, and I'll have your guts for garters. Well, don't just stand there; get the hell out of here! If those pastries are ruined, it's coming out of your wages, not mine!"

Saxon grunted something vaguely placating, and headed for the side gate. The men-at-arms didn't even look at him, just at the white coat. Saxon timed his pace carefully, not too slow and not too hurried, and tucked his chin down against his chest, as though trying to keep the rain out of his face. As he neared the gate, one of the men-at-arms stirred suddenly, and Saxon's heart jumped.

"Stay on the path," said the man-at-arms in a bored monotone, as though he'd said it before many times, and knew he'd have to say it a great many more times before the day was over. "As long as you stay on the path the alarms won't go off. If you do set off an alarm, stay where you are till someone comes to get you."

Saxon grunted again, and passed between the two men-at-arms. He braced himself for a last-minute shout or blow, but nothing happened. He strode quickly along the gravel path, speeding up his pace as much as he dared. The path led him through the wide-open grounds to a door at the rear of the House. He followed slow-moving white coats into the kitchens, put down his tray with the others, and leaned against a wall to get his breath back and wipe the rain from his face, surreptitiously taking in the scene as he did so. The kitchen was bigger than some houses he'd known, with ovens and grills on all sides, and a single massive table in the middle of everything, holding enough food to feed a medium-sized army. The air was full of steam and the smells of cooking, and a small battalion of servants bustled noisily back and forth, shouted at impartially by the three senior cooks. A single guard was leaning easily against the far door, gnawing on a pork rib and chatting amiably with a grinning servant girl. Saxon smiled. Just what the doctor ordered. He headed straight for the guard, oozing confidence and purpose, as though he had every right to be there, and people hurried to get out of his way. He came to

a halt before the guard and coughed meaningfully. The guard
looked at him.

"Yeah? You want something?"

"Through here," said Saxon crisply. "You'd better take a
look at this."

He pushed open the door behind the guard, stepped through,
and held the door open for the guard to follow him. The guard
shrugged, and smiled at the servant girl. "Don't you move,
little darling. I'll be back before you know it. And don't talk
to any strange men. That's my job." He stepped out into the
corridor, and Saxon pulled the door shut behind him. The guard
glared at him. "This had better be important."

"Oh, it is," said Saxon. "You have no idea." He looked
quickly around to be sure no one was looking, then briskly
kneed the guard in the groin. The guard's eyes bulged, and he
bent slowly forward. His mouth worked as he tried to force
out a scream and couldn't. Saxon took him in a basic but
very efficient stranglehold, and a few seconds later lowered
the unconscious body to the floor. It was good to know he
hadn't lost his touch. He dragged the body over to a cupboard
he'd spotted, and yanked it open. From now on, speed was of
the essence. Anyone could come along, at any moment. The
cupboard proved big enough to take both of them easily, and
he took the opportunity to change his white coat and beggar's
rags for the guard's honour outfit and chain mail. Leaving the
door open a crack provided all the light he needed. The mail
fit tightly in all the most uncomfortable places, but it would do.
He kicked the guard spitefully for being the wrong size, and
strapped the man's sword to his own hip. He wished briefly for
a mirror, and then pushed open the cupboard door and stepped
out into the corridor. A passing servant stopped in his tracks
and stared blankly at Saxon.

"Excuse me . . . this is probably a silly question, but what
were you doing in the cupboard?"

"Security," said Saxon darkly, closing the door. "You can't
be too careful."

He met the servant's gaze without flinching, and the man
decided to continue about his business and not ask any more
stupid questions. Saxon grinned at the servant's departing
back. It was his experience that people will believe practically anything you care to tell them, as long as you say it

firmly enough. He fingered the bone medallion he'd found on the guard, and which was now hanging round his own neck. Presumably this was the charm that protected the guard against the House's protective wards. With it, he should be able to go anywhere he wanted. Of course, if it wasn't the charm, or the right charm, he was about to find out the hard way. He shrugged. Whatever happened, he'd think of something. He always did.

He strode leisurely through the House as though he belonged there, nodding to people as they passed. They nodded back automatically, seeing only his uniform, sure he must have a good reason for being where he was. Saxon smiled inwardly, and studied his surroundings without seeming to do so. Everywhere he looked there was luxury, in the thick carpets and antique furniture, and the portraits and tapestries covering the walls. And so much space. He remembered the single room where his sister now lived, and his fury burned in him.

He had to find the two Kings. He needed to see them, study their faces, look into their eyes. He wanted to know the people he was going to destroy. There was no satisfaction in taking vengeance on faceless people, on titles and positions rather than individuals. He wanted this first act of revenge to be entirely personal. He stepped out of a side corridor into a high-ceiling hall, and stopped to get his bearings. Servants scurried back and forth around him, intent on their various missions. He couldn't just stand around watching without appearing conspicuous. So, when in doubt, be direct. Saxon stepped deliberately in front of a hurrying footman, and gave the man his best intimidating scowl.

"You; where are the Kings?"

"Fourth floor, in the main parlour, sir. Where they've been for the past two hours."

There had been more than a hint of insolence in the footman's tone, so Saxon cranked up his scowl another notch. "And how do you know I'm not some terrorist spy? Do you normally give away vital information to the first person who walks up to you and asks? Shape up, man! And stay alert. The enemy could be anywhere."

Saxon stalked off in the direction of the stairs, leaving a thoroughly confused and worried footman behind him. He threaded his way through the bustling crowd, nodding briskly to the few guards he passed. He'd almost reached the stairs when a guard officer appeared out of nowhere right in front of him, and he had to stop or run the man down. The officer glared at him, and Saxon remembered just in time to salute him. The officer grunted and returned the salute.

"What the hell do you think you're doing, appearing on duty looking like that? Your uniform's a disgrace, your chain mail looks like it was made for a deformed dwarf, and that was the sloppiest damn salute I've ever seen. What's your name and your unit?"

Oh, hell, thought Saxon wearily. *I don't need this. I really don't.*

He glanced quickly around to be sure no one was looking and then gave the officer a vicious punch well below the belt. All the color drained out of the officer's face, and his legs buckled. Saxon grabbed him before he fell and quickly walked him across the hall and back into the side corridor. He shook his head woefully at a passing guest.

"Don't touch the shellfish."

The guest blinked, and hurried on his way. Saxon waited a moment till the corridor was deserted, and then knocked the officer out with a crisp blow to the jaw. It was only a matter of a few seconds to stuff him into the cupboard along with the first guard. He considered for a moment whether to swap his outfit for the officer's, but decided against it. Officers tended to stand out; the rank and file drew less notice. He hurried back down the corridor into the hall, and ran straight into another officer. This time he remembered to salute. The new officer returned it absent-mindedly.

"I'm looking for Major Tiernan. Have you seen him?"

"No, sir. Haven't seen him all day."

"What do you mean, you haven't seen him all day? This is your commanding officer we're talking about! What's your name and unit?"

Oh, hell.

"If you'll follow me, sir, I think I can take you right to the Major."

Back in the side corridor, Saxon finished stuffing the unconscious officer into the cupboard, and forced the door shut. He'd better not run into any more officers, or he'd have to find another cupboard. He set off again at a brisk walk, with a very determined expression that he hoped suggested he was going somewhere very important and shouldn't be detained. He flexed the fingers of his right hand thoughtfully. There was one thing to be said for his new strength: when he hit someone they stayed hit. He doubted the two officers and the guard would be waking up for a good few hours yet. More than enough time for him to take his vengeance on the two Kings and depart.

The main parlour turned out to be full of people trying to look important. The two Kings sat in state at the back of the room, surrounded by an ever-shifting mob of courtiers, local Quality, and guards. Any assassin trying to get close to the monarach's would probably have been trampled underfoot in the crush long before he got anywhere near his targets. Politicians and military mixed more or less amicably around the punch bowl, while merchants and nouveau riche Quality hovered desperately on the edges of conversations, angling hopefully for introductions to the right people. Polite conversation provided a steady roar of noise, easily drowning out the string quartet murdering a classical piece in the corner. No one even noticed Saxon's entrance. He took up a position by the door, not too far from the buffet table, and studied the layout of the room. No one paid him any attention. He was just another guard.

He watched the two Kings for a time. They didn't look like much. Take away their crowns and their gorgeous robes of state, and you wouldn't look at them twice in a crowd. But those two men, both in their late forties, were symbols of their countries and the Parliaments that governed them. A blow struck against them would be heard across the world. But of even more importance was the Peace Treaty, standing on display in a simple glass case between the two Kings.

There were two copies of the Treaty, standing side by side under the glass; one for each Parliament. Two sheets of pale-cream parchment covered with the very best copperplate calligraphy, awaiting only the Kings' signatures to make them law. Saxon smiled slowly. He flexed his leg, and felt the leather canister press against his bare skin. Inside the canister were two sheets of pale-cream parchment, carefully rolled, and protected by padding. From a distance, they looked exactly like the Treaty. And once Saxon had swapped them for the real

Treaty, no one would be able to tell the difference. At least, not until it was far too late.

Saxon had put a great deal of thought into his first act of vengeance. It wasn't enough just to hurt those in authority; they had to be publicly humiliated. His two sheets of parchment were covered with copperplate calligraphy, but a minor avoidance spell which Saxon had purchased from the son of one of his old contacts would ensure that no one studied the text too closely. The spell was too subtle and too minor to set off any security alarms and would fade away completely in a matter of hours anyway, but by then the damage would have been done. Both the Kings would have put their signatures, and thereby their Parliaments' approval, to a Treaty that declared the authorities of both countries to be corrupt, incompetent, and complete and utter bastards without a single trace of human feeling. The text went on like that for some time, in increasingly lengthy and insulting detail. Saxon had written it himself in a fury of white-hot inspiration, and was rather proud of it.

And the Kings were going to sign it. Right there in public, with everyone watching. They'd never live it down. When word got out, as it inevitably would, as to exactly what they'd put their names to, a shock wave of incredulous laughter would wash across Outremer and the Low Kingdoms. The more the authorities tried to suppress and deny the story, the more people would flock to read or listen to pirated copies of the false Treaty, and the wider the story would spread. The first part of Saxon's vengeance would have begun. More practical jokes and humiliations would follow, and no one would be safe from ridicule. Powers that would stand firm against intrigue and violence were helpless when it came to defending themselves against derisive laughter. It's hard to be scared of someone when their very appearence is enough to start you giggling. Saxon's grin broadened. After today, both the Kings and their Parliaments were going to be laughingstocks.

He looked around one last time, and let his hands drift casually into his trouser pockets, reaching for the smoke bombs he'd put there. One to go into the open fire, and the second for an emergency exit, if necessary. Under cover of the smoke and chaos, and while the security people were busy protecting the Kings from any attack, it would be child's play for him to open the glass case and make the substitution. The real parchments would disappear into his leather canister, and it would all be over before the smoke cleared. And afterwards it should be easy enough for a single guard to disappear in all the confusion.

It was a superb plan; simple but elegant. Nothing could go wrong.

Daniel Madigan stood openly in the street under a rain avoidance spell, watching Champion House from the middle of a crowd of onlookers waiting patiently for a glimpse of the two Kings. Horn and Eleanour Todd stood on either side of him, watching the crowd. Just in case. The young killer Ellis Glen stood beside Todd, shifting impatiently from foot to foot. They'd been watching the House for the best part of an hour, waiting for a signal from the traitors inside the House. The signal would tell them that the protective wards had been temporarily lowered, and then the fun could begin. But until then, they could only wait and watch. Even with the sorcerer shaman Ritenour working for him, Madigan wasn't prepared to take on the kind of magical defences the Kings' sorcerers would have set up. He hadn't made his reputation by being stupid. Or impatient.

Ritenour himself stood a little away from his new associates. Their constant aura of suppressed violence disturbed him. To his eyes, the House was surrounded by an ever-shifting aurora of lights and vibrations, flaring here and there with deadly intent. The magic within him stirred at the sight of it. He looked thoughtfully at the terrorists. He still wasn't sure why he was there. The more he thought about what Madigan had planned, the less tempting the money seemed. He could still leave. Ritenour had no loyalty to anyone save himself, let alone anything as nebulous as a Cause. And he didn't trust fanatics, particularly when it came to their paying their bills. But when all was said and done, he was intrigued, curious to see if Madigan could bring off his plan. And perhaps, just perhaps, he stayed with Madigan because he knew the terrorist would kill him if he tried to back out now.

"Can't keep still for a moment, can you?" said Horn to Glen, as the young man shifted his position yet again. "Like a big kid, aren't you, Alice?"

"Don't call me that," said Glen. He was blushing despite himself, but his eyes were cold. "I've told you; my name is Ellis."

"That's what I said, Alice. It's a nice name; suits a good looker like you. Tell you what: you do good in there today and I'll get you a nice big bunch of flowers and a ribbon for your hair. How about that?"

"If you don't shut up, I'm going to kill you, Horn. Right here and now."

"Now, Alice, behave yourself, or I'll have to spank you."

Glen's hand dropped to the sword at his side, and Todd glanced at Horn. "That's enough. Leave the boy alone."

Glen shot her a look of almost puppyish adoration and gratitude, and looked away. Horn chuckled.

"I think he fancies you, Eleanour. Isn't that nice? All girls together."

Todd glared at him, and Horn looked away, still chuckling. He didn't say anything more. Much as he enjoyed teasing Glen and challenging Todd's authority, he knew he could only push it so far before Madigan would step in. Horn wasn't stupid enough to upset Madigan. Over anything. He glanced surreptitiously at Eleanour Todd. Before Madigan brought her into the group, he'd been second-in-command, Madigan's voice. And if something were to happen to her, he might be again. Of course, he'd have to be very careful. If Madigan even suspected he was plotting something against another member of the group . . . The thought alone was enough to stop him chuckling, and he went back to studying the House.

Glen stared straight ahead of him, not really seeing the crowd or the House. He could feel the warmth of the betraying blush still beating in his face, and his hands had clenched into fists at his sides. The need to cut and thrust and kill was almost overpowering, but he held it back. If he let it loose too soon, Madigan would be disappointed in him, and Glen would have cut off his own hand rather than disappoint Madigan. He had turned Glen's life around, given him a Cause and a purpose. Told him that his talent for death was a skill and an asset, not something to hide or be ashamed of. Madigan understood his dark needs and bloody dreams, and had taught him to control and channel them. Now he killed only at Madigan's order, and the joy was that much sweeter.

He wondered if Eleanour had seen him blushing. He worshipped her almost as much as he did Madigan, though for different reasons. He'd kill for Madigan, but he'd die for Eleanour. She was everything he dreamed of being—a cool professional killer who stood at Madigan's right hand, his trusted support and confidante. She was also heart-stoppingly beautiful, and on the few occasions when she actually smiled at him, he walked around in a daze for minutes on end. He'd never told her how he felt, of course. He'd seen the way she looked at Madigan. But still he dreamed. And it was only in his dreams that it occurred to him that Eleanour might look more kindly on him if Madigan wasn't around any longer. . . .

Bailey strode through the crowd to rejoin his associates, and people hurried to get out of his way. His huge frame was intimidating, even when he was trying his best to be inconspicuous. Ritenour was glad to see the big man back again, even though he couldn't stand the fellow. Madigan had sent the warrior out on reconnaissance almost an hour ago, and the long wait had been wearing at everyone's nerves. Everyone except Madigan, of course. Bailey ground to a halt before Madigan, and nodded briefly.

"Everything's set. The men are all in position, awaiting your signal to begin."

"Are you sure we can trust these men?" said Ritenour. "If they let us down, or turn against us, we're dead."

"Relax, shaman," said Madigan easily. "These are professional fighting men, every one; a hundred of the very best, gathered and placed under contract outside Haven so as not to drawn unwelcome attention. We can trust them to fight and die like any other mercenary, particularly on the wages they've been promised."

"I'd have thought you'd be happier with fanatics, ready to die for their Cause."

"I don't want men who can die; I want men who can win. That's enough questions for now, shaman. We have work to do."

"If you'd take the time to fill me in on what's happening, I wouldn't have to keep asking questions."

"You know all you have to. Now be quiet. Or I'll have Bailey remonstrate with you."

Ritenour looked at the huge warrior looming over him, and decided there was nothing to be gained by pushing Madigan any further. He had to know more about the terrorists' plans if he was to know the best time to cut and run, but that could wait. He had no intention of leaving without his money, anyway, and he also had to be sure that Madigan was in no position to come after him. He gazed haughtily up at Bailey, and turned his back on him. The huge warrior chuckled quietly. Ritenour pointedly ignored him, and fixed his attention on Champion House. A light flared briefly in an upper window. There was a slight pause, and then it flashed again. Madigan nodded calmly.

"About time, Sir Roland. Bailey, give the signal. The wards are finally down, and we can proceed."

Bailey waved his hand over his head, and the mercenaries appeared from everywhere, with swords and axes in their hands. They came from among the gawking crowd, from the beggars at the main gate, and from every side street and alleyway. They were in a multitude of disguises, but all of them wore the identifying black iron torc of the mercenary on their wrist. They howled a deafening mixture of battle cries, and threw themselves at the various gates in the House's outer walls. The honour guards fought well and valiantly, but were quickly overwhelmed by the sheer number of their attackers. The mercenaries hurdled their twitching bodies and raced on into the grounds.

Madigan led his people through the panicking crowd, and approached the main gate. A small band of guards had slammed the gate in the mercenaries' faces, and were somehow still holding their ground behind the gate's heavy steel framework. Madigan looked at Ritenour, who nodded quickly. He gestured at the guards and spoke a minor Word of Power. The guards fell screaming to the ground as the blood boiled like acid in their veins. Steam rose from their twisting bodies as the acid ate holes in their flesh. Ritenour gestured again, and the gate swung open, pushing the guards' bodies out of the way. Madigan led his people through the open gate and into the grounds, smiling quietly at the chaos his mercenaries had caused.

A small army of guards and men-at-arms spilled out of the House and stared wildly about them, confused and disorientated because the security wards had failed them. The mercenaries fell upon them like starving wolves, and blades flashed dully in the rain. The air was full of screams and war cries, and blood pooled thickly on the sodden ground. Madigan cut down the first defender to get in his way with a single stroke of his sword, and passed on without slowing. Bailey strode at his side, wielding his great sword with casual, professional skill. No one could stand against his strength and skill, and only the desperate or the foolish even tried. Horn and Eleanour Todd busied themselves opening up a bloody path for Madigan to walk through. Glen fought where he would, cutting down opponents as fast as he could reach them. His face was wild and horribly happy, and his chain mail was thickly spattered with other men's blood. He was always in the thick of the fighting, but no one could touch him. He killed wherever his eyes fell, and it was never enough. Ritenour hurried to keep up with the others, saving his magic as much as he could. He was going to need all his power for the horrible thing Madigan wanted him to do later.

Men-at-arms and honour guards threw themselves at the advancing terrorists, and fell back dead and dying. All across the grounds the defenders were being killed or beaten back, and mercenaries were streaming into the House itself. Madigan led his people through the open front door, and into the entrance hall. He paused just long enough to congratulate the mercenaries who were guarding the door, and then led his people quickly through the panic-filled corridors, ignoring the screaming servants who scattered before the terrorists' bloody blades like startled geese. A small group of men-at-arms tried to ambush them in an open hall, and the terrorists quickly closed around Madigan to protect him. Bailey scattered the men-at-arms with wide sweeps of his great sword, and Glen and Eleanour Todd cut them down with savage efficiency. The last remaining man-at-arms tried to turn and run, and Horn disembowelled him with a casual sideways sweep of his sword. The man sank to his knees, and tried to stuff his bloody guts back into his stomach. The terrorists left him sitting there, and continued on their way. Ritenour hurried along in the rear, fighting for breath but not wanting to be left behind. Here and there the House's defenders still struggled with Madigan's mercenaries, but they were clearly outnumbered and outmatched. Blood and gore soaked the thick pile carpets and spattered the priceless tapestries.

Finally they came to the main parlour on the fourth floor, and Madigan stood for a moment in the doorway, smiling round at the terrified guests. The guards and men-at-arms in the room were all dead, the bodies left to lie where they had fallen. Twenty mercenaries surrounded the guests with drawn swords, and a small pile of mostly ceremonial swords and daggers at one side showed that the prisoners had already been disarmed. Madigan nodded approvingly, and walked unhurriedly into the room, flanked by Horn and Eleanour Todd. He stopped before the two Kings, sitting stiffly in their chairs with knives at their throats, and bowed politely. His voice was smooth and assured and only lightly mocking.

"Your Majesties, I do beg your pardon for this intrusion. Allow me to assure you that as long as you and your guests behave yourselves, there is no reason why most of you shouldn't leave this room alive. Please don't delude yourselves with any thought of rescue. My men now control this House and its surrounding grounds. Your men are dead."

"You won't get away with this!" A grey-haired General from the Outremer delegation stepped forward, ignoring the swords that moved to follow him. His uniform had been pressed within an inch of its life, and his right breast bore ribbons from a dozen major campaigns. His face was flushed with anger, and his eyes met Madigan's unflinchingly. "By now this whole area is surrounded by enough armed men to outnumber your little army a hundred times over. You don't have a hope in hell of getting out of here alive. Surrender now, and I'll see you get a fair trial."

Madigan nodded to Horn, who stepped forward and plunged his sword into the General's belly. There were muffled screams from some of the ladies, and gasps from the men. The General looked down at the sword unbelievingly. Horn twisted the blade, and blood poured down between the General's legs. He groaned softly and sank to his knees. Horn withdrew the blade, and the General fell forward onto the bloody carpet. Over by the door, Glen giggled quietly. Madigan looked calmly about him.

"I trust there'll be no more outbursts. Any further unpleasantness will be dealt with most firmly."

No one said anything. The General was breathing heavily as blood pooled around him, but no one dared approach him. Ritenour took advantage of the pause to surreptitiously study four bodies in sorcerer's black that had been dumped unceremoniously in a pile by the door. Their faces were pale, their eyes bulged unseeing from their sockets, and their lips were tinged with blue.

Poison, thought Ritenour approvingly. *No wonder the Kings' sorcerers were unable to maintain the House's wards or defend against the mercenaries' attack. Madigan's pet traitors must have doctored their wine.*

He looked up quickly as a mercenary came running into the room and whispered at length to Bailey. The big man nodded, and moved forward to murmur in Madigan's ear. The terrorist smiled and turned back to face his reluctant audience.

"You'll no doubt be relieved to hear that the authorities have been informed of your plight and negotiations for your release will soon begin. Now, I suppose you're wondering what this is all about. It's really very simple. Everyone here will be released unharmed when the authorities agree to meet my demands, which are very reasonable under the circumstances. I want one million ducats in gold and silver, carts to transport it, and a ship waiting at the docks to carry us away from Haven. I also want a number of political prisoners freed from jails in the Low Kingdoms and Outremer. A list of names and locations will be provided."

King Gregor of the Low Kingdoms leaned forward slightly, careful of the knife at his throat. His narrow, waspish features did little to hide the anger boiling within him, but when he spoke his voice was calm and even. "And if our respective Parliaments should refuse to go along with your demands; what then?"

King Louis of Outremer nodded firmly, imperiously ignoring the knife at his throat. His unremarkable face had the constant redness that comes from too much good food and drink, but his smile was unflinchingly arrogant, and his eyes were full of a cold, contemptuous fury. "They won't pay. They can't afford to give in to terrorist scum. Not even for us." His smile widened slightly. "If we'd been the Prime Ministers you might have got away with it. But our Parliaments won't pay a single penny for us, or release a single prisoner. They can't afford to look weak, or they'd end up a target for every terrorist group with a grudge or a Cause."

"I hope for your sake that you're wrong," said Madigan calmly. "If my demands are not met before the deadline I've set, I'll have no choice but to begin by killing your guests, one at a time, and sending out the bodies to convince the authorities I mean business. If that doesn't impress them, I'll start sending out pieces of your royal anatomy. I think I'll begin with the teeth. They should last a while." He looked away from the silent Kings and smiled at the assembled guests, who shrank before his cold gaze. "Do make yourselves comfortable, my friends. We're in for something of a wait, I fear, before Haven's authorities can get their scattered wits together enough to begin negotiations. Remember: as long as you behave yourselves, you'll be well treated. Annoy me, and I'll have my men hurt some of you severely, as an example to the others. And please; put all thoughts of rescue out of your minds. You're mine now."

He looked at Horn and Todd. "Take them into the adjoining rooms in small groups, and have the mercenaries search them thoroughly. I don't want anyone harbouring any nasty surprises. Strip them if necessary, and confiscate anything that even looks dangerous." He looked back at the white-faced guests. "Anyone who wishes to give up their little secrets now, to avoid any unpleasantness, is of course welcome to do so."

There was a pause, and then several men and a few of the ladies produced hidden knives and dropped them on the floor. Two mercenaries quickly gathered up the weapons and put them with the other confiscated blades. Madigan waited patiently, and one lady pulled a long hat pin from her hair and offered it to the nearest mercenary, who took it with a grin and a knowing wink. The lady ignored him. Wulf Saxon raised his hand politely. Madigan looked at him.

"If you want to visit the jakes, you'll have to wait."

"I have a document container strapped to my leg," said Saxon. "I don't want it confused for a weapon."

"Then I think we'd better have a look at it, just to be sure," said Madigan. "Drop your trousers." Saxon looked around him, and Madigan smiled. "We're all friends together here. Now take them off, or I'll have someone take them off for you."

Saxon undid his belt, and lowered his trousers with immense dignity. Madigan approached him, and prodded the leather canister with the tip of his sword. Saxon didn't flinch.

"What's in the container?" said Madigan, not looking up.

"Documents," said Saxon vaguely. "I'm a courier."

"Take it off and give it to me."

Saxon did so, as slowly as he dared. He'd hoped that by revealing the canister openly, he could bluff them into thinking it was unimportant and therefore not worth opening, but he couldn't refuse a direct order from Madigan. Not if he wanted to keep his teeth where they were. On the other hand, he couldn't afford to hand over the fake Treaties. They'd break the avoidance spell easily, once they realised what it was, and once they read the parchments they'd be bound to ask all sorts of awkward questions. And whatever happened then, his chance of vengeance would be gone. Terrorists! He'd planned for anything but that. He still had his smoke bombs, but it was a long way to the door, and the solitary double windows overlooked a hell of a long drop to the unforgiving flagstones below. Even he might not survive a fall of four stories. Besides, both the House and the grounds were apparently occupied by mercenaries. There could be a whole army out there for all he knew. And there were definite limits to his new strength and speed . . . especially with his trousers round his ankles.

He handed the leather canister over to Madigan as casually as he could. There was a way out of this. There had to be. A dozen possible stratagems ran through his mind as Madigan opened the canister, looked briefly at the parchments, and then turned the receptacle upside down and shook it, to check there was nothing else inside but the padding. He sniffed, unimpressed, and dropped the canister and parchments onto the buffet table. Saxon almost gaped at him. The terrorist obviously considered him completely harmless and unimportant. The nerve of the man! Saxon was so outraged, he almost forgot to be relieved about the parchments. He'd make the terrorist pay for this insult. He didn't know how yet, but he'd think of something. In the meantime . . . He coughed loudly.

"Excuse me, but can I pull my trousers back up?"

"Of course," said Madigan. "We're not barbarians."

Saxon pulled his pants back up, and forced the belt shut, regretting once again that he couldn't have found a larger guard to steal a uniform from. It suddenly struck him that it was only a matter of time before Madigan's people discovered the guard and the two officers he'd stuffed into the closet. And Madigan didn't look the type to suffer mysteries long. Saxon scowled mentally. The sooner he figured out a way to shake off the terrorists and disappear, the better. Not that he had any intention of leaving Champion House just yet. No one insulted him and ruined one of his scams and got away with it. He had his reputation to think of. The Kings could wait. Madigan and his terrorists were going to rue the day they ever crossed Wulf Saxon.

Ritenour found himself a comfortable chair, and gave some serious attention to the plateful of food he'd gathered from the buffet. Nothing like hard work to give you a good appetite. He offered a chicken leg to Bailey, but the big man ignored him, presumably too professional to allow himself to be distracted while on duty. Idiot. Ritenour took a healthy bite from the chicken leg, and chewed thoughtfully as he studied his fellow conspirators.

Glen was almost falling over himself trying to impress Bailey with accounts of his part in the storming of Champion House. Bailey was listening indulgently, though his gaze never left the captives. Madigan and Todd were talking quietly together. Ritenour still wasn't sure about them. Sometimes they seemed like partners, or even lovers, but at other times Madigan treated her as just another follower. Horn was watching the two of them covertly, clearly jealous of the attention Todd was getting from Madigan. Ritenour filed the thought away for future reference. It might come in handy to have something divisive to use against his new associates. They were all too eager to give everything for their precious Cause, for his liking. Ritenour had no intention of giving anything that mattered for anybody's Cause.

He thought again of what Madigan wanted him to do, down in the cellar, and the parlour seemed suddenly colder.

4

Something in the Dark

Hawk waded slowly through dark, knee-high water in the sewers under the Westside, and tried hard not to recognise some of the things that were floating on the surface. Fisher moved scowling at his side, holding her lantern high to spread the light as far as possible. She kept a careful eye on the flame. If it flickered and changed color, it meant the gases in the air were growing dangerously poisonous. There were supposed to be old spells built into the sewers to prevent the build-up of such gases, but judging by the smell, they weren't working too well. Hawk wrinkled his nose and tried to breathe only through his mouth. If the air had been any thicker, he could have cut it with his axe.

He glared about him, searching the low-ceilinged tunnel for signs of life, but everything seemed still and quiet. The only sounds came from the SWAT team splashing along behind him, and Fisher cursing monotonously under her breath. The lantern's golden light reflected back from the dark water and glistened on moisture running down the curved brick walls, but it didn't carry far down the tunnel, and the shadows it cast were lengthened and distorted by the curving brickwork. Hawk glowered unhappily, and pressed on through the filthy water and the stench. It was like moving through the bowels of the city, where all the filth and evil no one cared about ended up.

Jessica Winter plodded along just behind the two Guards, looking around her with interest. If the smell bothered her, it

121

didn't show in her face. Hawk smiled slightly. Winter wasn't the sort to admit to any weakness, no matter how trivial. Barber and MacReady brought up the rear, ploughing steadily along in Winter's wake. Barber carried his sword at the ready, and studied every side tunnel and moving shadow with dark suspicion. MacReady held the other lantern, his eyes thoughtful and far away. Nothing much bothered MacReady, but then if Storm's explanation about his charmed life was right, he didn't have much to worry about. Storm . . . Hawk scowled. While they were all up to their knees in it and gagging on the stench, the sorcerer was probably sitting in some nice dry office with his feet up, following it all with his Sight and grinning a lot. He couldn't go with them, he'd explained in a voice positively dripping with mock disappointment, because the terrorists had raised the House's defensive wards again, and no sorcerer could even approach Champion House without setting off all kinds of alarms.

Hawk's scowl deepened. The situation got more complicated every time he looked at it. The city negotiators had been talking earnestly with the terrorists from the moment they made their first demands, but so far they hadn't got anywhere. The terrorists wouldn't budge an inch in their demands, and the city Council couldn't agree to meet them because both Parliaments were still arguing over what to do. Sorcerers were working in relays passing messages back and forth across the two countries, but so far nothing had been decided. Some factions were pressing for a full-scale assault on Champion House, arguing that a powerful enough force could smash through the House's defences and reach the hostages before the terrorists even knew what was happening. Fortunately for the hostages, no one was listening to these people. Apart from the obvious danger to the two Kings, most of the hostages were extremely well-connected—socially, politically, or economically—and those connections were making it clear to both Parliaments that they would take it very badly if any kind of force was used before every other avenue had been investigated.

So the negotiators talked and got nowhere, the city men-at-arms trained endlessly for an attack they might never make, and the Brotherhood of Steel told anyone who'd listen that this insult to the honour guards they'd provided would be avenged in blood, whatever happened. It wasn't clear whether the Brotherhood was referring to the terrorists or the people who wouldn't let them send in a rescue force, and no one liked to ask. On top of all that, the city's sorcerers couldn't do a damned thing to help because the House's wards were apparently so powerful it would have taken every sorcerer in the city working together to breach them, and the terrorists had threatened to kill both Kings if the wards even looked like they were going down. Champion House was an old house, with a great deal of magic built into its walls. It had been built to withstand a siege, and that was exactly what it was doing.

The city Council listened to everyone, had a fit of the vapours, threw its collective hands in the air, and called in the SWAT team. Wild promises and open threats were made. And that was why Hawk was up to his knees in stinking water and wishing he was somewhere else. Anywhere else. A study of the House's architectural plans revealed it had been built directly over the ruins of an old slaughterhouse (the Westside hadn't always been fashionable), and supposedly there were still tunnels leading from the cellar straight into the sewers. So, theoretically it should be possible for the SWAT team to break into the cellar from the sewers without being noticed. The wards were worn thin down there, for some reason Storm didn't understand, and could be breached by a small force that had been suitably prepared.

Hawk had pressed Storm on this point, but the sorcerer had been unusually evasive. He just insisted that he could keep any alarms from going off, and that was all that mattered. And then he looked away, and said quietly that the cellar had originally belonged to another, even older building, and the slaughterhouse had been built on its ruins. He didn't know what the original building had been, but just making mental contact with the cellar had made his skin crawl. Storm didn't tell Hawk to be careful. He didn't have to. All of which hadn't exactly filled Hawk with confidence, but as Winter kept pointing out, she was the team leader, and she was determined to go in. So they went in.

Hawk studied the sewer tunnel as he trudged along, and supposed he ought to be impressed. There were said to be miles of these tunnels, winding back and forth under the better parts of the city before carrying the wastes out to sea. Of course such tunnels were expensive, which is why you only found them beneath the better parts of the city. Everyone else had to make do with crude drains, runoffs, and sinkholes. Which is why you always knew which way the downmarket areas of the city were, especially when the wind was blowing. The thought made Hawk aware of the sewer's stench again, and he made a determined effort to think about something else. He and the rest of the team had been given the House's plans and the sewers' layout as a mental overlay before they left, and he could tell they were getting close to the right area. The tunnels leading up to the cellar weren't actually marked on either set of plans, but they had to be around here somewhere.

Hawk smiled sourly. Actually, there were lots of things about the sewers that weren't on any map. Half the sorcerers and alchemists in Haven flushed their failed experiments down into the sewers, producing an unholy mixture of chemicals and forces that gave nightmares to anyone who thought about it too much. Oversized rats were the least of the unpleasant things said to prowl the sewer darkness. There were cobwebs everywhere, strung across the walls and beaded here and there with moisture. Hanging strands of slimy gossamer twitched occasionally as wafts of warm air moved through the tunnels. In places the webs became so thick they half blocked the tunnels, and Hawk had to cut his way through with his axe. Sometimes he found the remains of dead rats and tiny homunculi cocooned in the webbing, along with other things he couldn't identify, and wasn't sure he wanted to. He tried hard not to think about Crawling Jenny, or how big a spider would have to be to produce such webs.

He'd never liked spiders.

Fisher moved in close beside him, so that they could talk quietly without being overheard. "I once talked with one of the maintenance men whose job it is to clean out these tunnels twice a year. He said there wasn't enough money in the world to get him to come down here more often than that. He'd seen things, heard things. . . ."

"What sort of things?" said Hawk, casually.

Fisher moved in even closer, her voice little more than a murmur. "Once, they found a blind angel with tattered wings, from the Street of Gods. They offered to guide it out, but it wouldn't go. It said it was guilty. It wouldn't say what of. Another time, the slime on top of the water came alive and attacked them. Someone smashed a lantern against it, and it burst into flames. It rolled away into the darkness, riding on top of the water, screaming in a dozen voices. And once, they saw a spider as big as a dog, spinning a cocoon around something even larger."

"Anything else?" asked Hawk, his mouth dry.

Fisher shrugged. "There are always stories. Some say this is where all the aborted babies end up, neither living nor dead. They crawl around in the tunnels, in the dark, looking for a way out and never finding it."

"If you've got any more cheerful stories, do me a favour and keep them to yourself," said Hawk. "They're just stories. Look, we've been down here almost an hour now, and we haven't seen a damned thing so far. Not even a rat."

"Yeah," said Fisher darkly. "Suspicious, that."

Hawk sighed. "Whose stupid idea was this, anyway?"

"Yours, originally."

"Why do you listen to me?"

Fisher chuckled briefly, but didn't stop frowning. "If there aren't any rats, it can only be because something else has been preying on them." She stopped suddenly, and Hawk stopped to look at her. She cocked her head slightly to one side, listening. "Hawk, can you hear something?"

Hawk strained his ears against the quiet. The rest of the team had stopped too, and the last echoes from their progress through the water died away into whispers. The silence gathered around them like a watchful predator, waiting for them to make a mistake. Fisher held her lantern higher, her hand brushing against the tunnel roof, but the light still couldn't penetrate far into the darkness. Winter moved forward to join them.

"Why have we stopped?"

"Isobel thought she heard something ahead," said Hawk.

"I did hear something," said Fisher firmly.

Winter nodded slowly. "I've been aware of something too, just at the edge of my hearing. Sometimes I think it's behind us, sometimes out in front."

"There's something out there," said MacReady flatly. "I can feel its presence."

They all looked at him. "Any idea what it is?" asked Hawk.

"No. But it's close now. Very close."

"Great. Thanks a lot, MacReady." Hawk reached out with his mind to Storm, using the mental link the sorcerer had established with the team before they left. *Hey, Storm. You there?*

For the moment, Captain Hawk. The closer you get to the House's wards, the harder it is for me to make contact.

Can you tell what's ahead of us in the dark?

I'm sorry, Captain. My Sight is useless under these conditions. But you should all be wary. There's a lot of magic in Champion House, old magic, bad magic, and its proximity to the sewers is bound to have had unfortunate effects on whatever lives there.

A lot of help you are, sorcerer. Hawk broke the contact, and hefted his axe. "Well, we can't go back, and according to the plans, there's no other way that'll get us where we're going. So we go on. And if there *is* anything up ahead, we'd better hope it's got enough sense to stay out of our way."

"Everyone draw their weapons," said Winter crisply. "And Hawk, since you're so keen to make all the decisions, you can lead the way."

"You're so good to me," said Hawk. "Let's go, people."

He led the way forward into the dark, feeling Winter's angry look burning into his back. He didn't mean to keep undermining her position as leader, but he wasn't used to taking orders. And he couldn't wait around and keep quiet while she made up her mind. It wasn't in his nature. Fisher waded along beside him, holding her lantern in one hand and her sword in the other. The rest of the team ploughed along behind them, spread out enough not to make a single target, but not so far apart they could be picked off one at a time without the others noticing. The silence pressed in close around them, weighing down so heavily it was almost like a physical presence. Hawk had an almost overpowering urge to shout and yell, to fill the tunnel with sound, if only to emphasise his presence. But he didn't. He had an unsettling feeling his voice would sound small and lost in this vast network of tunnels, no matter how loudly he shouted. And apart from that, there was also the rumour he'd heard that any loud sound in the tunnels never really died away. It just echoed on and on, passing from tunnel to tunnel, growing gradually quieter and more plaintive but never fully fading away. Hawk didn't like the idea of any part of him being trapped down here in the dark forever, not even just his voice.

After a while, it seemed to him he could hear something moving in the tunnel up ahead, a sound so faint and quick he could only tell it was there by the deeper silence that came when it stopped. His instincts were clawing at his gut, urging him to get the hell out of there while he still could, and he clutched the haft of his axe so tightly his fingers ached. He made himself loosen his grip a little, but the faint sounds in the dark wore at his nerves like sandpaper. He took to checking each new side tunnel thoroughly before he'd let the others pass it, torn between his need for action and the urgency of their mission, and the necessity of not allowing himself to be hurried. Hurried people made mistakes. He couldn't help the hostages if he got himself killed by acting carelessly.

The sounds grew suddenly louder and more distinct and he stopped, glaring ahead into the gloom. The others stopped with him, and Fisher moved in close beside him, her sword at the ready. Something was coming towards them out of the darkness, not even bothering to hide its presence anymore, something so large and heavy its progress pushed the air before it like a breeze. Hawk could feel the air pressing against his face.

A dozen red gleams appeared high up in the gloom before him, shining like fires in the night. Hawk lifted his axe as a horrid suspicion stirred within him. The glaring eyes, the soft sounds, and everywhere he looked, the endless webbing. . . . Oh hell, no. Anything but that. The blazing eyes drew closer, hovering up by the tunnel roof, and then the huge spider burst out of the darkness and lurched to a stop at the edge of the lantern light, its eight spindly legs quivering like guitar strings. It swayed silently before them, the top of its furry body pressing against the roof, its legs splayed out into the water and pressing against the tunnel walls. The vast oval body all but filled the tunnel, its thick black fur matted with water and slime. Its red eyes glared fiercely in the lantern light, watchful and unblinking. Thick gobbets of saliva ran from its twitching mandibles. Hawk stood very still. There was no telling what sudden sound or movement might prompt it to attack.

What the hell, he thought firmly. *You can handle this. You've faced a lot worse in your time.*

That was true, but not particularly comforting. Truth be told, he'd never liked spiders, and in particular he'd never liked the sudden darting way in which they moved. If he found one in the jakes, he usually called for Isobel to come and get rid of it. Of course, she was so softhearted she couldn't bear to kill a helpless little insect, so she just dumped it outside, whereupon it immediately found its way back inside again to have another go at terrorizing him. He realised his thoughts were rambling, and brought them firmly back under control. He could handle this. He looked surreptitiously back at the others, and was a little relieved to see that they looked just as shaken as he was.

"Well?" he said steadily. "Anyone got any ideas?"

"Let's cut its legs off, for a start," said Barber. "That should ruin its day."

"Sounds good to me," said Fisher. "I'll go for the head. Hack its brain into mincemeat, and it's got to lie down and die. Hasn't it?"

"Strictly speaking," said Hawk, "it doesn't appear to have a head. The eyes are set in the top part of its body."

"All right, I'll go for the top part of its body, then. God, you can be picky sometimes, Hawk."

"That's enough!" hissed Winter sharply. "Keep your voices down, all of you. I don't want it panicked into attacking before we're ready to handle it. Or hasn't it occurred to you that the bloody thing is hardly going to just stand there and watch while you step forward and take a hack at it? If it can move as fast as its smaller cousins, we could be in big trouble."

"It might also be poisonous," said MacReady.

They all looked at him. "Something that big doesn't need to be poisonous," said Fisher, uncertainly.

"Are you willing to bet your life on that?" asked MacReady.

"We're wasting time," said Winter. "While we're standing around here arguing, the terrorists could be killing hostages. We've got to get past this thing, no matter how dangerous it is. We need someone to hold the creature's attention while Barber and Fisher attack its weak spots. Hawk, I think it's time we found out just how good you are with that axe."

Hawk nodded stiffly. "No problem. Just give me some room."

He moved slowly forward, the scummy waters swirling about his knees. The tunnel floor was uneven, and he couldn't see where to put his feet. Not exactly ideal fighting conditions. The spider's huge body quivered suddenly, its legs trembling, and Hawk froze where he was. The serrated mandibles flexed silently, and Hawk took a firmer grip on his axe. He stepped forward, and the spider launched itself at him, moving impossibly fast for its bulk. He braced himself, and buried his axe in the spider's body, just above the mandibles. Thick black blood spattered over his hands, and he was carried back three or four feet by the force of the spider's charge before he could brace himself again. He could hear the SWAT team scattering behind him, but couldn't spare the time to look back. The spider shook itself violently, and Hawk was lifted off his feet. He clung desperately to his axe with one hand, and grabbed the mandibles with the other, keeping them at arm's length from his body. At his side, Barber cut viciously at the creature's nearest leg, but the spider lifted it out of the way with cat-quick reflexes. Barber stumbled, caught off balance by the force of his own blow, and the leg lashed out and caught him full in the chest, sending him flying backwards into the water. He disappeared beneath the surface, and reappeared coughing and spluttering but still hanging onto his sword.

Fisher cut at the spider's eyes with the tip of her sword, and it flinched back, dragging Hawk with it as he tried to tear his axe free. The spider's body had seemed as soft as a sponge when he hit it, but now the sides of the wound had closed on the axehead like a living vise. He braced one foot against the tunnel wall and pulled hard with both hands, putting his back into it. The axe jerked free with a loud, sucking sound and he fell back into the water, just managing to keep his feet under him. The spider reared up over him, and he swung his axe double-handed into the creature's belly. The heavy weapon sank into the black fur, the force of the blow burying the axe deep into the spider's guts. Thick blood drenched Hawk's arms and chest as he wrenched the axe free and struck at the belly again.

Barber coughed up the last of the water he'd swallowed and staggered back into the fight. Winter was trying to cut through the spider's front legs, but it always managed to pull them out of reach at the last moment, and she had to throw herself this way and that to avoid the legs as they came swinging viciously back. Barber chose his moment carefully, and cut at one leg just as it lashed out after Winter. His blade sank deep into the spindly leg and jarred on bone. He pulled the sword free and cut again, and the leg folded awkwardly in two, well below the joint.

The spider lurched to one side, and Fisher scrambled up on top of it, grabbing handfuls of the thick fur as she went. She thrust her sword in between the glaring red eyes again and again, burying the blade to the hilt. The edge of the sword burst one of the eyes and its crimson light went out, drowned in black blood. The spider reared beneath her, slamming her against the tunnel roof and trying to throw her off. She hung on grimly, probing for the creature's brain with her sword. Barber and Winter cut through another leg between them, and the spider collapsed against the tunnel wall, thrown off balance by its own weight. Hawk cut deeply into the spider's belly above him, kneeling in the water to get more room to swing his axe. Blood and steaming liquids spilled over him as he hacked and tore at the creature's guts. Barber severed a third leg, and Fisher slammed her sword into a glaring red eye. The spider reared up, crushing Fisher against the tunnel roof, and then collapsed on top of Hawk. He just had time to see the great bulk coming down on top of him, and then the spider's great weight thrust him down beneath the surface of the water and held him there.

The spider's last breath went out of it in a long shuddering sigh, its mandibles clattering loudly, and then it was still. The light went out of its remaining eyes, and black blood spilled out into the filthy water. Winter and Barber leaned on each other for support while they got their breath back. Fisher clambered slowly down off the spider's back, wincing at the bruises she'd got from being slammed against the tunnel roof. She dropped back into the water, and looked around her.

"Where's Hawk?"

Winter and Barber looked at each other. "I lost track of him in the fight," said Winter. "Mac, did you see what happened to him?"

MacReady looked at Fisher. "I'm very sorry. Hawk was trapped beneath the water by the spider when it collapsed."

Fisher looked at him speechlessly for a moment, then demanded, "Why the hell didn't you say something? We can still get him out! There's still time. Help me, damn you!"

She splashed back through the water and tried to grab the spider's side to lift it, but her hands just sank uselessly into the spongy mass. Barber and Winter moved in on either side of her to help, but even when they could find a hold, they couldn't lift the spider's body an inch. They couldn't shift the immense weight without leverage, and the soft yielding body wouldn't allow them any.

"There's nothing you can do, Isobel," said MacReady. "If there was, I'd have done it. I'm sorry, but it was obvious Hawk was a dead man from the moment the spider collapsed on top of him."

"Shut up!" said Fisher. "And get over here and help, damn you, or I swear I'll cut you down where you stand, charm or no bloody charm!"

MacReady shrugged, and moved in beside Barber. Fisher sank her arms into the spider's body up to her elbows, and strained upwards with all her strength, but the body didn't move. She tried again and again, hauling at the dead weight till her back screamed and sweat ran down her face in streams, but it was no use. Finally she realised that the others had stopped trying and were staring at her compassionately. She stumbled back from the dead spider, shaking her head slowly at the words she knew were coming.

"It's no good," said Barber. "We can't lift it, Isobel. We'd need a dock crane just to shift the bloody thing. And it's been too long anyway. He's gone, Isobel. There's nothing more we can do."

"There has to be," said Fisher numbly.

"I'm sorry," said Winter. "He was a good fighter, and a brave man."

"You couldn't stand him!" said Fisher. "You thought he wanted your stupid command! If you hadn't sent him in first, on his own, he might still be alive!"

"Yes," said Winter. "He might. I'm sorry."

Storm! yelled Fisher with her mind. *You're a sorcerer! Do something!*

There's nothing I can do, my dear. This close to the House, my magic is useless.

"Damn you! Damn you all! He can't die here. Not like this."

They stood for a while in the tunnel, saying nothing.

"It's time to go," said Winter finally. "We still have our mission. The hostages are depending on us. Hawk wouldn't have wanted them to die because of him."

"We can't just leave him here," said Fisher. "Not alone. In the dark."

"We'll send someone back for him later," said Barber. "Let's go."

The spider's back pressed upwards suddenly, and the whole body lurched sideways. The SWAT team stumbled backwards, lifting their swords again. *It can't be alive,* Fisher thought dully. *It can't be alive when Hawk is dead.* The spider's back protruded suddenly in one spot and then burst apart as a gore-streaked axehead tore through it. A bloody hand appeared after the axe, and then Hawk's head burst out beside it, gulping great lungfuls of the stinking air. The SWAT team stared at him uncomprehendingly, and then Fisher shrieked with savage joy and scrambled up on top of the spider again. She cut quickly at the torn hide with her sword, opening the hole wider. Barber and Winter climbed up beside her, and between them they hauled Hawk out of the spider's body and helped him clamber down into the water again. Fisher clung to him all the way, unable to let go, as though afraid he might vanish if she did. He was covered in blood and gore from head to toe, but none of it seemed to be his. He was still breathing harshly, but he found the strength to hug her back, and even managed a small, reassuring smile for her.

"What the hell happened?" she said finally. "We'd all given you up for dead!"

Hawk raised a sardonic eyebrow. "I demand a second opinion."

Fisher snorted with laughter. "All right, then; why didn't you drown?"

Hawk grinned. "You should have known I don't die that easily, lass. When the damned thing collapsed on top of me, the weight of its body forced me through the hole I'd made in its guts, and I ended up inside it. Turned out the thing was largely hollow, for all its size. There was just enough air in there to keep me going while I cut my way through its body and out the top. It was hard going, and the air was getting pretty foul by the end, but I made it." He took a deep lungful of the tunnel air. "You know, even this stench can smell pretty good if you have to do without it for a while."

Fisher hugged him again. "We tried to lift the spider off you, but we couldn't budge it. At least, most of us tried. MacReady had already given you up for dead. He wouldn't have helped at all if I hadn't made him."

·"That right?" Hawk gave MacReady a long, thoughtful look. "I'll have to remember that."

MacReady stared back, unconcerned. Winter cleared her throat loudly. "If you're feeling quite recovered, Captain Hawk, we ought to get a move on. The hostages are still depending on us, and they're running out of time."

The atmosphere in the parlour was getting dangerously tense, and Saxon was getting worried. There'd been no word on how negotiations were going, but whatever the terrorists' deadline was, it had to be getting closer. Madigan had disappeared with his people some time back, leaving twenty mercenaries to watch the hostages. Talking wasn't allowed, and the mercenaries had taken an almost sadistic pleasure in denying the hostages food or drink while taking turns at stuffing their own faces. Time dragged on, and the mercenaries grew bored while the hostages grew restless. Sooner or later, someone on one side or the other was going to do something stupid, just to break the monotony. Which would be all the excuse the mercenaries needed to indulge in a little fun and games. . . .

Saxon smiled coldly. Whatever happened, he wasn't going to make any trouble. The terrorists could kill every man and woman in the room, and he wouldn't give a damn. These people represented all the vile and corrupt authority that had made Haven what it was. He was in no real danger himself. He had a way out, just in case things started getting really out of hand. He knew Champion House well from his earlier days, when he'd been a rising politician and much courted by those seeking patronage or influence with the Council. What he knew, and presumably the terrorists didn't, was that the House was riddled with secret doors and hidden passageways, a holdover from the House's original owners, who'd raised the fortune needed to build Champion House by being Haven's

most successful smugglers. Apparently the passages, with their
magically warded walls, had come in handy more than once
for concealing goods and people from investigating customs
officers who were outraged at being denied their rightful cut.

As far as Saxon knew, the passages were still there, unless
they'd been discovered and blocked off during the years while
he was away. Either way, if he remembered correctly, there
was a concealed door right there in the parlour, not too far
away. All he had to do was press a section of the panelling
in just the right place, the wall would open, and he'd be gone
before the mercenaries knew what was happening. That was
the theory, anyway. But he didn't think he'd try it until he
had no other choice. The way his luck had been going, the
secret door would probably turn out to be nailed shut and
booby-trapped.

The tension was so thick on the air now, he could practically
taste it. The two Kings were sitting stiffly but not without
dignity, trying to set a good example, but no one was paying them much attention. The military types were watching
the mercenaries like hawks, waiting for someone to make a
slip. The Quality were pointedly ignoring the mercenaries, as
though hoping they might go away once they realised how
unwelcome they were. The merchants stood close together and
kept a hopeful watch on the closed door. They'd given up on
trying to bribe the mercenaries, but they obviously still thought
they could make some kind of deal with Madigan or one of
his people. Saxon knew better. He knew fanatics when he saw
them, and this bunch worried the hell out of him. It was clear
they had their own agenda, and if they were as committed to
their Cause as they seemed, once they'd started they wouldn't
turn aside for hell or high water. You'd have to kill them all
to stop them.

Saxon glanced again at the hidden door, and his hand tightened around the smoke bomb he'd palmed while he was being
searched. If trouble broke out, he was off, and to hell with all
of them. Whatever the terrorists were up to, it was none of his
business.

The door slammed open and everyone jumped, including
most of the mercenaries. Eleanour Todd stood in the doorway with the young killer Glen at her side, and Saxon's

heart sank. He could tell from their faces that the deadline
had come and gone without being met. Todd looked calm,
almost bored, but there was an air of unfocused menace about
her, as though she was readying herself for some bloody
but necessary task. Glen was grinning broadly. Todd looked
unhurriedly about her, and the hostages stared back like so
many rabbits mesmerized by a snake.

"It seems your city Council has chosen not to take us seri-
ously," said Todd. "They have refused to meet our legitimate
demands. It's time we showed them we are not to be trifled
with. It's time for one of you to die."

She let her gaze drift casually over the hostages, and faces
paled when her gaze lingered for a moment before passing on.
People began to edge away from each other, as though afraid
proximity to the one chosen might prove dangerous. No one
raised a voice in protest. A few of the braver souls looked as
though they might, but one look from Glen was all it took to
silence them. Saxon held the smoke bomb loosely in his hand,
and cast about for a good spot to lob it. He'd wait until Todd
had chosen her victim, and all eyes were on them, and then
he'd make his move.

Eleanour Todd finally stepped forward and smiled at a
young girl in the front row, not far from where Saxon was
standing. The girl couldn't have been more than fourteen or
fifteen, some merchant's daughter wearing her first formal
gown to an important function. She'd been vaguely pretty
before, but now sheer terror made her face ugly as she tried
to back away from Todd's smile. Her father stepped forward
to stand before her, opening his mouth to protest, and Todd hit
him with a vicious, low blow. He fell to the floor, moaning.
Glen strolled forward and kicked him casually in the face a
few times. The girl stared desperately around her for help, but
no one would meet her eyes. She turned back to Todd and held
herself erect with a pathetic attempt at dignity. She didn't know
she was whimpering quietly, and that her face was so pale her
few amateurish attempts at makeup stood out against her pallor
like a child's daubings.

"It's nothing personal," said Todd. "We always choose a
young girl for our first execution. Makes more of an impact.
Don't worry; it'll all be over before you know it."

"My name is Christina Rutherford," said the girl steadily. "My family will avenge my death."

"Your name doesn't matter, girl. Only the Cause matters. Now, will you walk or would you rather be dragged?"

"I'll walk. I just want to . . . say goodbye to my family and friends."

"How touching. But we don't have time. Glen; drag her."

His grin broadened, and Christina shrank away from him. She started to cry, and tears ran down her face as Glen grabbed her by the arm and pulled her towards the door. Saxon swore tiredly, and stepped forward to block their way.

"That's enough, Glen. Let her go."

"Get out of the way, guard, or we'll take you too."

"Try it."

Glen chuckled suddenly, and thrust Christina behind him. Todd took her firmly by the arms. Glen studied Saxon thoughtfully. "So; someone here's got some guts after all. I was hoping someone had. Now I get to have some fun. How far do you think you can run, hero, with your intestines dragging down around your ankles?"

His sword was suddenly in his hand, and he lunged forward incredibly quickly. Saxon sidestepped at the last moment, and the blade's edge just caressed the chain mail over his ribs as it hissed past. Glen stumbled forward, caught off balance, and Saxon brought his knee up savagely. Glen fell to his knees, the breath rattling in his throat. Saxon kicked him in the ribs, slamming him back against the wall. He leant forward and picked up Glen's sword, ignoring the unpleasant sounds behind him as the young killer vomited painfully. He turned to face Eleanour Todd, who had a knife at Christina's throat. The young girl was looking at him with the beginnings of hope. The mercenaries standing around the room were staring at him open-mouthed. Saxon flashed them his most confident politician's smile and then looked back at Todd.

"Let the girl go. We can talk about this."

"No," said Todd. "I don't think so." She drew the knife quickly across Christina's throat, and then pushed the girl away from her. She fell onto her knees, her eyes wide in horror. She tried to scream, but only a horrid bubbling sound came out. Blood ran thickly down her neck and chest, and she put her hands to her throat as though she could hold the wound together, but the blood gushed through her fingers. She held out a bloody hand to Saxon, but she was already dead by the time he took it. He lowered her body to the floor, then looked up at Todd. There was death in his eyes, but she didn't flinch.

"You bitch," Saxon said numbly. "You didn't have to do that."

"She wasn't important," said Todd. "And at least she died in a good Cause. Now it's your time to die, hero. Can't have the sheep getting ideas, can we?"

She gestured impatiently to the watching mercenaries, and they began to close in.

"I'll kill you for this," said Saxon flatly. "I'll kill you all."

He threw the smoke bomb onto the floor before him and it cracked open, spilling out thick clouds of choking black smoke that billowed quickly through the parlour. Todd lashed out with her sword but Saxon was already gone, sprinting for the hidden door. Mercenaries loomed out of the smoke in front of him and he smashed his way through, tossing them aside like broken dolls. The hostages were shouting and screaming, and some made a dash for the door. Saxon hoped some of them made it. He found the right stretch of panelling, hit it smartly in just the right place, and a section of the wall swung open on silent counterweights. He darted forward into the gloomy passageway, and a knife came flying out of nowhere to bury itself in the panelling behind him. He hurried on without looking back, and a sourceless glow appeared around him, lighting the way ahead. It was nice to know the passage's built-in magics were still functioning. He glanced back, and swore harshly as he saw the concealed door had jammed half shut, caught on the thrown knife. Todd would be sending mercenaries into the passage after him any time now. He grinned coldly. Good. Let them come. Let them all come. There were secrets in these passageways that only he knew about, and anyone foolish enough to come after him was in for some nasty surprises. And when they were all dead, he would go out into the House and kill Madigan and Todd and all the other terrorists.

They shouldn't have killed the girl. He'd make them pay for that.

Back in the parlour, the smoke was slowly starting to clear, but terrorists and hostages alike were still coughing helplessly and wiping tears from their smarting eyes. The mercenaries had rounded up the escaping hostages without too much trouble, and the situation was more or less back under control. Todd glared into the hidden passageway, and gestured quickly to two mercenaries. "Horse, Bishop; take five men and go in there after him. You needn't bother to bring all of him back; just the head will do. After that, check the passage for other concealed exits. I don't want anyone else suddenly disappearing on me. Move it!"

The two mercenaries nodded quickly, gathered up five men with a quick series of looks and nods, and led the way into the passage. Glen started to go in after them, but Todd stopped him.

"Not you, Glen. I need you here, with me."

"I want that bastard. No one does that to me and gets away with it."

"He won't get away. Even if he gets out of the passage, there's nowhere he can go. The House is full of our people."

Glen scowled unhappily. "I don't know, Eleanour. He's fast. I've never seen anyone move like that. And anyway, I want to kill him myself."

"Glen, we've got work to do. The guard can wait. He isn't important. Not compared to our purpose here. Now, get yourself another sword, and get the girl's body out of here. Show it to the city negotiators, and tell them we'll kill another hostage every half hour until our demands are met."

Glen looked at her, puzzled. "I thought the hostages were just a cover," he said quietly.

"They are," said Todd, just as quietly, "but as long as the city's concentrating on them, they won't be getting suspicious about what we're really up to. Now, do as you're told, Ellis; there's a dear."

Glen blushed at the endearment, and turned quickly away to bark orders at the mercenaries. The hostages watched silently as the girl's body was dragged out. Todd coughed suddenly as the smoke caught in her throat again.

"Somebody open those bloody windows!"

Horse and Bishop led their men cautiously down the narrow stone corridor of the secret passage, checking for other exits as they went. A sourceless glow had formed around them, enough to show them the way ahead, but it didn't carry far into the darkness. The rogue guard could be lurking just ahead of the light, waiting in the dark to ambush them, and they'd never know it until it was too late. Horse shook his head determinedly, pushing aside the thought. The guard had enough sense to keep running. He'd be long gone by now. But if he was dumb enough to be still hanging around, then he and Bishop would take care of him. They'd dealt with would-be heroes before, and in Horse's experience they died just as easily as anyone else. Particularly if you outnumbered them seven to one.

Horse was a large, heavily built man in his late twenties, with thick, raggedly cut black hair and a bushy beard. He'd fought in seventeen campaigns, for various masters, and had never once been on the losing side. Horse didn't believe in losing. In his experience, the trick to winning was to have all the advantages on your side, which was why he'd teamed up with Bishop. His fellow mercenary was the same age as he, a head or so taller, but almost twice Horse's size. It wasn't all muscle, but then, it didn't have to be. He wasn't the brightest of men either, but Horse was bright enough for both of them, and they both knew it. Besides, Bishop was very creative when it came to interrogating prisoners. Especially women. Horse grinned. Bishop stopped suddenly, and Horse stopped with him, glaring back at the other mercenaries when they almost ran into him.

"What is it, Bishop?" he said quietly.

"I'm not sure." The big mercenary fingered the heavy iron amulet he wore on a chain round his neck, and glowered unhappily into the gloom ahead. "Something's wrong, Horse. This place doesn't feel right."

"Have you seen something? Heard something?"

"No. It just doesn't . . . feel right."

The other mercenaries looked at each other, but Horse glared them into silence. He respected Bishop's hunches. They'd paid off before. He gestured to the two nearest men. "Check out this section. Inch by inch, if necessary."

The two men looked at each other, shrugged, and moved warily forward, swords at the ready. The light moved with them. There was still no sign of the rogue guard. The passageway was eerily silent, the only sound the scuffling of their boots on the plain stone floor. They'd gone about ten paces

before part of the floor gave slightly under one of the men's
feet, and there was a soft clicking noise. They both looked
down automatically, and consequently never saw the many
long, pointed wooden stakes which shot out of concealed vents
in both walls. The stakes slammed into the two men with brutal
force, running them through in a dozen places. They hung there
limply, their feet dangling, and blood pooled on the floor below
them. They didn't even have time to scream. There was another
soft click as the lever in the floor reset itself, and then the
stakes retracted silently into the walls. The two bodies sagged
slowly to the floor, the blood-slick wood making soft, sucking
noises as it slid jerkily out of the dead flesh. Bishop swore
slowly, his voice more awed than anything else.

"Booby trap," said Horse grimly. "And if there's one, you
can bet there are more. For all we know, the whole place could
be rigged with them."

"Then there's no point in going on," said one of the
mercenaries behind him. "Is there?"

"Do you want to go back and tell Todd that?" said Horse,
without bothering to look round. He smiled briefly at the
silence that answered him. "All right, then; we're going on. I'll
take the lead. Walk where I do, and don't touch anything."

He set off slowly, studying the ground before him carefully
before gradually lowering his foot onto it. Bishop followed
close behind him, all but treading on his heels. The other
mercenaries brought up the rear, grumbling quietly among
themselves. Horse glowered into the dark ahead of him. The
guard they were pursuing had to have known about the booby
traps and how to avoid them, which suggested he was no
ordinary guard. It had been obvious from the other hostages'
faces that they'd known nothing about the hidden passageway.
If they had, they'd have used it.

With the guard's special knowledge, he could avoid all the
traps and be anywhere in the House by now, but even so, they
had to press on. They might not be able to run down the man
himself, but at least they could identify the other hidden exits
and block them off.

There was a soft click from somewhere close at hand, and
Horse threw himself forward instinctively, Bishop at his side as
a heavy crash sounded behind them and a cloud of dust puffed
up, filling the passage. Horse clutched briefly at Bishop to

make sure he was all right, and then looked back. A huge slab of solid stone had dropped from the passage ceiling, crushing two of the mercenaries beneath it. Blood welled out from under the stone and lapped at the toes of Horse's boots. The sole surviving mercenary on the other side of the stone block was standing very still, his face white as a sheet. Horse called out to him, but he didn't answer. Horse called again, and the man turned and ran. Some of the light went with him as he fled down the passageway, and then a section of the floor dropped out from beneath his feet and he disappeared screaming into a concealed pit. There was a flash of shining blades, and then the trapdoor swung shut, cutting off his scream, and the passage was still and silent again.

"This place is a deathtrap," said Bishop.

"Yeah," said Horse. "But the guard got through alive. Probably somewhere out there in the dark right now, watching us and laughing."

"He's no ordinary guard, Horse. Did you see the way he flattened Glen? I didn't think anyone was faster than Glen."

"He's just one man. We can take him. And then you can show him some of your nasty little tricks with a hot iron."

"You're welcome to try," said Saxon.

The two mercenaries spun round to find Saxon standing behind them, just out of sword's reach. He was smiling. Horse could feel his heart beating hard and fast in his chest, but somehow he kept the shock out of his face. He lifted his sword, and Bishop did the same a second later. Saxon's sword was still in his scabbard, and his hand was nowhere near it.

"You shouldn't have come back," said Horse. "You're a dead man now. You're walking and you're breathing, but you're dead. And we're going to make it last a long time."

Saxon just smiled back at him, his eyes cold. "I've had a really bad day. You're about to have a worse one."

Bishop growled something indistinct, and launched himself at Saxon, his sword out before him, his great bulk moving with surprising speed. Saxon casually batted the sword blade aside, and slammed a fist into Bishop's side. The big mercenary stopped as though he'd run into a wall. The sound of his ribs breaking was eerily loud on the quiet. He stood hunched over before Saxon, breathing in short, painful gasps, trying to lift his sword and failing. Saxon hit him again, burying his fist in the man's gut up to his wrist. Blood flew from Bishop's mouth, and he sank to his knees. Horse looked at him incredulously. It had all happened so *fast*. He looked back at Saxon, his sword forgotten in his hand.

"Who are you?" he whispered.

"I'm Saxon. Wulf Saxon."

Horse tried for some of his usual bravado, but the words came out flat and empty. "You say it like it's supposed to mean something, but I've never heard of you."

Saxon shrugged. "I've been away for a while. People forget. But they'll remember, once I've reminded them a few times. You shouldn't have killed the girl, mercenary."

"That wasn't me. That was Todd."

"You stood by and let it happen. You're guilty. You're all guilty, and I'm going to kill every last one of you."

"What was she to you, Saxon? Your girlfriend? Family?"

"I never saw her before in my life."

"Then why . . . ?"

"She was so young," said Saxon. "She had all her life before her. She had friends and family who cared for her. And you took all that away." He leaned forward and took Bishop's head in his hands. The big mercenary shuddered, but hadn't the strength to pull away. Saxon looked at Horse.

"I'm going to send you back to the others with a message, mercenary. Be sure to tell them who sent it. Tell them Wulf Saxon is back."

A moment later, the passage was full of someone screaming.

Eleanour Todd paced up and down, scowling angrily, and the hostages shrank back from her as she passed. She didn't bother to hide her contempt for them. Nothing but sheep, all of them, shocked and terrified because their comfortable little world had been overthrown and the wolves had finally caught the flock undefended. They deserved everything that was going to happen to them. The guard had been the only one with any backbone. And that was the problem. It had been almost a quarter of an hour since she'd sent her mercenaries into the hidden passage after him, and there'd been no word from them since. There couldn't be that many passages to search, surely? She stopped herself pacing with an effort. The guard was only one man; there was nothing he could do to upset the plan. Nothing could go wrong now. But what the hell had happened to the mercenaries? Could they have got lost in the passages? She glared out over the hostages, taking a quiet satisfaction in the way their faces paled.

"Who can tell me about the hidden passageways?" she said flatly. The hostages looked at each other, but no one said anything. Todd let her scowl deepen into a glare. "Someone here must know something about the passageways. Now, either that someone starts talking, or I'm going to have my men pick out someone at random and we'll take turns cutting him or her into little pieces until someone else starts remembering things."

"Please believe me, no one here knows anything about the passageways," said Sir Roland. He stepped forward diffidently, and the crowd shrank back to give him plenty of room. "You see, the only people who might know anything are the House's actual owners, and they're not here. The whole Family moved out so we could have the place to ourselves."

Todd nodded unhappily. It figured Madigan's pet traitor would turn out to be the one with the answers, even if they weren't the ones she wanted. "So how did that guard know about them?"

"I don't know. He was one of a number of men the Brotherhood of Steel supplied us for use as honour guards. Perhaps he'd been here before and knew the Family. After all, the Brotherhood recruits from all the social strata."

Todd grunted, and dismissed him with a wave of her hand. Sir Roland bowed politely, and stepped quickly back into the crowd. There was a murmur of praise for his courage from the other hostages, but it died quickly away as the watching mercenaries stirred menacingly. Todd beckoned to Glen, who was lounging by the door, and he hurried over to her with his usual puppyish grin.

"The mercenaries I sent into the hidden passage have been gone too long," she said quietly. "Something must have happened. Take a dozen men and search the passageways from end to end. I want to know exactly what happened to Horse and his men, and I want that guard dead. Is that clear?"

"Oh, sure. But I won't need a dozen men."

"Take them anyway. There's something about that guard. . . ."

"I can take him," said Glen confidently. "I just wasn't ready for him last time."

"Take the men. That's an order. I don't want anything to happen to you."

Glen's face brightened. "You don't?"

"Of course not. You're a valuable member of our group."

Glen's face dropped, and he nodded glumly. "Don't worry," he said, for something to say. "Horse will probably have caught him by now. He's a good man."

"Horse? He couldn't catch the clap from a Leech Street whore. I should never have sent him. Now get a move on."

Glen winced slightly at her crudeness, and turned away to pick out his men. He wished she wouldn't talk like that. It wasn't fitting in a woman. And it seemed she still didn't see him as anything more than an ally. She never would . . . as long as Madigan was around. The thought disturbed him, and he pushed it aside, but it wouldn't go away entirely. He scowled. That guard had made him look bad in front of Eleanour. He'd make the bastard bleed for that. It was amazing how long you could keep the other party in a sword fight alive before finally killing them. Sometimes they even begged him to do it.

He liked that.

He chose his men quickly, impatient to be off, and sent them over to the opening in the wall to wait for him. He glanced back for one last look at Eleanour, and then stopped as he saw Bailey was talking to her urgently. From the expression on both their faces, it had to be something important, and bloody unwelcome news at that. He hurried back to join them. Bailey acknowledged his presence with a nod, but Eleanour ignored him, her gaze fixed on Bailey.

"Are you sure about this?"

"Of course I'm sure!" Bailey struggled to keep his voice low, but his eyes were angry. "Do you think I'd have come to you with something like this if I wasn't sure?"

"Keep your voice down. This isn't something we want the hostages to hear. It just seems impossible, that's all. How can we have lost twenty-seven men without anyone seeing anything?"

Bailey shrugged. "They were all found dead at their posts. No one even suspected anything was wrong until some of them didn't report in at the proper times. We did a check, and found twenty-seven of our people had been killed, all in the last twenty minutes or so."

"How did they die?" asked Glen, frowning.

"Some were stabbed, some were strangled. And two," said Bailey, his voice never wavering, "were torn literally limb from limb."

Todd and Glen looked at him for a moment, trying to take it in. Bailey shrugged, and said nothing. Todd glowered, her face flushing angrily as she tried to make sense of the situation.

"These deaths took place not long after the guard disappeared into the hidden passageways. There has to be a connection."

"One man couldn't be responsible for twenty-seven deaths," said Bailey. "Not in such a short time. And I saw the bodies that had been torn apart. Nothing human is that strong."

"All right," said Todd, "Maybe there was some kind of creature living in the passages, and he let it loose."

"If there was, then he's probably dead as well," said Glen. "Damn. Now I'll never know whether I could have taken him."

"Oh, stop whining, Glen! This is important." She didn't bother to look at Glen, her gaze turned inward as she struggled with the problem. So she didn't see the hurt in his face quickly give way to anger, and then disappear behind a cold, impassive mask. Todd glared once at the secret doorway, and then turned the glare on Glen and Bailey.

"We can't afford to have things going wrong this late in the game. We're spread too thin as it is. So, this is what we're going to do. Bailey, pass the word back that from now on our people are to work in groups of five or six, and under no conditions are they to let their partners out of their sight, even for a moment. And they're to check in every ten minutes, regardless. As soon as you've done that, take Glen and round up a dozen men and search those hidden passages from end to end. Don't come back until you've found the guard or the creature or some kind of answer. Got it?"

Bailey started to nod, and then turned away suddenly and looked at the opening in the wall. "Did you hear that?"

Todd and Glen looked at each other. "Hear what?" said Todd.

"There's something in the passage," said Bailey. "And it's coming this way."

"It could be Horse and his men," said Glen.

"I don't think so," said Bailey.

He drew his sword and headed towards the opening, followed quickly by Glen. Todd snapped orders to the mercenaries to watch the hostages closely, and then hurried after Glen, her sword in her hand. They stood together before the opening, blocking it off from the rest of the room, and strained their eyes against the gloom in the passageway. Slow, scuffing footsteps drew steadily closer. One man's footsteps. And then a glow appeared in the passage, and Horse came walking towards them out of the dark. His face was unnaturally pale, and his eyes were wild and staring. Drool ran from the corners of his mouth. Blood had splashed across the front of his clothes, soaking them, but there was no sign of any wound. In his hands he carried Bishop's head.

He came to a stop before Todd and the others, and his eyes were as unseeing as Bishop's. The severed head wore an expression of utter horror, and the mouth gaped wide, as though in an endless, silent scream. Some of the hostages were whimpering quietly, only kept from screaming by fear of what the mercenaries might do to them if they did. A few had fainted dead away. Even some of the hardened mercenaries looked shocked. Todd glanced quickly round, and knew she had to do something to take control of the situation before it got totally out of hand. She stepped forward and slapped Horse hard across the face. His head swung loosely under the blow, but when it turned back his eyes were focused on hers.

"What happened, Horse?" said Todd. "Tell me what happened."

"Wulf Saxon sends you a message," said Horse, his calm, steady voice unsettling when set against the horror that still lurked in his eyes. "He says that all the terrorists in this House are going to die. He's going to kill us all."

"Who the hell's Wulf Saxon?" said Glen, when it became clear Horse had nothing more to say. "Is he the guard? What happened to the rest of your men?"

"They're in the passages," said Horse. "The House killed

them. And then Saxon killed Bishop, and sent me back here with his message."

"Why did he cut off Bishop's head?" asked Bailey.

Horse turned slowly to look at him. "He didn't. He tore it off with his bare hands."

Glen recoiled a step, in spite of himself. Bailey frowned thoughtfully. Todd found her voice again and gestured to the two nearest mercenaries. "Take that bloody thing away from him, and get him out of here. Find an empty room and then grill him until you've got every detail of what happened. Do whatever it takes, but get me that information. Find the sorcerer Ritenour, and give him Bishop's head. Maybe he can get some answers out of that. Then get word to Madigan about what's happened, including the twenty-seven deaths. I know he gave orders he wasn't to be disturbed, but he's got to be told about this. I'll take full responsibility for disturbing him. Now move it!"

The two mercenaries nodded quickly, took Horse by the arms, and led him away. The hostages retreated quickly as he passed. Blood dripped steadily from the severed head in his hands, leaving a crimson trail on the carpet behind him. The hostages began to murmur among themselves, some of them clearly on the edge of hysteria. Todd glared at the other mercenaries. "Keep these people quiet! Do whatever it takes, but keep them in line. I'll be just outside if you need me for anything."

She nodded curtly for Bailey and Glen to follow her, and strode hurriedly out of the parlour and into the corridor. She shut the door carefully behind them, and then leaned back against it, hugging herself tightly. "What a mess. What a bloody mess! How could everything go so wrong so quickly? Everything was going exactly to plan, and now this. . . . At least now we know who killed the twenty-seven men. Wulf bloody Saxon, whoever or whatever he is."

"He used to be a city Councillor, but that was some time ago," said Bailey. "He was supposed to have died more than twenty years ago."

"Then what the hell's he doing here now, disguised as a guard?" said Todd. "And how come you know so much about him?"

"I knew him, long ago. But I don't see how it can be him.

He'd be my age now, in his late forties, and the guard was only in his twenties." Bailey paused suddenly. "About the age Saxon would have been when he died . . ."

They all looked at each other. "He hasn't aged . . . he's incredibly strong . . . and he's supposed to be dead," said Todd slowly. "I think we may have a supernatural on our hands."

"Oh, great. Now we're in real trouble," said Glen. "Want me to go get the sorcerer?"

"Let's not panic just yet," said Bailey. "We don't know that it's really Wulf Saxon. He could be using the name just to throw us. The Saxon I knew was never a killer."

"A lot can happen to a man when he's been dead for more than twenty years," said Todd sharply. "You're missing the point, Bailey, as usual. What Madigan has planned for this place is very delicate. We can't afford any magical interruptions. And we definitely can't afford to lose any more men, or we won't be able to hold the House securely. Damn this Saxon! He could ruin everything!"

"From what I remember of him," said Bailey. "I think he could."

Down in the cellar, the sorcerer shaman Ritenour strode unhappily back and forth, staring about him. The single lamp on the wall behind him cast a pale silver glow across the great stone chamber and glistened on the moisture running down the wall. The cellar was a vast open space, and Ritenour's footsteps echoed loudly on the quiet. The place had been a real mess until Madigan had had his men clear it out for the ritual, but Ritenour wasn't sure he wouldn't have preferred the cellar the way it was. It was too empty now, as though waiting for something to come and fill it.

It was painfully cold, and his breath steamed on the still air, but that wasn't why his hands were trembling. Ritenour was scared, and not just at the thought of what Madigan wanted him to do down here. All his instincts, augmented by his magic, were screaming at him to get out of the cellar while he still could. The House's wards interfered with his magic and kept him from Seeing what was there too clearly, for which he was grateful. Something was bubbling beneath the surface of reality, something old and awful, pushing and pressing against the barriers of time and sorcery that held it, threatening to break through at any moment. Ritenour could smell blood on the air, and hear echoes of screams from long ago. He clasped his trembling hands together, and shook his head back and forth.

I've torn the heart from a living child and stood over dying bodies with blood up to my elbows, and never once given a damn for ghosts or retribution. I've gone my own way in search of knowledge and to hell with whatever paths it took me down. So why can't I stop my hands shaking?

Because what lay waiting in the cellar knew nothing of reason or forgiveness, but only an endless hatred and an undying need for revenge. It was a power born of countless acts of blood and suffering, held back by barriers worn thin by time and attrition. It could not be harmed or directed or appeased. And it was because of this power that Madigan had brought him to Champion House.

Ritenour scowled, and wrapped his arms around him against the cold. He had to go through with it. He had to, because Madigan would kill him if he didn't, and because there was no way out of the House that Madigan hadn't got covered. It was at times like this that Ritenour wished he knew more about killing magics, but his research had never led him in that direction. Besides, he'd always known Madigan was protected by more than just his bodyguards.

There was a clattering on the steps behind him, and a mercenary appeared, staring down into the gloom. "Better get your arse back up here, sorcerer. We've got problems. Real problems."

He turned and ran back up the stairs without waiting for an answer. Ritenour took a deep breath to try and calm himself. He didn't want the others to be able to tell how much the cellar scared him.

A quiet sound caught his attention and he looked quickly around, but the cellar was empty again now that the mercenary had left. He smiled briefly. He'd been down there on his own too long. His nerves were getting to him. The sound came again, and his heart leaped painfully in his chest. He glared about him, wanting to run, but determined not to be chased out of the cellar by his own fear. His gaze fell upon a wide circular drain set into the floor, and the tension gradually left his body and his mind. The drain had clearly been built into the floor back when the cellar had been a part of the old slaughterhouse. Probably led directly into the sewers, and that was what he could hear, echoing up the shaft. He strolled casually over to the drain and looked down it. The yard-wide opening was blocked off with a thick metal grille, but there was nothing to be seen beyond it save an impenetrable blackness. As he stood there, he heard the quiet sound again, this time clearly from somewhere deep in the shaft. Ritenour smiled. Just nerves. Nothing more. He cleared his throat and spat into the drain. He listened carefully, but didn't hear it hit anything. He shrugged, and turned away. No telling how far down the sewers were. He supposed he'd better go back up and see what Madigan wanted. Maybe, if he was really lucky, Madigan had changed his mind about the ritual, and he wouldn't have to come back down here again after all.

Yeah. And the tides might go out backwards.

He strode stiffly over to the stairs and made his way back up into the House, away from the cellar. He wasn't hurrying. He wasn't hurrying at all.

Down in the sewers, at the bottom of the shaft that connected with the drain, Hawk look at the gob of spittle that had landed on his shoulder, and pulled a disgusted face. "The dirty bastard . . ."

"Count your blessings," said Barber, trying to hide a grin and failing. "He could have been looking for a privy."

"I don't know what you're making such a fuss about," said Fisher calmly. "You're already covered in blood and guts from the spider and God knows what else from the sewer water, so what harm's a little spittle going to do you?"

Hawk looked down at himself, and had to admit she had a point. He supposed he must have looked worse sometime in the past, but he was hard pressed to think when. "It's the principle of the thing," he said stiffly. "Anyway, it sounds like he's left, so we can finally get a move on. I thought he was never going to go. . . ."

He looked unenthusiastically at the opening above him. The cellar drain emptied out into the sewer through a broad circular hole in the tunnel ceiling. It was about three feet wide, and dripping with particularly repellent black slime that Hawk quickly decided he didn't want to study too closely. He looked back at Winter. "What was this, originally?"

"Originally, it carried blood and offal and other things down from the old slaughterhouse," said Winter offhandedly. "These days, Champion House uses it for dumping garbage and slops and other things."

"Other things?" repeated Hawk suspiciously. "What other things?"

"I don't think I'm going to tell you," said Winter. "Because if I did you'd probably get all fastidious and refuse to go, and we have to go up that shaft. It's the only way in. Now get a move on; we're way behind schedule as it is. It's quite simple; you just wedge yourself into the shaft, press hard against the sides with your back and your feet, and wriggle your way up. As long as you watch out for the slime, you'll be fine. It's not a long climb; only ten or twelve feet."

Hawk gave her a look, and then gestured for Fisher to make a stirrup with her hands. She did so, and then pulled a face as he set a dripping boot into her hands. Hawk braced himself, and jumped up into the shaft, boosted on his way by Fisher. It was a tighter fit than he'd expected, and he had to scrunch himself up to fit into the narrow shaft. His knees were practically up in his face as he set his feet against the other side and began slowly inching his way up. The others clambered in after him, one at a time, and light filled the shaft as MacReady brought up the rear, carrying his lantern. Fisher had put hers away so that she could concentrate on her climbing. As it turned out, one was more than enough to illuminate the narrow shaft, and emphasise how claustrophobic it was.

The slime grew thicker as they made their way up, and Hawk had to press his feet and back even harder against the sides to keep from slipping. He struggled on, inch by inch, sweat running down his face from the effort. A growing ache filled his bent back, and his shoulders were rubbed raw. Every time he shifted his weight, pain stabbed through him in a dozen places, but he couldn't stop to rest. If he relaxed the pressure, even for a moment, he'd start to slip, and he doubted he had the strength left to stop himself before he crashed into the others climbing below him. He pressed on, bit by bit—pushing out with shoulders and elbows while repositioning his feet, and then pressing down with his feet while he wriggled his back up another few precious inches. Over and over again, while his muscles groaned and his back shrieked at him.

"Not unlike being born, this, only in reverse," said Fisher from somewhere down below him, in between painfulsounding grunts.

No one had the breath to laugh, but Hawk managed a grin. The grin stretched into a grimace as muscles cramped agonizingly in his thighs, and he had to grit his teeth to keep from crying out. A pale light showed, further up, marking the end of the shaft and sparking the beginning of a second wind in Hawk. He struggled on, trying to keep the noise to a minimum just in case there was someone still in the cellar. If anyone was to take a look down the drain and spot them, they'd be helpless targets for all kinds of unpleasantness. He tried very hard not to think about boiling oil, and concentrated on maintaining an even rhythm so his muscles wouldn't cramp up again. As a result, when his head slammed into something hard and unyielding, he was taken completely by surprise and slid back a good foot or more before he could stop himself. He stayed where he was for a moment, his heart hammering, feeling very glad that he hadn't dropped onto the person below, and then he craned his neck back to get a look at what was blocking the shaft.

"Why have we stopped?" asked Winter, from somewhere below. "Is there a problem?"

"You could say that," said Hawk. "The top of the shaft's sealed off with an iron grille."

"Can you shift it?"

"I can try. But it looks pretty solid, and I don't have much room for leverage. Everyone stay put, and I'll see what I can do."

He struggled back up the shaft, braced himself just below the iron grille, and studied it carefully. There were no locks or bolts that he could see, but on the other hand there were no hinges either. Damned thing looked as though it had been simply wedged into place, and left to rust solid. He reached up and gave it a good hard push with one hand, but it didn't budge. He tried again, using both hands, but only succeeded in pushing himself back down the shaft. He fought his way back up again, set his shoulders against the grille, and heaved upwards with all his strength. He held the position as long as he could, but his strength gave out before the grille did, and he started sliding slowly back down the shaft. He used his aching legs to bring himself to a halt again, and thought furiously. They couldn't have come all this way, just to be stopped by a stubborn iron grille. There had to be a way to shift it.

An idea came to him, and he forced his way back up the shaft until he was right beneath the grille. He drew his axe, with a certain amount of painful contorting, and jammed the edge of the blade into the fine crack between the grille and the shaft itself. He braced himself again, took several deep breaths, and then threw all his weight against the axe's haft, using the weapon as a lever. The iron grille groaned loudly, shifted a fraction, and then flew open with an echoing clang.

Hawk grabbed the edge of the hole to keep from falling, and hauled himself painfully out into the cellar. He glared quickly about him, in case anyone had heard the noise, but there was no one else in the vast stone chamber. He crawled away from the hole and tried to stand up, but his legs gave way almost immediately, the muscles trembling in reaction to everything he'd put them through. He sat up, put his axe to one side, and set about massaging his leg muscles. His back was killing him too, but that could wait. He just hoped no one would come to investigate the noise. In his present condition he'd be lucky to hold off a midget with a sharpened comb. He shook his head, and concentrated on kneading some strength back into his legs.

Fisher hauled herself out of the drain shaft next, her back dripping with slime, and pulled herself over to collapse next to Hawk. They shared exhausted grins, and then helped each other to their feet as MacReady scrambled out of the drain, still clutching his lantern. For the first time, Hawk realised that there was already a lamp burning on the far wall. Considerate of someone. He frowned suddenly. It might be a good idea to get the hell out of the cellar before whoever it was came back for their lamp. Winter pulled herself out of the drain, waving aside MacReady's offer of help, and stretched painfully as she moved away from the shaft on slightly shaking legs. Barber was the last one up, and bounded out of the drain as though he did this sort of thing every day and twice on holidays. Everyone looked at him with varying degrees of disgust, which he blithely ignored, ostentatiously studying the cellar. Hawk sniffed. He never had liked showoffs.

"This is a bad place," said MacReady suddenly. "I don't like the feel of it at all."

"Oh, I'm sorry," said Hawk. "Hang on and I'll take it back to the store and get you another one. What do you mean, you don't like the *feel* of it?"

"Ease off, Hawk," said Winter. "Mac has a sensitivity to magic. I trust his hunches. Still, this used to be part of the old slaughterhouse, remember? There's bound to be a few bad resonances left over."

"It's more than that," said MacReady, without looking at her. "Contact Storm. See what he makes of this."

Winter shrugged. *Storm? Can you hear me?*

They waited, but there was no reply in their minds.

"Damn," said Winter. "I was afraid of that. Now we're in the House proper, the defensive wards are blocking him off from us. We're on our own."

"Terrific," said Hawk. "I already figured that out when he didn't offer to levitate us up the drain shaft."

"There's more here than just old slaughterhouse memories," said MacReady slowly. "There have always been stories about Champion House. Hauntings, apparitions, strange sightings; uneasy feelings strong enough to send people screaming out into the night rather than sleep another hour in Champion House. The place has been quiet the past year or so, ever since the sorcerer Gaunt performed an exorcism here, but all the recent activity has awakened something. Something old, and powerful.

"Did any of you ever wonder why Champion House has four storeys? Four storeys is almost unheard of in Haven, with our storms and gales. The amount of magic built into this House to keep it secure from even the worst storms staggers the imagination. But there had to be four storeys. The original owner insisted on it. According to legend, the owner said the House would need the extra weight to hold something else down."

"If you're trying to spook me," said Fisher, "you're doing a bloody good job. How come you never mentioned this before?"

"Right," said Hawk.

"I never really believed it before," said MacReady. "Not until I came here. Something's down here with us. Watching us. Waiting for its chance to break free."

"Mac," said Winter firmly, "stop it. When our mission is over, we can send a team of sorcerers down here to check things out, but in the meantime let's just concentrate on the job at hand, shall we? The sooner we're done, the sooner we can get out of here."

"You're not going anywhere," said a voice behind them.

The SWAT team spun round as one, automatically falling into defensive positions, weapons at the ready. The stairs leading from the House down into the cellars were packed with armed men, dressed in various clothing but all wearing the distinctive black iron torc of the mercenary on their left wrist. Their leader was a large, squarish figure with a barrel chest wrapped in gleaming chain mail. He grinned down at the SWAT team, raising an eyebrow at their generally filthy condition.

"One of my men came down here to collect the lamp the sorcerer left behind, and heard suspicious noises down the drain. So, being a good and conscientious lad, he came and told me, and I brought a whole bunch of my men with me, just in case. And here you are! The Gods are good to me today. I reckon Madigan will be good for a tidy little bonus once I turn you over to him. Now you can drop your weapons and walk out of here, or be dragged. Guess which I'd prefer." He looked them over one at a time, waiting for a response, and seemed a little shaken at their calm silence. His gaze stopped on Hawk, covered from head to foot in blood and gore, and for the first time his confidence seemed to slip. "Who the hell are you people?"

Hawk grinned suddenly, and a few of the mercenaries actually flinched a little. "We're the law," said Hawk. "Scary, isn't it?"

He launched himself forward, swinging his axe with both hands, and suddenly the mercenaries realised that while they were crowded together on the stairway they had no room in which to manoeuvre. They started to retreat up the stairs, pushing each other aside for room in which to draw their swords. Their leader levelled his sword at Hawk, but Hawk batted it aside easily and buried his axe in the man's chest. The heavy axehead punched clean through the chain mail, and the force of the blow drove the dead mercenary back against his men.

Hawk jerked his axe free and charged into the mass of
mercenaries, cutting viciously about him. Fisher and Barber
were quickly there at his side, with Winter only a second or
two behind them. Hawk burst through the crowd and blocked
off the stairs so that none of them could break free to warn
Madigan.

Winter and Fisher fought side by side, cutting down the
mercenaries one by one with cold precision, while Barber
spun and danced, his sword lashing out with incredible
speed, spraying blood and guts across the cold stone walls.
His face was casual, almost bored. Soon there were only two
mercenaries left, fighting back to back halfway up the stairs.
Winter ran one through, and the other immediately dropped
his sword and raised his arm in surrender. The SWAT team
leaned on each other, breathing hard, and looked thoughtfully
at the single survivor.

"We don't have the time to look after prisoners," said Barber.

"We can't just kill him in cold blood!" said Hawk.

Barber smiled. "Sure we can. I'll do it, if you're squeam-
ish."

He moved closer to the mercenary, and Hawk stepped forward to block his way. The prisoner looked at them both
frantically.

"Barber's right," said Winter slowly. "We can't take him
with us, and we can't risk him escaping to warn the others."

"He surrendered to us," said Hawk. "He surrendered to me.
And that means he's under my protection. Anyone who wants
him has to go through me."

"What's your problem, Hawk?" said Barber. "Got a soft spot
for mercenaries, have we? It didn't stop you from carving up
this young fellow's friends and colleagues, did it?"

"That was different," said Hawk flatly. "Isobel and I kill
only when it's necessary, to enforce the law. And the law
says a man who has surrendered cannot be killed. He has to
stand trial."

"Be reasonable, Hawk," said Winter. "This scum has already
killed the Gods know how many good men just to get in here,
and he was ready to stand by while defenceless hostages were
killed one by one! The world will be a better place without
him, and you know it. Talk to him, Fisher."

"I agree with Hawk," said Fisher. "I'll fight anyone dumb enough to come at me with a sword in his hand, but I don't kill helpless hostages. And isn't that what he is? Just like the ones we've come to rescue?"

"I don't have time for this!" snapped Winter. "Barber, kill that man. Hawk, Fisher; stand back and don't interfere. That's an order."

"Come here, friend," said Barber to the sweating mercenary. "Co-operate, and I'll make it quick and easy. If you like, I'll give you back your sword."

He stopped as Hawk and Fisher stood side by side between him and the mercenary. "Back off," said Fisher flatly.

"We only kill when we have to," said Hawk to Winter, though his eyes never left Barber. "Otherwise, everything we do and everything we are would be meaningless."

"You've got soft, Hawk," said Barber, his voice openly contemptuous. "Is this the incredible Captain Hawk I've heard so much about? Sudden death on two legs, and nasty with it? One should never meet one's heroes. They're always such a disappointment in the flesh. Now get out of my way, Hawk, or I'll walk right through you."

Hawk grinned suddenly. "Try it."

At which point the mercenary took to his heels and ran up the stairs as though all the devils in Hell were after him. Hawk and Barber both charged after him, with Fisher close behind.

"Stop him!" yelled Winter. "Damn you, Hawk, he mustn't get away, or all the hostages are dead!"

Barber pulled steadily ahead of Hawk as they pounded up the stairs. Hawk fought hard to stay with him, but it had been a long, hard day. His stamina was shot to hell, and his legs were full of lead after climbing up the drain. Fisher ran at his side, struggling for breath. Somehow they managed to at least keep Barber and the mercenary in sight. There was a door at the top of the stairs, standing slightly ajar, and Hawk felt a sudden stab of fear as he realised that if the mercenary could get to it first, he could slam it in their faces and lock them in the cellar while he spread the alarm. Winter would be right. He would have thrown the hostages' lives away for nothing. His face hardened. No. Not for nothing.

The mercenary glanced back over his shoulder, saw Barber gaining on him, and found an extra spurt of speed from somewhere. He'd almost reached the door when it flew open suddenly, and Wulf Saxon stepped through to punch the mercenary out. He flew backwards into Barber, and the two of them fell sprawling in a heap on the stairs. Hawk and Fisher stumbled to a halt just in time to avoid joining the heap, and looked blankly up at Saxon. He smiled at them charmingly.

"I take it you're here to rescue the hostages. So am I. From the look of things, I'd say you needed my help as much as I need yours."

They bundled the unconscious mercenary into a convenient closet on the ground floor, and then found an empty room to talk in. MacReady stood in the doorway, keeping an eye out for Madigan's patrols, while the rest of the SWAT team sank gratefully into comfortable chairs, ignoring his visible irritation. Saxon leaned casually against the mantelpiece, and waited patiently for them to settle themselves. Barber and Hawk had exchanged some pointed looks, but had declared an unspoken truce for the time being. They listened silently with the rest of the team as Saxon brought them up to date on what had been happening in Champion House. Fisher whistled admiringly when he finally stopped.

"Twenty-seven men in twenty minutes. Not too shabby, Saxon. But the last time I saw you, you'd just escaped from Messerschmann's Portrait, stark naked and mad as a hatter, and were busily attacking everything in sight. What happened?"

Saxon smiled. "I wasn't really myself at the time. I'm a lot calmer now."

"You still haven't explained where you got that honour guard's uniform from," said Winter. "You're not telling us you came by that honestly, are you?"

"We've got about five minutes before Madigan kills the next hostage," said Saxon. "Let's save the interrogation till later, shall we? They've already killed one girl; I'm damned if I'll stand by and let them murder another. Now, I'm going to stop Madigan, with or without your help, but it seems to me the hostages' chances for survival would be a lot better if you were involved. Right?"

"Right," said Hawk, getting to his feet. "Let's do it."

"I'm the leader of this team, dammit!" Winter jumped to her feet and glared at Hawk. Then she turned to face Saxon.

"If you want to work with us, you'll follow my orders. Is that clear?"

"Oh, sure," said Saxon. "But first, may I suggest you swap your clothes for those of the mercenaries you just killed? I don't know what you people have been doing, or what that stuff is you have all over you, but it's bound to raise awkward questions. Besides, you all smell quite appalling, and there's always the chance we might want to sneak up on someone. Now let's hurry, please. Some poor hostage is running out of time."

Winter nodded stiffly, and led the SWAT team back into the cellar to change their clothes. Saxon stayed at the top of the stairs and watched the corridor for Madigan's people. Typical Guards. Here he was trying to help, and they were trying to nail him for stealing an honour guard's uniform. Typical. The last he'd heard, when someone wanted to join the Guard they made him take an intelligence test—and if he failed, he was hired. Still, they had their uses. He'd use them to get the hostages clear, but then he was going after Todd and Madigan, and to hell with anyone who got in his way, mercenary or Guard.

The SWAT team came back up out of the cellar, wearing their new clothes, and Saxon had to hide a smile. Despite a lot of swapping back and forth, their new clothes mostly fitted where they touched. They each wore their black iron torcs ostentatiously, in the hope other mercenaries would look at them first, and the clothes second. They'd cleaned themselves up with spit and handkerchiefs as best they could, but it hadn't been all that successful, especially in Hawk's case. But given the look on Hawk's face, Saxon didn't think too many people would challenge him about it.

"All right, this is the plan," said Winter finally. "We haven't time for anything complicated, so we'll make it very basic. Our mission is to rescue the hostages, so their safety comes first. We'll split into two teams. Team One will infiltrate the parlour, as mercenaries. Team Two will cause a diversion outside. When the real mercenaries go to investigate, Team One will kill those mercenaries remaining in the room and then barricade the parlour, thus sealing off the hostages from the terrorists. Team Two will then get the hell out of Champion House, and tell the army to come in and clean this place up. Anyone have any problems with that? Hawk?"

"Yeah," said Hawk evenly. "When the terrorists figure out what's happening, they're going to hit the parlour with everything they've got. How the hell is Team One supposed to keep the hostages alive until the army gets there?"

"You'll think of something," said Winter. "According to your file, you and Fisher specialise in last-minute miracles. Besides, you'll have Barber to help you."

Hawk looked at Fisher. "I just knew she was going to say that. Didn't you just know she was going to say that?"

"What's this about a file?" said Fisher. "Did you know we were in a file?"

"What kind of diversion did you have in mind?" asked Saxon. "These men are professionals. I've got them all nicely stirred up, but they wouldn't leave their posts guarding the hostages for just anything."

"They'd abandon their own families for a chance at you," said Winter. "You've scared them, and mercenaries don't like being scared. Don't worry, Saxon; you'll make excellent bait for our trap."

Never trust a bloody Guard, thought Saxon, nodding politely to Winter. "Shall we go? The deadline for the hostages must be getting dangerously close."

"Of course. If Madigan chooses the wrong hostage to kill, there could be all kinds of political repercussions. Let's go."

"You're all heart, Winter," said Saxon.

They made their way through the largely deserted House without attracting too much attention. The mercenaries were watching for attacks from outside rather than from within, and only those in the parlour knew what Saxon actually looked like. Winter hurried along, saluting officers with brisk efficiency and glaring at anyone who tried to speak to her. Saxon strolled along beside her as though he owned the place. The rest of the team did their best to look unobtrusive, while still keeping their hands near their weapons at all times. They reached the main parlour without being challenged, and Winter, Saxon, and MacReady hung back at the end of the corridor to let the others go on ahead.

Hawk looked at Barber. "I'll handle the talking. Right?"

"Sure," said Barber. "That seems to be what you're best at."

Hawk gave him a hard look, and then strolled casually up to the mercenary at the parlour door. "Any trouble inside?"

"No, they're quiet as mice. Why? You expecting trouble?"

"Could be. Madigan will be here in a minute to select the next victim. We're here to help make sure things go smoothly this time."

"Glad to have you," said the mercenary, pushing open the parlour door. "You heard what that rogue guard did to us?"

"Yeah. Better keep an eye open; he might turn up here again."

"I hope he does," said the mercenary grimly. "I hope he does."

Hawk and Fisher strolled casually into the parlour and took up positions by the buffet table. Barber leaned against the wall by the door. Hawk's stomach rumbled loudly at such proximity to food, but he ignored it, trying to take in as much of the situation as he could without being too obvious about it. There were sixteen mercenaries, scattered round the room in twos and threes, and fifty-one hostages, including the two Kings. Most of the hostages looked scared and thoroughly cowed, but there were a few military types here and there who looked as though they might be useful when the action started.

Hawk frowned slightly. Once the mercenaries in the parlour realised they were under attack, the odds were they'd try and grab the most important hostages to use as bargaining points; and that meant the two Kings. They had to be protected at all costs. Winter had been very specific about that. According to her orders, all the other hostages were expendable, as long as the two Kings came out of it safe and sound. Hawk had nodded politely to that at the time, but as far as he was concerned the Kings could take their chances with everyone else. They knew the job was risky when they took it. Still, it might be a good idea to get a message to them, so that their own people could protect them once the fighting started.

He nodded for Fisher to stay where she was, and headed casually towards the two Kings at the back of the room. Team One was now pretty much in position: Barber by the door, ready to slam and barricade it, Fisher covering the middle of the room, and Hawk by the Kings. Everything was going according to plan, which made Hawk feel distinctly nervous. In his experience, it was always when a scheme seemed to be going especially smoothly that Lady Fate liked to step in and really mess things up. Still, he had to admit he couldn't see what could go wrong this time. They'd covered every eventuality. He stopped before the two Kings, and gave them his best reassuring smile. Both monarchs ostentatiously ignored him, while the nearby Quality glared at him with undisguised loathing. Hawk coughed politely, and leaned forward as though studying the Kings' finery.

"Don't get too excited," he murmured, his voice little more than a breath of air, "but help has arrived. When the excitement starts, don't panic. It's just part of a diversion to lure away the mercenaries. My associates and I will take care of those who remain, and then barricade the room and hold it until help arrives from outside. Got it?"

"Got it," said King Gregor, his lips barely moving. "Who are you?"

"Captain Hawk, Haven SWAT."

"How many of you are there?" said King Louis of Outremer quietly.

"Only three here in the room, but there are more outside, ready to start the commotion."

"No offence, Captain Hawk," said King Gregor, "but it's going to take a lot more than three men to hold this room against a concerted attack."

Hawk smiled. "I was hoping you might be able to suggest a few good men we could depend on when things start getting rough."

King Gregor nodded slowly. "I think I might be able to help you there, Captain."

He gestured surreptitiously for a young noble to approach him. The noble looked casually around to see if any of the mercenaries were watching, and then wandered unhurriedly over to stand beside King Gregor. He glanced at Hawk, and then looked again, more closely. King Gregor smiled.

"Exactly, my young friend. It seems we're about to be rescued, and this gentleman is one of our rescuers. But he could use a little help. Alert those with the stomach for a little action, would you, and tell them to stand by."

"Of course, Your Majesty. We've been waiting for something like this to happen." Sir Roland bowed slightly to the two Kings, looked hard at Hawk, and moved back into the crowd. Hawk looked carefully around, but the mercenaries didn't seem to have noticed the brief, muttered conversations. Very slack, but mercenaries functioned best as fighting men, not prison guards. He checked that Fisher and Barber were still in position, and let his hand rest impatiently on the axe at his side. Surely something should have happened by now. What were they waiting for outside? He looked around him to see how the young noble was getting on with his search for support, and then froze as he saw the man talking openly with a group of mercenaries by the double windows. The mercenaries looked straight at Hawk, and the noble gave him a smile and a mocking bow. Hawk swore, and drew his axe.

"Isobel, Barber; we've been betrayed! Get Team Two in here, and then barricade the door and hold it. Move it!"

He charged at the two nearest mercenaries, and cut them down with swift, vicious blows while they were still trying to work out what was going on. The hostages screamed, and scattered this way and that as mercenaries ploughed through them to get to Hawk. He grinned broadly, and went to meet them with his axe dripping blood. Barber yelled out the door to Team Two, and then had to turn and defend himself against a concerted attack by three mercenaries. His sword flashed brightly as he spun and thrust and parried with impossible grace and speed, holding off all three men at once and making it look effortless. Fisher tried to get to him, to keep the door open for Team Two, but was quickly stopped and surrounded by more mercenaries. She put her back against the nearest wall and cut viciously about her with her sword, manoeuvring constantly so that the mercenaries got in each other's way as often as not.

The parlour was full of the din of battle, punctuated by screams and shouts from the hostages, but the noise grew even louder as Team Two finally burst in through the open door. Winter and Saxon tore into the scattered mercenaries like an axe through rotten wood, and for a moment it seemed as though the reunited SWAT team might have the advantage, but only a few seconds later a crowd of mercenaries streamed through the open door, led by Glen and Bailey. The room quickly filled to its limit, and the sheer press of numbers made fighting difficult, but the terrorists didn't shrink from cutting a way through the defenceless hostages to get at their opponents. Some of the hostages tried to help their rescuers, grappling barehanded with the mercenaries, but others worked openly with Sir Roland to help the soldiers. Screams filled the air, and the rich carpets were soaked with blood and gore.

Glen launched himself at Barber as he cut down the last of his three assailants, and the two swordsmen stood toe to toe, ignoring everything else, caught up in their own private battle of skill and speed and tactics. Hawk made his way slowly through the chaos to fight at Fisher's side, and they ended up together with their backs to the double windows. Hawk fought furiously, trying to open up some space around him so that he could use his axe to better advantage, but there were just too many mercenaries, and more were pouring through the door every minute.

Winter ducked and weaved and almost made it out the door a dozen times, but always at the last moment there was someone there to block the way. She fought on, desperate to break away. She had to get word out of the House that the SWAT team's mission was a failure. Saxon ploughed through the soldiers, dodging their blows easily and breaking skulls with his fists. He snatched up one opponent, and tried to use him as a living club with which to beat the others, but there wasn't enough room. He threw the unconscious body aside, and flailed about him with his fists and feet, grinning widely as blood flew on the air, and well-armed mercenaries fell back rather than face him. But for all his efforts, he was still outnumbered and surrounded, and it was all he could do to hold his ground. MacReady stood alone in a corner, unable to escape or intervene, but protected by his magic from any personal danger. Mercenaries kept trying to seize him, only to end up dead or injured as MacReady's charm turned their attacks back against them. Even the hostages were afraid to go near him, though their numbers kept him blocked off from the only exit.

Glen and Barber cut and stamped and thrust, grinning humourlessly as they panted and grunted with every moment. Sweat ran down their faces as they both tried every trick they knew, only to see their moves blocked or countered by the other's skill or speed. Finally a mercenary bumped into Barber from behind, throwing him off balance for a fraction of a second, and that was all Glen needed. He lunged forward with all his weight behind it, and his sword slammed between Barber's ribs and punched bloodily out of his back. Barber sank to his knees, fighting for breath as blood filled his lungs, and tried to lift his sword. Glen put his foot against Barber's chest and pushed him backwards, jerking out his sword as he did so. Barber fell on his back, blood filling his mouth. There was no pain yet, held off for the moment by shock, and his mind seemed strangely clear and alert. He rolled awkwardly onto his side and channelled all his will into his sole remaining talent: the ability to move unseen and unheard. He crawled towards the door, where Winter was fighting fiercely, leaving a trail of his own blood behind him on the thick pile carpet, and neither the mercenaries nor the hostages paid him any attention. He grinned crazily, feeling blood roll down his chin. He'd get out of there and hole up somewhere till the army stormed the place. He'd done all that could be expected of him. As far as he was concerned, the fight was over. And then a shadow fell across his path, and he sensed someone leaning over him. A quiet voice spoke right next to his ear.

"Nice try. But I know that trick too."

Glen thrust his sword through the back of Barber's neck, skewering him to the floor. Blood gushed out of Barber's mouth in a seemingly endless flow.

Winter hit Glen from behind, slamming him against the wall and knocking the breath out of him. She drew back her sword for a killing thrust but then had to turn and run as mercenaries burst out of the milling crowd after her. She glanced briefly at Barber's unmoving body, and then sprinted out the door and down the empty corridor, not daring to look back at her pursuers. All thoughts of plans and revenge were forgotten for the moment, her mind filled only with the need to survive. She ran on, from corridor to corridor, never slowing, long after her pursuers had given up and turned back.

Hawk and Fisher were backed right up against the double windows, facing a solid block of mercenaries. None of them seemed particularly anxious to get within sword's range and risk their lives unnecessarily. There were more than enough of them to block off any hope of escape, and they were happy to settle for that. Hawk and Fisher stood side by side, weapons at the ready, using the opportunity to get their breath back. They had a strong feeling there might not be another.

Bailey ploughed through the crowd towards Saxon, using his great size to open up a path before him. Hostages and mercenaries alike hurried to get out of his way, reacting as much to the grim determination in his face as his imposing size. Saxon spun round to face the new threat, not even breathing hard. There was blood on his hands and his clothing, and none of it was his. Bailey bore down on Saxon, swinging his great sword with both hands. Saxon waited till the last minute, and then ducked easily under the blow and sank his fist into Bailey's gut. The fist drove clean through Bailey's chain mail and brought him to a sudden halt, as though he'd run into a wall. He convulsed as the fist plunged on, burying itself in his gut, and the heavy sword slipped from his numb hands. Bailey felt the strength go out of his legs and deliberately slumped forward, trying to bring Saxon down with the sheer weight of his huge frame. Saxon stopped Bailey's fall and picked him up easily, as though the huge mercenary weighed practically nothing, and threw him against the nearest wall.

Bailey hit the wall hard, the impact driving all the breath out of him. Ribs cracked audibly, driving spikes of pain into his side, and his eyesight faded out for a moment, but somehow he got his feet under him again, and his hands curled into fists before him. Saxon stepped forward and drove his fist into Bailey's stomach, crushing it between his fist and the wall. Blood flew from Bailey's mouth, and he collapsed as the last of his strength went out of him. He sat with his back against the wall, looking unflinchingly up at Saxon as he raised his fist for the final blow that would crush Bailey's skull. And then Saxon hesitated, and lowered his fist. He crouched down before the huge man and looked at him thoughtfully. The watching hostages and mercenaries made no move to intervene. Bailey stared back at Saxon, breathing slowly and painfully.

"Finish it. I'm dying anyway. Feels like you broke something important inside."

"Who are you?" said Saxon. "I feel like I ought to know you."

Bailey smiled, and blood ran from the corners of his mouth. "It's been a long time, Wulf. Twenty-three years, since you ran out on us."

Saxon looked at him for a long moment, and then his blood ran cold as he saw the ghost of familiar features in Bailey's battered and weather-worn face. "No . . . Curt? Is that you, Curt?"

"Took you long enough, Wulf. Or had you forgotten all about your baby brother?"

"They told me you were dead!"

Bailey smiled again. "They said the same about you. But I recognized you the first moment I saw you, pretending to be a guard. You haven't changed at all, Wulf."

"You have. Look at the size of you. Dammit, Curt, you were always such a scrawny kid. . . . Why the hell did you fight me? We're family."

"No," said Bailey flatly. "You stopped being family when you ran out on us. These people are my family now. I would have killed you if I could. But you always were a better fighter than me. Finish it, Wulf. Don't let me die slow, if there's a spark of honour left within you."

"Curt, don't make me do this. I can't let you go, not after finding you again. Don't leave me here alone."

"Selfish as ever, Wulf. Do it, damn you! Put me out of my misery! You owe me that much."

Bailey coughed harshly, spraying blood across Saxon's face. Saxon brushed it away with his sleeve, and then reached out tenderly and took Bailey's head in his hands. "Rest easy, brother."

He snapped Bailey's head round sharply, and there was a loud crack as the neck broke. Saxon released him, and Bailey slumped back against the wall and was still. Saxon looked at him for a long moment, and then reached out and closed his brother's eyes. He rose clumsily to his feet, and looked around him, and the mercenaries shrank back from the rage and despair in his eyes. He strode over to the hidden door in the wall, still wedged half-open, and disappeared into the concealed passageway. No one made any move to stop him, or follow after him.

By the time Madigan and Ritenour appeared on the scene, shortly afterwards, the fighting was over. The hostages had been rounded up and put under guard again, Hawk and Fisher stood at bay before the windows, and MacReady watched calmly from his corner. Madigan looked at the dead and injured lying scattered across the room, and beckoned to Glen, who hurried over to join him, grinning broadly.

"What happened?" said Madigan.

"Local SWAT team tried for a rescue," said Glen. "One's dead, two ran away, including that bastard Saxon, and we've got the other three boxed in. They're not going anywhere. I thought you'd want to talk to them before we killed them."

"Quite right," said Madigan, smiling at him briefly. "You've done well, Glen. Now have the bodies removed, and see to the wounded."

Glen frowned. "Does that include the hostages?"

"Of course. They'll die when I decide, not before." He nodded for Ritenour to accompany him, and strode unhurriedly over to MacReady. "And who might you be?"

"John MacReady, negotiator for the Haven SWAT team. I assure you there's no need for any further violence. If we could just sit down somewhere and talk, I'm sure we could find a way out of this situation."

"That's very kind of you," said Madigan. "But I really have no need for a negotiator. I like the situation the way it is." He looked across at Glen. "Kill this one."

"You can't," said MacReady quickly. "I cannot be harmed."

Madigan looked at Ritenour. "Is that right?"

"Normally, yes." Ritenour looked at MacReady, and smiled. "But, unfortunately for him, there's so much magic built into these walls it's quite simple for me to put aside the charm that protects him. He's all yours, Madigan. But I should cut off the head, just to be sure."

"An excellent suggestion." Madigan nodded to Glen. "Cut off his head."

Glen gestured to two mercenaries, who grabbed MacReady by the arms and dragged him out of his corner. At first it seemed he couldn't believe it, but then he began to struggle and shout as they forced him onto his knees in front of Glen. They held him easily. Glen raised his sword, took careful aim, and brought it down in a long, sweeping stroke. The blade bit deeply into the back of MacReady's neck, and blood spurted over a wide area. He heaved against the mercenaries' hands, and almost got his feet under him before they forced him down again. Glen struck again and again, hacking at MacReady's neck like a woodsman with a stubborn tree trunk. Many of the hostages cried out, or turned their faces away as MacReady's screams gave way to horrid sounds. Glen's sword cut through at last, and MacReady's head rolled away across the carpet, the mouth still working though the eyes were glazed. The two mercenaries dropped the twitching body, stepped back, and tried to wipe some of the blood from their clothes. Glen wiped the sweat from his forehead, and grinned at Madigan.

"Never actually beheaded a man before. Hard work, that. Executioners always make it look so easy."

"I imagine the wooden block makes a lot of difference," said Madigan. "Remove the head and the body. Burn the body, but give the head to the city negotiators, so they can see what happens to those foolish enough to try and stage a rescue." He turned away and looked at Hawk and Fisher, staring grimly at him from their place before the double windows. "And now, finally, we come to you. The infamous Captains Hawk and Fisher. I always thought you'd be taller. No matter. I think we'll make your deaths last a little longer, as an example to those who would dare defy me. I wish I had more time, to allow for some real inventiveness, but even so, I promise you you'll beg for death before I'm done." He turned to the nearest mercenary. "Heat some irons in the fire." He smiled at Hawk and Fisher. "I've always been a traditionalist in such things." He gestured for his men to come forward. "Disarm them, and then strip them."

Hawk glanced over his shoulder, out the windows. Madigan smiled. "Don't even think about it, Captain. We're on the top floor, remember? It's four storeys, straight down. The fall would undoubtedly kill you both."

Hawk put away his axe, and gestured for Fisher to do the same. He grinned back at Madigan, his single eye burning coldly. "Better a quick death than a slow one. Right, Isobel?"

"Right, Hawk. Burn in hell, Madigan."

Hawk turned and kicked the windows open. The mercenaries surged forward. Hawk took Fisher's hand in his, and together they jumped out of the windows, and disappeared from sight.

5

At Play in the Fields
of the Lord

Madigan looked at the open windows for a moment, and then shrugged and turned away. "A pity. Now I'll never know whether or not I could have broken them. Still, that's life. Or in their case, death."

"Shall I take the irons out of the fire, sir?" asked the mercenary by the fireplace.

Madigan considered the matter briefly, and then shook his head. "No, leave them there. You never know; someone else might annoy me. In the meantime, send someone down to recover Hawk and Fisher's bodies, and then deliver them to the city negotiators. When they ask how their famous Captains died, you can tell them that the illustrious Hawk and Fisher leapt to their deaths rather than face me."

Madigan dismissed the mercenary and the subject with a wave of his hand, and moved away to stare thoughtfully down at Bailey's body. The big man looked somehow even larger in death, despite the blood and the limply lolling head. Glen was crouching beside him, staring into Bailey's empty face as though waiting for him to explain what had gone wrong. A lock of Bailey's hair had fallen across his eyes, and Glen tucked it back out of the way with an almost gentle touch. He realised Madigan was standing over him, and looked up quickly, expecting some scathing comment at such a show of weakness. Instead, to his surprise, Madigan crouched down beside him.

"It's not wrong to grieve, boy. We've all lost friends and loved ones. That's what brought most of us into the Cause in the first place. You'll get your chance to avenge him."

"He always looked out for me," said Glen. "Taught me how to work as part of a team. I wish I'd listened to him more now."

"I wonder what they talked about," said Madigan.

Glen looked at him, puzzled. "Who?"

"Bailey and the man who killed him, Wulf Saxon. They talked for a moment, before Saxon broke Bailey's neck. If I can find the time, I think I'll have Ritenour call up Bailey's spirit, and ask him. It might be important. Saxon is becoming dangerously meddlesome." He realised Glen was staring at him, shocked. "Is something wrong, Ellis?"

"Bailey's dead. He died for us! It isn't right to disturb his rest."

Madigan put his hand on Glen's shoulder. "He died for the Cause, because he knew nothing was more important than what we plan to do here tonight. He'd understand that sometimes you have to do unpleasant things because they're necessary. We took an oath, Ellis, remember? All of us. *Anything for the Cause.*"

"Yes," said Glen. "Anything for the Cause." He got to his feet and sat on the edge of the buffet table while he cleaned the blood from his sword with a piece of cloth. He didn't look at Madigan or Bailey.

Madigan sighed quietly, and moved to the other end of the table, where the sorcerer Ritenour was dubiously sampling some of the more exotic side dishes. He picked up a wine bottle to study the label, and Madigan produced a silver hip flask and offered it to him. "Try some of mine. I think you'll find it a far superior vintage to anything you're likely to find here. Whoever stocked this House's cellar had a distinctly pedestrian palate."

Ritenour took the flask, opened it, and sniffed the bouquet cautiously. His eyebrows rose, and he studied Madigan with a new respect. "You continue to surprise me, Daniel. It's hard to picture you sampling vintages in between the kidnappings and assassinations."

Madigan shrugged easily. "Every man should have a hobby."

Ritenour poured a healthy measure into a glass, and then stopped and looked at Madigan suspiciously. "Aren't you joining me, Daniel?"

"Of course," said Madigan. He took back the flask, found himself a glass, and filled it almost to the brim. He rolled the wine in the glass to release the bouquet, savoured it for a moment, and then drank deeply. He sighed appreciatively, and then lowered the glass and looked coldly at the sorcerer. "Really, Ritenour, you don't think I'd poison my own wine, do you? Particularly a fine vintage like this."

Ritenour bowed slightly. "My apologies, Daniel. Old habits die hard."

"A toast, then. I think we're ready to begin the final phase. To success!"

They both drank deeply, and Madigan took the opportunity to look around the room. Most of the hostages were still in shock from the sudden death and violence, and the dashing of their hopes of rescue, but some were clearly seething with anger at being betrayed by those they'd thought they could trust. Violence was bubbling just below the surface, and several of the mercenaries were watching the situation carefully, swords at the ready. Sir Roland and his fellow conspirators had been herded off to one side by the mercenaries, at their own request, and now stood close together, their faces wearing an uneasy blend of self-righteousness and apprehension. Some of them looked to Madigan for support, but he just looked back impassively. The traitors had done as he'd expected, but their usefulness had passed. They were expendable now. Just like everyone else.

As he watched, the crowd of hostages suddenly parted as the two Kings strode forward together to glare at the traitors. A thin line of mercenaries kept the two groups apart with raised swords. King Gregor of the Low Kingdoms ignored them, fixing Sir Roland with a burning gaze. The traitor stared back unflinchingly, with mocking self-assurance.

"Why?" said King Gregor finally. "Why did you betray us? I trusted you, Roland. I gave you wealth and position and favour. What more could you want?"

"Power," said Sir Roland easily. "And a great deal more wealth. I'll have both, once Outremer and the Low Kingdoms are at war. My associates and I had been planning for some

time on how best to take advantage of a small, carefully
controlled war on our outer borders, and we weren't about to
abandon all our plans just because both Parliaments suddenly
got cold feet. War is too important to the right sort of people
to be left to politicians."

"You won't get away with this," said King Louis of Outremer,
his voice calm and quiet and very dangerous. "There's nowhere
you can go, nowhere you can hide, that my people won't find
you. I'll see you dragged through the streets by your heels
for this."

Sir Roland smiled arrogantly. "You're in no position to
threaten anyone, old man. You see, you don't really understand what's going on here. To begin with, you can forget
about being ransomed. Madigan doesn't give a damn about
the money. Like us, he's in favour of war, so he's planned an
atrocity so shocking that war will be inevitable, once carefully
planted rumours have convinced both sides that the other is
really to blame."

"What . . . kind of atrocity?" said King Gregor.

"You're going to be executed, Your Majesty," said Sir
Roland. "You, and King Louis, and all the other hostages,
save for those few like myself, who can be trusted to tell the
story in the right way. Isn't that right, Madigan?"

"In a way," said the terrorist. He looked at Ritenour, ignoring Sir Roland's angry, puzzled gaze. "It's time, sorcerer. Have
you absorbed enough magic from the House?"

"Yes," said Ritenour, putting down his empty glass and
patting his mouth delicately with a folded napkin. "It's been
a slow process. I couldn't risk hurrying it, or the build-up
of power would have been noticed by those monitoring the
situation from outside. But your hostage negotiations brought
me the time I needed. I'm ready now. We can begin."

"Begin?" snapped Sir Roland. "Begin what?" He started
toward Madigan, and then stopped as the mercenaries raised
their swords threateningly. "What is this, Madigan? What is
he talking about?"

Madigan looked at him calmly. "You didn't really think I'd
settle for just the Kings and a handful of hostages, did you?
That wouldn't have had nearly enough impact. No, traitor,
my hatred for the Low Kingdoms and Outremer Parliaments
requires a more extravagant gesture than killing two political

figureheads and a crowd of toadying hangers-on. I'm going to destroy your whole city. Starting with everyone in this House. Do it, sorcerer."

Ritenour grinned, and gestured sharply. An oppressive weight fell across the room, crushing everyone to their knees, except for Madigan, Glen, and Ritenour. Hostages and mercenaries alike screamed and cursed and moaned in horror as the life drained slowly out of them. A few tried to crawl to the door, dragging themselves painfully across the rich pile carpet, but Glen moved quickly to block their way, grinning broadly. The victims clawed and clutched at each other, but one by one their eyes glazed and their breathing slowed, and the sorcerer Ritenour glowed like the sun. Stolen lives boiled within him, the mounting energy pressing against his controlling wards, and he laughed aloud as his new power beat within him like a giant heart. The glow faded away as his control firmed, and he looked slowly around him. Lifeless bodies covered the floor from wall to wall. Mercenaries in their chain mail, hostages in their finery, and the two Kings, staring up at the ceiling with empty eyes. Ritenour wanted to shout and dance and shriek with glee. He looked triumphantly at Madigan, who bowed formally. Over by the doorway, Glen was giggling. They all looked round sharply as they heard hurried footsteps approaching down the corridor outside, and then relaxed as Horn and Eleanour Todd appeared in the doorway. Horn and Todd looked briefly at the bodies on the floor, and then nodded to Madigan.

"Everyone inside Champion House's walls is now dead, Daniel," said Todd briskly. "Everyone but us, of course."

Horn laughed. "You should have seen the mercenaries' faces when the spell hit them! Dropped like flies, they did."

"We'll have to move fast," said Todd, ignoring Horn. "The mercenaries out in the grounds are unaffected, but it won't be long before the city sorcerers watching this place realise something's happened. They'll hold off for a while out of caution, but once they realise there's no longer any contact with anyone inside the House, they'll come charging in here like a brigade of cavalry to the rescue."

"They'll be too late," said Madigan calmly. "By the time they've worked up their courage, the ritual will have taken place. And then it will be too late for many things."

Horn chuckled quietly, brimming with good humour as he stirred a dead body with his foot. "You know, in a few minutes we're going to do what no army's been able to do for centuries. We're going to destroy the city of Haven, and grind it into the dust. They'll write our names in the history books."

"If we don't get a move on, they'll write it on our tombstones," growled Todd.

Madigan raised a hand, and they fell silent. "It's time, my friends. Let's do it."

Down below the parlour's double windows, Hawk was clinging grimly to the thick, matted ivy that covered the ancient stone wall. Fisher was clinging equally grimly to his waist, and trying to dig her boots into the greenery. Hawk clenched his hands around the ivy, and dug his feet deeper into the thick, spongy mass. For the moment it was holding his weight and Fisher's, but already he could hear soft tearing sounds as parts of the ivy pulled away from the wall. Fisher tested the mass of leaves under her feet with some of her weight, and when it held she cautiously transferred her hands to the vines, one at a time, taking care not to throw Hawk off balance as she did so. They both froze where they were for a moment, and struggled to get their harsh breathing back under control.

"Tell me something," said Fisher. "Did you know this ivy was here when you jumped out the window?"

"Oh sure," said Hawk. "I saw it when I looked out the windows that first time. Mind you, I was only guessing it would hold our weight. But it looked pretty thick. Besides, under the circumstances we didn't have much choice. Didn't you know about the ivy?"

"No. I just assumed you had something in mind. You usually do."

"I'm touched. You want your head examined, but I'm touched."

They grinned at each other, and then looked carefully about them.

"All right, clever dick, what do we do now?" said Fisher.

"There's a window directly below us. We climb down, break the glass with as little noise as possible, and climb in. And we'd better do it quickly, before some bright spark up above thinks to look out the window to see where we landed."

They slowly clambered down the thick carpet of green leaves, which creaked and tore under their weight, but still clung stubbornly to the wall. Hawk wondered vaguely if perhaps the magic in the House's walls had somehow affected the vines as well, but didn't have time to dwell on the matter. He was pretty sure they couldn't be seen against the ivy in the evening gloom, but once someone discovered their bodies weren't where they were supposed to be, all hell would break loose. He pushed the pace as much as he dared, but while it was only a few more feet down to the third-floor window, it seemed like miles.

He grabbed at another strand of ivy as he lowered himself towards the window, and it came away in his hand. He swung out away from the wall, holding desperately on with his other hand, suddenly all too aware of the long drop beneath him. He tried to pull himself back towards the wall, and the vine creaked threateningly. Fisher saw what was happening and reached out a hand to grab him. She couldn't reach him, and pushed herself further out from the wall. The whole mass of ivy beneath her ripped away from the wall, and she fell like a stone. Hawk snatched at her as she fell past him, and grasped her hand in his. She jerked to a halt and swung back towards the wall. Her feet thudded to a halt beside the third-floor window, but there was no ivy within reach of her free hand or her feet, which she could use to stabilize herself. She hung beneath Hawk, twisting and turning, and his mouth gaped soundlessly in agony as her weight pulled at his arm, threatening to tear it from its socket. The vine he clung to jerked and gave under his other hand as their combined weight pulled it from the old stone wall bit by bit.

"Drop me," said Fisher.

"Shut up," said Hawk quickly. "I've got you. You're safe."

"You've got to let me go, Hawk," said Fisher, her voice calm and steady. "If you don't, our weight is going to rip the ivy right off that wall, and we're both going to die."

"I won't let you go. I can't."

"If you die, who's going to avenge me? Do you want those bastards to get away with it? Do it, Hawk. While there's still time. Just tell me you love me, and let go. Please."

"No! There's another way! There has to be another way." Hawk thought furiously as the ivy jerked and trembled beneath his hand. "Isobel, use your feet to push yourself away from the wall. Get yourself swinging, work up a good momentum, and then crash right through the bloody window!"

"Hawk," said Fisher, "That is the dumbest plan you've ever come up with."

"Have you got a better idea?"

"Good point. Brace yourself, love."

Hawk set his teeth against the awful pain in his shoulder, and clutched desperately at the ivy as though he could hold it to the wall by sheer willpower. Sweat ran down his face, and his breathing grew fast and ragged. Fisher pushed herself away from the wall, swinging out over the long drop, back and forth, back and forth. It seemed to take forever to build up any speed, like a child trying to get a swing moving on its own. She could hear Hawk panting and groaning above her, and she could tell both their hands were getting dangerously sweaty. She pushed hard against the wall, swinging out and away, and then twisted her arm slightly so that she was flying back towards the window. The heavy glass loomed up before her, and she tucked her knees up to her chest. Her heels hit the glass together, and the window shattered. She flew into the room beyond, and fell clumsily to the floor as Hawk's hand was jerked out of hers by the impact. She scrambled to her feet and was there at the window to catch him as he half climbed, half fell through the window. They clung to each other, shaking and trembling and gasping for breath.

"Drop you?" said Hawk, eventually. "Did you really think I'd do a dumb thing like that?"

Fisher shrugged. "It seemed a good idea at the time. But your idea was better. For a change."

"I will rise above that remark. Go and take a look out the door. The amount of noise we made crashing in here, someone must have heard us."

Fisher nodded, and padded over to the door, sword in hand. She eased it open a crack, looked out into the corridor, and then looked back at Hawk and shook her head. He nodded, and collapsed gratefully into the nearest chair.

"I hate heights."

"You needn't think you're going to sit there and rest," said Fisher mercilessly. "We haven't got the time. We've got to figure out what the hell we're going to do next. Our original plan was based on us having the element of surprise, and we've blown that. So what do we do? Get the hell out of here, tell the Council we failed, and they'd better start getting the ransom money together? Or do we stick around, and see if maybe we can pick off the terrorists one by one?"

"No," said Hawk reluctantly. "We can't risk that. They'd just start executing the hostages, in reprisal. Standard terrorist tactic. But, on the other hand, we can't afford to leave just yet. We need more information about what's going on here." He frowned suddenly, and looked intently at Fisher. "You know, we could be all that's left of the SWAT team. Barber and MacReady are dead, Winter's hiding somewhere in a panic, and Storm's trapped outside, unable to reach us. Whatever happens now, it's down to us."

Fisher smiled and shrugged. "As usual. Mind you, Saxon's still around here somewhere. At least, I suppose he is. He disappeared during the fighting."

Hawk sniffed. "Yeah, well, Saxon didn't exactly strike me as being too stable, even at the best of times. Hardly surprising, I suppose, after spending all those years trapped in the Portrait. I just hope he hasn't had a relapse, ripped all his clothes off, and reverted back to the way he was when we first met him. That's all we need."

"I don't know," said Fisher. "If nothing else, a naked, blood-thirsty madman stalking the corridors would make one hell of a distraction." Hawk gave her a hard look, and she laughed. "I know; don't tempt Fate. Come on, get up out of that chair. We've got work to do."

Hawk hauled himself out of the chair, stretched painfully, and together they moved silently over to the door and slipped out into the corridor, weapons at the ready. It was completely deserted, and deathly quiet. They moved cautiously down the corridor, and up the stairs to the next floor, but there was no trace of movement anywhere. Hawk scowled unhappily. They ought to have run across some kind of patrol by now. Madigan hadn't struck him as the type to overlook basic security measures. He and Fisher hurried down the empty corridors, impelled by a strange inner sense of urgency, the only sound the quiet scuffling of their feet. They rounded a corner and then stopped abruptly as they discovered the first bodies. Two mercenaries lay sprawled on the floor, their bulging eyes fixed and sightless. Hawk and Fisher looked quickly about them, but there was no sign of any attackers. Hawk moved quickly forward, and knelt by the bodies to examine them while Fisher stood guard.

"Could it have been Saxon?" said Fisher quietly. "After all, he killed twenty-seven mercenaries before he joined up with us."

"I don't think so," said Hawk. "I can't find any wound, any cause of death. This stinks of magic."

"Maybe Storm finally broke through the House's wards and decided to help."

"No. He'd have contacted us by now, if he could. And the only other sorcerer in this place belongs to Madigan."

They looked at each other. "Double cross?" said Fisher finally. "Maybe they had a falling out."

"Could be," said Hawk. He got to his feet again, and hefted his axe thoughtfully. "I think we'd better head back to the main parlour and see if we can get a look at what's happening there. I'm starting to get a really bad feeling about this."

They padded quickly down the corridor. As they made their way through the fourth floor they came across more and more bodies, and by the time they reached the corridor that led to the main parlour they were running flat out, no longer caring if anyone saw or heard them. They slowed down as they approached the parlour, stepping carefully around the dead mercenaries lying scattered the length of the hall. The parlour door stood open, and the air was still and silent as a tomb. Hawk and Fisher moved forward warily, weapons held out before them, and peered in through the doorway. The dead lay piled together, hostage and mercenary, so that it was almost impossible to tell them apart. Hawk and Fisher checked the room with a few quick, cursory glances, but it was obvious the killers were long gone. They examined some of the bodies for signs of life, just in case, but there were no survivors, and nothing to show how they died. There was no trace of Madigan or any of his people among the bodies, but they'd expected that. And then they found the two Kings, and the heart went out of them.

"So it will be war, after all," said Fisher dully. "We failed, Hawk. Everything we've done has been for nothing. Why did they do it? Why did they kill them all?".

"I don't know," said Hawk. "But one thing's clear now; the situation isn't what we thought it was. Madigan never had any interest in the ransom money, or any of his other demands. He had his own secret agenda, and the hostages were just window dressing. A distraction, to keep us from guessing what he was really up to."

"But why kill his own men, too?" said Fisher. "He's left the House practically undefended. It doesn't make sense!"

"It has to, somehow! Madigan's not stupid or insane. He always has a reason, for what ever he's doing."

Hawk! Fisher! Storm's voice crashed into their minds like thunder, and they both winced. *Listen to me! You must get down to the cellar immediately! Something's happening down there. Something bad.*

What kind of something? snapped Hawk. *We've got our own problems. The Kings and the hostages are all dead.*

Forget them! Ritenour's getting ready to perform a forbidden ritual. No wonder Madigan chose him; he's a shaman as well as a sorcerer.

Fisher looked at Hawk. "What's a shaman?"

"Some kind of specialised sorcerer, I think. Deals with spirits of the dead, stuff like that." *Storm! Talk to us; what's happening down in the cellar? Is it part of Madigan's plan?*

Yes. They're going to open the Unknown Door.

What?

Run, damn you! Get to the cellar while there's still time. A storm is building in the Fields of the Lord, and the beasts are howling, howling. . . .

Down in the cellar, Ritenour was on his knees, painstakingly drawing a blue chalk pentacle on the floor. Glen and Eleanour Todd watched with interest, while Madigan stood a little apart, his gaze turned inward. Horn padded up and down at the base of the stairs, scowling impatiently. He didn't trust Ritenour, and deep down he didn't trust the spell to do what it was supposed to. Madigan had explained the plan to him many times, and he still didn't really understand it. He had no head for magic, and never had. His scowl deepened. It was bad enough they were depending on untried magic to destroy Haven, but they were also dependent on Ritenour, and Horn didn't trust that shifty-eyed kid-killer any further than he could throw him.

It had all seemed different, up in the main parlour. He'd been happy and confident and full of enthusiasm for the plan, then. But now he was down in the gloom of the cellar, the only illumination a single lamp on the wall, and his mood had changed, darkened. He didn't like the cellar. The place felt bad; spoiled, on some elemental level. He shuddered suddenly, and made a determined effort to throw off the pessimistic mood. Everything was going to be fine. Madigan had said so, and he understood these things. Horn trusted Madigan. He had to, or nothing in his life had meaning anymore.

He deliberately turned his back on the sorcerer, and scowled nervously up the stairs. He kept thinking he heard movement somewhere up above, just beyond the point where the light gave way to an impenetrable darkness. It was just nerves. There couldn't be anyone there. The sorcerer had killed them all. For a moment his imagination showed him dead bodies rising to their feet and stumbling slowly through the House, making their way down to the cellar to take a hideous revenge on those who had killed them. Horn shook his head, dismissing the thought. He'd killed many men in his time, and none of them had ever come back for revenge. It took a lot of magic to resurrect the dead, and the only sorcerer in Champion House was Ritenour. Horn breathed deeply, calming himself. Not long now, and then the ritual would be under way. Once started, nothing could stop it. And his long-awaited vengeance on Outremer would finally begin. He looked round sharply as Ritenour rose awkwardly to his feet, his knees making loud cracking sounds in the quiet.

"Is that it?" said Horn quickly. "Can we start now?"

"We're almost ready," said Madigan, smiling pleasantly. "How long have you been my man, Horn?"

Horn frowned, thrown for a moment by the unexpected question. "Six years. Why?"

"You've always obeyed my orders and followed my wishes. You swore the oath to me. Anything for the Cause. Remember?"

"Sure I remember." Horn looked at Madigan warily. This was leading up to something, and he didn't like the feel of it. "You want me to do something now? Is that it?"

"Yes, Horn. That's it. I want you to die. Right here and now. It's an important part of the ritual."

Horn gaped at him, and then his mouth snapped shut and set in a cold, straight line. "Wait just a minute. . . ."

"Anything for the Cause, Horn. Remember?"

"Yeah, but this is different! I joined up with you to avenge my family. How can I do that if I'm dead? If you need a sacrifice, take that weird kid, Glen. You don't need him anyway, as long as you've got me."

Madigan just stared at him calmly. Horn began to back away, a step at a time. He looked to Eleanour Todd for support, but she just stared at him, her face cold and distant. Glen looked confused. Horn raised his sword, the lamplight shining on the blade.

"Why me, Madigan? I'm loyal. I've always been loyal. I've followed you into combat a hundred times. I would have died for you!"

"Then die for me now," said Madigan. "Trust me. It's necessary for the ritual, and for the Cause."

"Stuff the Cause!"

Horn turned and ran for the stairs. Madigan looked at the sorcerer. Ritenour smiled, and gestured briefly with his left hand. Horn crashed to the floor as something snatched his feet out from under him. The impact knocked the breath out of him, and his sword went flying from his numbed hand. He tried to get his feet under him, but something took him firmly by the ankles and began to drag him back towards the sorcerer waiting in his pentacle. He saw again the mercenaries dying slowly as Ritenour drained the life out of them, and he panicked, thrashing wildly and doubling up to beat at his own ankles with his fists. None of it made any difference. He tried to grab at the floor to slow himself down, but his fingernails just skidded across the worn stone. He snarled soundlessly, wriggled over onto his back, pulled a knife from a hidden sheath, and threw it at Ritenour. The sorcerer stepped to one side at just the right moment, and the knife flew harmlessly past his head. Horn was almost at the edge of the pentacle when he opened his mouth to scream. Ritenour gestured sharply, and life rushed out of Horn and into the sorcerer. What would have been a scream came out as a long, shuddering sigh as Horn's lungs emptied for the last time.

Glen looked at Horn's body, and then at Madigan. "I don't understand. Why did he have to die? Did he betray us?"

"No," said Madigan patiently. "Weren't you listening, Ellis? His death was a necessary part of the ritual. Just as yours is, and Eleanour's."

"No!" said Glen immediately. "Leave Eleanour out of this! I don't know what's going on here, but you never mentioned any of this before. And you can bet I wouldn't have come anywhere near you if you had. You're crazy, Madigan! Come over here, Eleanour; we're getting out of this madhouse. Damn you, Madigan! I believed in you! I thought you believed in me."

"Do be quiet, Ellis. Eleanour's not going anywhere, and neither are you."

He turned to Eleanour Todd, and Glen threw himself at Madigan, his sword reaching for the terrorist's heart. Madigan went for his sword, but it was already too late. Ritenour raised his hand, knowing even as he did so, that the spell wouldn't work fast enough to save Madigan. But even as Glen made his move, Eleanour Todd's blade swept out to deflect his, and then swept back to cut Glen's throat. He dropped his sword and fell to his knees. His hands went to his throat, as though trying to hold shut the wound, and blood poured between his fingers. He looked up at Eleanour, standing before him with his blood dripping from her sword, and mouthed the word *Why?*

"Anything for the Cause, Ellis," said Eleanour Todd.

Glen fell forward as the sorcerer's spell sucked out what was left of his life. Todd looked down at the still figure and shook her head.

"I was hoping it wouldn't come to that, Eleanour," said Madigan, sheathing his sword. "He liked you, you know."

"Yes. I know." Todd returned her sword to its scabbard and smiled at Madigan. "My turn now, my love."

"Are you ready?"

"Oh yes. I've been waiting for this ever since we first discussed it." She took a long, shuddering breath, and let it out again. "After all this time, my parents will finally be avenged. Do it, sorcerer." She smiled widely at Madigan. "No regrets, Daniel. And . . . it's all right that you never loved me. I understand."

Ritenour gestured, and the life went out of her. Madigan caught her as she fell forward, and lowered her gently to the floor.

"So you did know, after all. I'm sorry, Eleanour. But there was never room in my life for you." He looked at Ritenour. "Two willing sacrifices. That was the last ingredient of the ritual, wasn't it?"

"That's right," said Ritenour carefully. "She'll count as one, but you'll have to be the other. Or everything we've done so far will have been for nothing."

"Take it easy, sorcerer. I've no intention of backing out. I just want to see the ritual begin. I've waited a long time for this moment, and I want to savour it. You start the ball rolling, and I'll tell you when I'm ready."

Ritenour shrugged, and turned away. He took up a position in the exact centre of the pentacle and began a low, strangely cadenced chant accompanied by quick, carefully timed gestures. A vicious headache was pounding in his left temple, and he was feeling uncomfortably hot and sweaty. Probably the close air in the cellar. He'd never liked confined spaces. He made himself concentrate on what he was doing, but after all the work he'd put into memorizing the spell he could have practically done it in his sleep.

The blue chalk lines of his pentacle began to glow with an eerie blue light, and the air outside the lines seemed to ripple as though in a heat haze. A sudden rush of excitement swept through him, leaving him giddy. He could feel the forces building around the pentacle. He'd known of this spell for years, but had never dreamed that one day he'd be able to use it. Of course, it could still go wrong. If Madigan was getting cold feet . . .

He shot a quick glance at the man, but Madigan was just sitting quietly not far away, with his back to the wall, watching the ritual. Madigan would come through eventually. He wasn't the type to back down, once he'd set his mind to something. Everyone said so. Ritenour smiled. It'd be his name they'd remember now, not Madigan's. When this was all over and he was safely away from the ruins of what had once been Haven, he'd be both rich and famous, as the sorcerer who dared to open the Unknown Door.

Madigan blinked as sweat ran down his forehead and into his eyes. He was feeling very weak now, and he'd had to sit down before his legs betrayed him. The poison was taking hold of him. It was quicker than he'd expected, but hardly surprising. The wine in his hip flask had held enough poison to kill a dozen men. Which was, of course, why he'd insisted Ritenour share it with him. There was no way he was going to let the sorcerer run free after this was all over, boasting about his part in it. This was going to be remembered as Madigan's greatest triumph. No one else's.

Madigan had given his life to the Cause, to the destruction of Outremer, but he wasn't the man he used to be, and he knew it. He'd been a legend in his time, but the best days of his legend were gone, lost in the past, and other, newer names had appeared to replace his. No one doubted his loyalty to the Cause, but among those who mattered it was whispered more and more that he was getting old and cautious, slowing down. So the money went to younger men, and he had to find support for his plans where he could. But after this night, his legend would be secure. He'd already planted rumours in all the right places, so that when the investigators finally came to sift through the rubble of the city, word would already be going round that he was the one responsible. The rumours would blame both sides for hiring him, of course, and as the outrage mounted, the right people would quietly fan the flames until war was inevitable.

Madigan smiled as the sorcerer shot another quick glance at him. Probably thought he had cold feet, or second thoughts. Fool. He wasn't afraid to die. Better to die at the height of his fame, at his greatest moment, than to grow old and bitter watching his schemes collapse for lack of funding, or lack of skill. The Cause would go on without him, and that was all that really mattered. Poor Eleanour had never understood. The Cause had been friend and lover and religion to him, and he had never wanted anyone or anything else in his life.

He watched the sorcerer work, smiling slightly. Madigan knew he wouldn't live to see the opening of the Unknown Door, but it was enough to know that his own willing death would open it. The sorcerer would live a little longer, since he'd drunk less of the wine, but when he finally saw the horror he'd helped to unleash, he'd probably be glad of an easy death. Because once the Door had been opened, no one in this world could shut it again. No one.

Madigan smiled and closed his eyes.

• • •

Hawk and Fisher ran through the fourth floor, heading for the stairs. The bodies of the fallen mercenaries seemed to watch them pass with horrified, unmoving eyes. Hawk started counting the bodies, but had to give up. There were too many. He scowled furiously as he pounded down the stairs to the third floor, pushing his pace a little to keep up with Fisher. Why the hell had Madigan killed his own people, as well as the hostages? Hawk knew better than to expect honour or loyalty among terrorists, but even so, to wipe out his own people on such a scale suggested a coldness on Madigan's part that was more frightening than any number of dead bodies. And even apart from that, didn't the man feel the need for any protection anymore? Whatever he and his pet sorcerer were involved with down in the cellar, surely he still needed some protection, if only to keep them from being interrupted at the wrong moment. Unless whatever they were planning was so powerful that nothing could stop it once it had been started . . .

Hawk didn't like the turn his thoughts were taking. It was becoming clearer all the time that this whole business had been very carefully planned, right from the beginning. Which suggested the deaths had also been planned. But why? What could Madigan have hoped to gain from such a massacre? Power. That had to be the answer. Some sorcerers could use stolen life energy to power spells that couldn't otherwise be controlled. But what kind of ritual could Madigan and Ritenour be contemplating, that needed so many lives to make it possible?

Something's happening down there. Something bad.

He and Fisher had just reached the bottom of the second flight of stairs when Fisher stopped suddenly and leaned against the banisters, breathing hard. Hawk stopped with her, and looked at her worriedly. He was usually the first to run out of breath, as Isobel never tired of reminding him. On the other hand, she hated to be coddled.

"You all right, lass?" he said carefully.

"Of course I'm all right," she muttered. "Don't be too obvious about it, but take a look around. I thought I saw something moving, down the corridor to your right. Could be someone Madigan left here to guard his back."

"Good," said Hawk. "I'm in the mood to hit someone."

"I'd be hard pressed to remember a time when you weren't, Captain Hawk," said Winter, as she stepped out of the shadows of the corridor. She looked angrily at both Captains. "What kept you? I've been waiting here for ages. I take it Storm has contacted you? Good; then you know as much about the situation as I do. Which is, essentially, damn all, except that it's bloody urgent we get to the cellars. Let's go."

She set off down the stairs to the next floor, without looking back to see if they were following. Hawk and Fisher exchanged a brief look, shrugged more or less in unison, and went after her. Hawk felt he ought to say something, but was damned if he knew what. The last he'd seen of the SWAT team's leader, she'd been running from the parlour in a blind panic with half a dozen mercenaries right behind her. Hawk couldn't honestly say he blamed her. The odds against her had been overwhelming, and she'd just seen her strongest team member cut down as though he was nothing. Hawk would have run too, if he and Isobel hadn't been trapped by the windows.

But she'd panicked, and she knew that they'd seen it. Which could lead to all sorts of problems. Panic was hard for some people to acknowledge, never mind deal with. Winter was the sort who prided herself on her courage and self-control, and that pride would make dealing with her problem that much harder. Hawk had seen this kind of thing before. She'd come up with all kinds of rationalizations that would let her believe she hadn't really panicked, and that way she wouldn't have to think about it. But put her under real stress again, and there was no telling what she might do. Given the situation they were heading into, Winter could be a disaster waiting to happen. As though she could feel his gaze on her back, Winter suddenly began talking, though she was still careful not to look back at Hawk or Fisher.

"I thought I was the only one left and the rest of the team were dead. I shook off my pursuers easily enough, and went to ground till they gave up looking for me. I used the time to put together a plan that would get me safely out of the House. It was imperative that I get word to the Council that our mission was a failure, and they couldn't count on us to save the Kings. Then . . . something happened. After our narrow escape from the creatures of power in Hell Wing, I'd taken the precaution of removing a suppressor stone from Headquarters' Storeroom.

I thought we might need protection against magic at some point on this case, and the stone has always worked well for me in the past, even if it has fallen out of favour at the moment. Anyway, the stone suddenly started glowing brightly, and the House seemed to shake. I braced myself, but the stone protected me from whatever magic it was. The glow soon faded away, but I thought it best to lie low until I had some idea of what had happened. Then Storm contacted me, told me that Mac was dead and you were still alive, and that our mission wasn't over yet."

"Did Storm tell you what was happening down in the cellar?" said Fisher, when Winter paused for a moment.

"Not really. Just that the sorcerer Ritenour was up to something nasty. It doesn't matter. We'll stop him. The Kings may be dead, but we can still avenge them."

"It may not be as simple as that," said Hawk carefully. "According to Storm, the whole city may be in danger from what Madigan has planned."

"Storm worries too much," said Winter. "There are any number of powerful sorcerers in the city, not to mention all the Beings on the Street of Gods. You're not telling me that between them they couldn't handle anything Ritenour can come up with. After all, what could one shaman sorcerer call up that all the Powers and Dominations in Haven couldn't put down?"

"Good question," said Fisher. "And if we don't get to the cellar in time, I have an awful suspicion we're going to find out the hard way."

Winter sniffed, but increased her pace. Hawk and Fisher hurried after her. Winter was careful always to keep just a little ahead of them, so they wouldn't see her face. She'd managed to stop herself trembling, but she knew that if they got a good look at her face, they couldn't help but see the fear that was still there. She'd been afraid before, but never like this. She'd never run from anything in her life before, but she'd run from the parlour. It wasn't just the number of mercenaries, though that had been part of it. No; it had been the speed, the almost casual way in which Barber had been killed. He'd always been so much better than her, and Madigan's man had swept him aside as though he were nothing. And then Saxon was gone, and Mac and Hawk and Fisher had been cornered, and all she could think of was that she had to get out of there, *out of there*!

She'd hidden from her pursuers in the back of a dusty little cupboard, underneath a pile of old clothing she'd pulled over herself. She'd concentrated on the thought that it was vital she didn't get caught, that she had a responsibility to stay free so she could get a message out to the Council. But when she finally heard the mercenaries depart, and it was time to leave, she couldn't bring herself to leave the safety of the cupboard. She stayed there, in the dark, curled into a ball and trembling violently, clutching the suppressor stone in her fist like a child's lucky charm. After a while, a long while, Storm's voice came to her, telling her that Hawk and Fisher were still alive, and that the mercenaries were dead, and she was finally able to leave her hiding place. She wasn't alone after all, and she had a chance for revenge. It didn't matter what Madigan and Ritenour were doing down in the cellar; she was going to kill them both. They would pay for the murders of the two Kings, and for the theft of her courage and conviction.

She strode along, looking neither left nor right, and bit at the inside of her cheeks until they ached, to keep her teeth from chattering. She couldn't afford to let Hawk and Fisher see how badly Madigan had got to her. She was the leader of the SWAT team. She had to lead.

Winter led the way down the steps into the cellar, moving quietly and confidently, her sword held out before her. Hawk and Fisher followed close behind, keeping a wary eye on her. If Winter had a plan of attack, she hadn't seen fit to confide in them. Hawk found that worrying; normally Winter was full of herself over that kind of thing, and couldn't wait to impress everyone with her latest plans and strategies. Perhaps this time she didn't have a plan, and was just playing it by ear. If she was, Hawk for one didn't blame her. He hadn't got a clue what to do for the best. On the other hand, the only actual fighter in the cellar was Madigan, according to Storm, and they outnumbered him three to one. But on the other hand, Madigan was a first-class swordsman and had with him a sorcerer who was probably brimming over with stolen power and just looking for a target to use it on. Which would seem to argue against a frontal attack. Personally, Hawk favoured sneaking up on them from behind, and taking out both of them with his axe before they even knew what was happening. Hawk was a great believer in keeping things simple and to the point.

Winter eased to a stop at the point where the stairway curved round a long corner before leading down into the cellar itself. Hawk and Fisher stopped too, and listened to the silence. There wasn't a sound to be heard, but a strange, eerie blue light flickered across the wall below them. Hawk looked at Fisher, who shrugged. Winter stared at the flickering light for a long moment, and then moved slowly forward, keeping her shoulder pressed against the inner wall so as to stay hidden in the shadows. Hawk and Fisher moved silently after her. As they eased around the corner, the vast stone chamber swung gradually into view, and Hawk swore to himself as he saw the sorcerer Ritenour, standing in the middle of a glowing pentacle. They were too late. Whatever the ritual was, it had already started. The eerie blue light that blazed from the lines of the pentacle filled the cellar, and gave the sorcerer's skin the look of something that had been dead for a week. In between the stairway and the pentacle lay Glen and Todd, both dead. Madigan was sitting on the floor with his back against the wall, his eyes closed. Hawk thought for a moment he might be dead too, but his hopes were quickly dashed as he realised the terrorist's chest was still rising and falling. *Pity,* thought Hawk. *It would have simplified things no end.* Fisher leaned in beside him, looked at Madigan, and raised an eyebrow. Hawk shrugged. Maybe the man was asleep. He'd had a busy day.

The air in the cellar had a tense, brittle feel, as though any loud noise or sudden movement might shatter it like glass and reveal what lay behind it. The blue light clung to the wall like lichen, and the solid stone seemed to stir and seethe with slow, viscous movements. Shadows flickered here and there, come and gone in an eye blink, though there was nothing in the cellar to cast them. Ritenour began chanting in an unfamiliar tongue, but his voice seemed strangely quiet, as though it had crossed some great distance to reach them. He turned slowly in a circle, widdershins, slowly against the course of the sun's path right to left, light to darkness. Hawk could see his eyes were tightly shut. Possibly to help him concentrate, or possibly because he was afraid of what he might see if he opened them. Hawk moved down a step for a better look, and then stopped abruptly. His stomach muscles tensed, and sweat broke out on his forehead. He felt as though he were looking out over some vast, unimaginable gulf. The cellar seemed to be stretching, with Madigan and Ritenour moving slowly away from the stairs, until the gap between them seemed horribly great and impossible to cross. Fisher grabbed Hawk by the arm, and he all but jumped out of his skin. She gestured that she and Winter were moving back up the stairs round the curve of the wall, and Hawk nodded quickly. He looked back at the cellar, and then away again, and followed Fisher and Winter back up into the concealing shadows. He realised he was breathing too quickly, and made himself take several deep breaths to calm himself down.

They stopped just beyond the curve, and Hawk leaned in close to Winter, keeping his voice little more than a murmur. "We've got to do something while we still can. Things down there are getting out of hand fast."

"I'm open to suggestions, Captain," said Winter sharply. "In order to stop the ritual we have to get to Ritenour, but as long as he stays within the pentacle we can't touch him. It'll knock us out if we even get too close to it."

"What about your suppressor stone?" said Hawk.

"Burned out by whatever happened earlier."

"No problem," said Fisher. "Hawk can throw an axe like you wouldn't believe. He can cut the wings off a fly at twenty paces, and if flies had other things he could cut them off too. Right, Hawk?"

"More or less," said Hawk. "My axe is rather special, and it should cut through any magical protection, but I've still got to get within throwing range. An axe is too heavy to throw accurately over any distance. And you can bet once any of us step out into plain sight, Madigan is going to come up off that floor like a cat with a thorn up its arse and carve whoever's there into bite-sized chunks. I saw him fight in the parlour. He's good, Winter. Very good."

"We can handle him," said Winter confidently. "You get into a position where you can throw your axe, and Fisher and I will keep Madigan occupied."

"Right," said Fisher. "We kill Madigan, you kill the sorcerer, and then we all get the hell out of here. Simple as that."

"I'm afraid not," said Madigan calmly. "It's a good plan, and it might even work, though I hate to think what might happen to your precious city if the forces Ritenour is working with were to break free. But it's all immaterial. To get to him you have to get past me. And you're not that good. Any of you."

He was standing at the foot of the stairs, looking up at them, and his smile was a death's-head grin. He looked pale and drawn and ill, but his back was straight and the sword in his hand was quite steady.

Hawk and Fisher ran down the stairs and circled around him, weapons at the ready. He moved easily to follow them, never letting either of them entirely out of his sight. He laughed softly, charged with energy, as though all the strength he'd ever had was his again, gathered for just this moment. He laughed at them, and in that harsh, mocking sound there was no trace of weakness, or thought of failure. His eyes burned in his gaunt face, and every move he made was calm, calculated, and very deadly.

It's like he knows we can't win, thought Hawk. *That whatever happens, he's already won.*

He pushed the thought aside, and moved warily forward. Madigan was all that stood between him and Ritenour, and no matter how good he was, Madigan was only one man. Hawk had faced a hell of a lot worse in his time. He swung his axe in a vicious arc, and Madigan's sword was in just the right place to deflect it. The return thrust had Hawk jumping desperately back, and Fisher darted in quickly to draw Madigan's attention. Their swords clashed again and again in a flurry of sparks, but Fisher was the one who was forced to retreat. Hawk tried to circle round behind Madigan, but the terrorist drove him back with a flurry of blows that took all of Hawk's skill to counter.

Hawk and Fisher threw themselves at Madigan, but neither of them could touch him. He moved as though inspired, parrying and striking back with a tireless energy. His strength was incredible, his speed bordering on inhuman. He thrust and cut and parried with a simple economy of movement that was too brutal to be truly graceful, but somehow he was always in just the right place to block a blow or strike at his opponent's weakness. Hawk was hard put to save himself a dozen times over, and blood ran thickly down his side from a blow he hadn't seen coming till it was almost too late. If he or Fisher had been fighting alone they would have been dead by now, and all of them knew it. Madigan was never where he should be, and their weapons swept harmlessly past him again and again while his sword crept gradually closer with every attack. Madigan had been a legend in his day, and there in the cellars under Champion House, it was his day again, for a while. Hawk and Fisher fought on determinedly, grunting with the effort of their blows and fighting for breath, but Madigan just smiled at them, his eyes wild and fey, his time come round again in the last minutes of his life.

Ritenour's chant grew louder as he shuffled round and round in his pentacle, eyes squeezed shut as though against a blinding light. The air in the cellar grew steadily more tense, and an alien presence slowly permeated the stone chamber, pressing relentlessly against the barriers that held it back from reality and the waking world.

Winter watched the fighting from the foot of the stairs, unable to move. There was no point in trying to help. Hawk and Fisher were much better fighters than she, and Madigan was making them look like fools. If she even raised a sword against him, he'd kill her. She thought about trying to sneak past him to try and get to Ritenour, but she'd seen what happened when Hawk tried to circle round Madigan. The terrorist had blocked him off without even trying. There was nothing she could do. Nothing.

Think, dammit, think! You're supposed to be the tactician, the one with plans and strategies for every contingency. There's always something you can do!

And of course there was. The answer came to her in a flash of inspiration, and she knew she had to act on it immediately, while she still had the courage. Because if she stopped and thought about it, she'd come up with all kinds of reasons not to do it. She ran forward, her sword held high above her head, and threw herself at Madigan. He spun round impossibly quickly, and his sword plunged into her stomach and out her back. Winter dropped her sword and forced herself along the blade until she could grab his sword arm with both hands. He tried to break her grip, but her hands had closed like vises. She smiled at him. There was blood in her mouth, and it rolled down her chin as she spoke.

"Did you think you were the only one prepared to die for what they believe in?"

Madigan snarled at her and backed desperately away, dragging her with him, but Hawk's axe came swinging round in a wide arc out of nowhere and smashed into his rib cage. Bones broke and splintered, and the force of the blow drove him to his knees, crying out in pain and shock. Winter sank down with him, still smiling. Their eyes met for a moment, sharing hatred, and then the light went out of Winter's eyes and she slumped forward.

Hawk jerked his axe free in a gusher of blood, and Madigan cried out again as the pain cleared his head. He clung somehow to his sword as he lurched to his feet, avoiding Fisher's sword with desperate speed. Blood was pouring from the gaping wound in his side, but he ignored it. He was dying anyway, and the knowledge gave him strength. He bolted for the stairs, blood spilling onto the ground as he ran. A slow numbness crept through his body as the poison began to win out over his need and desperation. He could no longer feel his hands or his feet, and the strength was draining out of his legs. He forced himself on, concentrating on the flaring pain in his side to keep his head clear. He coughed painfully, and blood filled his mouth. He spat it out, and glanced back over his shoulder. Hawk and Fisher were pounding up the stairs after him.

He laughed giddily. Let the fools chase him. While they were preoccupied with him, Ritenour was completing the ritual. All he had to do was buy the sorcerer a little more time, and he'd spite Hawk and Fisher yet. He was glad he hadn't killed them, after all. He wanted them alive when the Unknown Door opened, so that they could see what he'd let loose on their precious city. He wanted them to know they'd failed, before they died screaming, in agony and despair. He laughed breathily, ignoring the pain and the blood, and then Wulf Saxon appeared on the steps before him. Madigan snarled at him and lunged forward, his sword still steady in his numb hand. Saxon slapped the blade aside and hit Madigan in the face with all his strength. The blow picked Madigan up and threw him back down the stairs, almost crashing into Hawk and Fisher. They pressed back against the wall, and Madigan slid and tumbled the rest of the way down the steps and back into the cellar. He lay still at the bottom of the stairs, his head at an unnatural angle, his neck broken.

Hawk and Fisher ran back down the stairs, and stood staring
down at Madigan's body. Hawk stirred it with his boot, and the
head lolled limply from side to side. And then Madigan's eyes
snapped open, and Hawk fell back a step, his heart jumping
painfully. Fisher raised her sword and stood ready to strike.
Madigan stared up at them, and his mouth stretched slowly in
a ghastly grin.

"You've achieved nothing. Won nothing. I was dying anyway. I've beaten you. Beaten you all. Your precious city's
going to burn, and everyone and everything you ever cared
for is going down into Hell. You lose, heroes! You lose!"

Hawk lifted his axe and brought it sweeping down with all
his strength behind it. The razor edge sliced through Madigan's
neck and bit deeply into the stone floor beneath. The terrorist's
head rolled away across the floor, still smiling. Hawk glared
down at the twitching body, and jerked his axe out of the floor
as though he meant to strike at the body again. Fisher grabbed
him by the arm.

"Forget about him, Hawk! We still have to stop the sorcerer.
He made us forget the bloody sorcerer!"

They spun round to stare at Ritenour, standing fixed and
frozen in his pentacle. His eye sockets were empty, and bloody
trails down his face showed where the eyes had melted and
run. *He must have finally opened his eyes and looked,* thought
Hawk numbly.

Saxon appeared out of the shadows of the stairway and came
to stand beside Hawk and Fisher. He started to ask what was
going on, but his voice dried up as he stared at the sorcerer.
Power beat on the still air like the wings of an enormous bird,
and the gathering presence swept through their minds like an
icy wind. It was very close now. Countless, unblinking eyes
watched hungrily from the borderlands of reality, driven by an
ancient hatred and an unwavering purpose.

Hawk shook his head violently, and looked across at the
sorcerer, who had fallen to his knees inside his pentacle.
The light from the chalk lines was almost blinding now. On
some basic level beyond his understanding, Hawk could sense
the stolen life energy pouring out of the sorcerer and passing beyond reality, to where the presence was waiting. He
tried to lift his axe, but his arm seemed far away, and the

sounds in his head roared and screamed, drowning out his thoughts.

Saxon stepped forward, and the air seemed to press against him as though he were wading through deep water. Hawk and Fisher were as still as statues, though sweat ran down their empty faces, and sudden tremors ran through them as they fought to lift their weapons. Saxon concentrated on the sorcerer in his pentacle. There was no one to help him; he was on his own, as he had been ever since he left the Portrait. He pressed on, putting everything out of his mind except the pentacle, as it drew nearer step by step. Something was screaming. Something was howling. The air stank of blood and death. The blazing blue lines of the pentacle flared up before him as he lashed out with his fist. The cellar shuddered like a drumhead, but the pentacle held. Saxon struck at it again and again, calling up every last vestige of his unnatural strength, but though the blazing light shuddered and trembled beneath his blows, it would not fall.

And then something bright and shining flashed past him, and Ritenour lurched suddenly forward, Hawk's axe buried between his shoulder blades. His hands came back to paw feebly at the axe's haft, and then he fell, face down, and lay still, one outflung hand crossing a line of the pentacle. The blinding blue light snapped off in an instant, and Saxon lurched forward to kneel at the sorcerer's side. Ritenour turned his head and looked up at him with his bloody eye sockets.

"Listen. Can you hear them? The beasts are here. . . ."

The breath went out of him. He was dead, and the last part of the ritual was complete. The Unknown Door swung open a crack, and the presence slammed through into reality, throwing aside the barriers of time and space, life and death. And what had waited for so long for revenge was finally loose in the world.

From out of the shadows of the slaughterhouse, from the time of blood and pain and horror, the beasts returned. Thousands upon thousands of animals, butchered and torn apart in the bloody cellar by men who laughed and joked as they killed. And from every scream and every death, and all the long years of suffering, came a legacy of hatred that drew upon the strange magics in that place, derived in turn from the unnatural building that had been replaced by the slaughterhouse. The small souls gathered together into something larger and more powerful that would not rest, but waited at the borders of the spirit lands, determined to return and take vengeance for what had been done to them. And finally, after all the many years, the willing and unwilling sacrifices of the forbidden ritual had opened the Unknown Door, and the beasts surged forward, using Ritenour's stolen life energies to manifest themselves once again in the lands of the living. The beasts had returned, and they would have their revenge.

Champion House trembled on its foundations, and jagged cracks split open the massive stone walls. The restraining magics built into the stone were ripped apart and scattered in a moment, and all the souls of all the many animals went rushing out into the city, a spiral of raging energy that swept outward from the House, leaving madness and devastation in its wake. Herds of scarlet-eyed cattle thundered through the narrow streets, trampling fleeing crowds underfoot. Blood soaked their hooves and legs, but it was never enough. Weapons tore and cut at them, but they felt no pain and took no hurt. They were dead, beyond fear or suffering anymore, and nothing could stop them now. They crushed men and women against walls, and tossed the broken bodies effortlessly on their splintered horns. Blood ran down the curving horns and disappeared into gaping holes in the cattle's skulls, made by sledgehammers long ago. The herd thundered on, and behind them their lesser cousins tore and worried at the bodies of the fallen, as even the mildest of creatures gloried in the taste of human flesh and blood. Sheep and lambs buried their faces in ripped-open guts, and blood stained their woollen muzzles as they bolted down the warm meat.

The soulstorm of raging spirits roared through the city, driving people insane with its endless cry of blood and pain and horror. Centuries of accumulated suffering and abuse were turned back upon their ancient tormentors, and men and women ran wild in the streets, screaming and howling with the voices of animals. Many killed themselves to escape the agony, or killed each other, driven by a fury not their own. There were islands of sanity in the madness, as isolated sorcerers and Beings from the Street of Gods struggled to hold back the soulstorm, but they were few and far between.

In the great prison of Damnation Row, cell doors burst from their hinges and blood ran down the walls. Shadows prowled the narrow corridors with glowing eyes, ignoring locks and bars, and prisoners and prison staff alike fell to cruel fangs and claws. Inmates grew hysterical in their cells and turned on their cellmates, tearing at them viciously, like creatures that had been penned together too long in battery cages, and had never forgotten or forgiven.

At Guard Headquarters the doors were locked and the shutters closed, but still beasts rampaged through the building, and no one could stand against them. Guards fought running battles where they could, gathering together in groups to protect each other, and Guard sorcerers roared and chanted and raised their wards, but the beasts were everywhere and would not be denied.

The Council chambers rang to the sound of a hundred hoofbeats as wild-eyed horses thundered back and forth through the corridors and meeting rooms. Desks and chairs were overturned, and the great round ceremonial table was split from end to end. People ran before the raging herd until their breath gave out or their hearts burst in their chests and it was not enough, never enough.

Down in the Docks the waters boiled as things came crawling up out onto the harbourside, clacking claws and waving antennae a dozen times the size they were in life. Death changes all things, and rarely for the better. They had grown as their hatred grew, and people ran screaming before them as they clattered across the Docks on their huge, segmented legs.

Around the great houses and mansions of the Quality dark shadows gathered, pressing against hastily erected wards with remorseless strength, and both those inside and outside knew it was only a matter of time before the wards fell.

Prayers went up on the Street of Gods, to all the many Beings and creatures of Power that resided there, but none of them answered. The beasts could not enter the Street of Gods, and that was all that mattered. The Gods had turned their faces away, for a time. They would not interfere. They understood about hatred and revenge.

Restaurants became abattoirs, and kitchens ran with blood. Death filled the streets, and buildings shook and shattered at the violence of the soulstorm. Fires broke out all over Haven, and there was no one to stop them. And from every street and every house and every room, came the howling of the beasts.

In the cellar under Champion House, Hawk and Fisher and Saxon huddled together inside the pentacle, and watched dark formless shapes drifting around the perimeter, never quite crossing the palely-glowing blue chalk lines. Storm's voice had told them to shelter inside the pentacle, and had raised its glowing wards around them, but that had been a long time ago, and they hadn't heard from him since. At least it seemed a long time. It was hard to be sure of anything anymore. Screams of dying animals echoed back from the blood-spattered walls. There was a quiet clattering from steel hooks and chains that hung on the air, reaching up into an unseen past. Torsos and heads hung on the chains and hooks, long dead but still suffering. Blood fell from the ceiling in sudden spurts and streams, steaming on the cold air.

Hawk would have closed his eye against the grisly sights, but when he did he saw visions of what was happening in Haven, and that was worse. He saw the buildings fall and the fires mount, and watched helplessly as the people he had sworn to protect died screaming in pain and anguish and horror. He clutched his axe until his hands ached, but he didn't leave the pentacle. He didn't need a vision to show him what would happen if he did. He looked at Fisher, kneeling beside him. Her face was drawn and gaunt, but her mouth was set and her gaze was steady. She saw he was looking at her worriedly, and squeezed his arm briefly. Saxon sat with his back to them, ignoring everything, lost in his private world of regrets and self-recriminations. He didn't answer when Hawk or Fisher spoke to him, and eventually they gave up. They sat up a little straighter as Storm's voice crashed into their minds again.

Can you hear me? Are you still all right?

Depends on how you define all right, said Hawk roughly. *We're still trapped in this pentacle, we're still surrounded by blood and madness, and Saxon's still out to lunch. That sound all right to you?*

Trust me, Captain; it's worse out here. The city's being torn apart, and the people massacred. Some of us are fighting back, but it's all we can do to hold our ground. There are centuries of accumulated hatred running loose in the streets. I've never seen such concentrated malevolent power. . . .

Are you saying there's nothing we can do? said Fisher. *That it's hopeless?*

No. There is something. If you're willing.

Of course we're willing! snapped Hawk. *We can't just sit here and watch Haven being destroyed! Tell us what to do, sorcerer. And you'd better make it fast. The pentacle's lines aren't burning anywhere near as brightly as they were.*

There's only one solution, Captain. The beasts must be comforted, and the Unknown Door must be closed. Two people died willingly to open the Door; it will take two more willing sacrifices to close it.

Hawk and Fisher looked at each other. *Let me get this straight*, said Hawk. *You want us to kill ourselves*?

Yes. Your souls will pass through the Unknown Door into the Fields of the Lord, the spirit land of the animals. Once there, you must make peace with the unquiet spirits of the beasts. Maybe then they will return to their rest, and the Door will close behind them.

Maybe? said Fisher. *Did I just hear you say* maybe? *You want us to kill ourselves, and you're not even sure it will work?*

It's the only hope we've got.

Then why don't you do it?

I can't get to Champion House, and the ritual must take place where the Unknown Door was opened.

Great, said Hawk. *It's all down to us, again. What are these spirit lands like, anyway? And are we going to end up trapped there, or do we go on to our own . . . spirit lands?*

I don't know. To my knowledge, no one has ever passed beyond the Unknown Door and returned to tell of it.

"This gets better by the minute," growled Fisher. *All right, Storm, you've said your piece. Now shut up and let us think for a minute.*

Hawk and Fisher sat for a while in silence, looking at each other. Dark shadows pressed close against the lines of the pentacle, and the air was thick with the stench of blood and offal.

"I never thought we'd die like this," said Hawk finally. "I never really expected to die in my own bed, but I always hoped it would be a lot further down the line than this. At the very least, I wanted it to be on my feet, fighting for something I believed in."

"You believe in the city," said Fisher. "And its people. Just like me. You said it yourself; we can't sit back and do nothing. And at least this way, we get to die together. I wouldn't have wanted to go on without you, Hawk."

"Or me, without you." Hawk sighed, and put his axe down on the floor beside him. He patted it once, like an old dog that had served well in its time, and smiled at Fisher. "A short life, but an interesting one. Right, lass?"

"You got that right. We squeezed a lifetime's love and adventure into our few years together. We can't really complain. We came close to dying many times in the Forest Kingdom, during the long night. Everything since then has been borrowed time anyway."

"Yeah. Maybe. I'm not ready to die, lass."

"No one ever is."

"There's so much I wanted to do. So many things I wanted to tell you, and never did."

Fisher put her fingertips against his lips to hush him. "I knew them anyway."

"Love you, Isobel."

"Love you, Hawk."

They clasped each other's hands and smiled tenderly. A kind of peace came over them, not unlike the relief one feels after finally putting down a heavy burden.

"How shall we do it?" said Hawk. His mouth was dry, but his voice was more or less steady. "I couldn't stand to see you suffer. I could . . . kill you quickly, and then throw myself on your sword."

"I couldn't ask you to do that," said Fisher, her eyes gleaming with tears she wouldn't let go. "Let the sorcerer do it. He probably knows all kind of ways to kill from a distance."

"Yeah. He strikes me as that type." They shared a small smile. Hawk looked out into the darkness. "Spirit land of the animals . . . Never occurred to me that all animals would have souls."

"Makes sense, when you think about it. I had a dog once, when I was a kid. Died in an accident, when I was twelve. He was never what you'd call bright, but I was always convinced

I'd meet him again, after I died. He had too much personality to just disappear."

Hawk nodded slowly. "So; one last adventure together, then."

They both jumped as Saxon turned suddenly and glared at them. "You were just going to go and leave me behind, I suppose?"

"What the hell are you talking about?" said Hawk. "You don't have to die. Storm said it only needed two willing sacrifices. And that's us."

"He also said the beasts have to be comforted, and from the way they've been acting, they're going to take a hell of a lot of persuading. Which is where I come in. No offence, but you two aren't exactly known for your diplomatic skills. I, on the other hand, have years of experience as a politician and con man. I could persuade a blue whale it could fly, and teach it to loop the loop while it was up there. I'm coming too. You need me."

"Think about what you're saying," said Fisher. "It's one thing for us to die; we're not leaving anyone behind. But what about you? Don't you have any friends, family?"

"My family are all dead," said Saxon. "And I don't know my friends anymore. There's no one and nothing I'll regret leaving behind. This city isn't the one I remember. Haven was always a cesspit, but it was never this bad."

"It's still worth saving," said Hawk. "There are villains and bastards beyond counting, but most of the people in Haven are good people, just trying to get through their lives as best they can, protecting their family and friends, and looking for what love and comfort they can find along the way."

"I know," said Saxon. "That's why I'm coming with you."

"You don't have to do this," said Fisher. "Hawk and I . . . It's our job. Our duty."

"This is my city," said Saxon. "My home. Much as I loathe it sometimes, it's still my home, and I couldn't bear to see it destroyed. I'm really not afraid of dying. I was dead for twenty-three years anyway. At least this time, I'll have died for something that mattered. Now let's get on with it. While our nerve still holds out."

"Sure," said Hawk. *Have you been listening, sorcerer?*
Yes. I'm here.

Then do it.
Goodbye, my friends. You will not be forgotten.

Elsewhere in the city the sorcerer Storm spoke a Word of Power, and Hawk and Fisher and Saxon slumped forward. They sprawled limply on the cold stone floor, and their breathing slowed and then stopped as the life went out of them. They died together, and the blue lights of the pentacle flickered and collapsed, until there was only darkness in the cellar.

There were fields and meadows that stretched away into an endless horizon. A forest stood to one side, full of sunlit glades and dark, comforting shadows. A river ran, bright and sparkling, and the riverbanks were honeycombed with holes and warrens. The summer sky was soft and blue, with grey-tinged clouds that promised soothing rain for the evening. The sun was fat and warm, and the air lay heavily upon the earth like the height of summer, when the heat warms your bones and makes all thoughts calm and drowsy, and winter seems so far away it may never come again. Insects murmured on the quiet, and butterflies fluttered by like animated scraps of color. A gentle breeze stirred the long grass, rich with the scent of earth and grass and living things. And everywhere, the beasts at play, running and hiding, jumping and tumbling, chasing and being chased with never a care or worry for predators or the fall of night. The land was theirs, and nothing could hurt them ever again.

Hawk and Fisher and Saxon stood together on the bank of the river, and felt no need to move. They were where they were, and for a long time in that timeless summer morning, that was enough. Hawk's face bore no scars, and he had both his eyes again. Fisher's scars were gone too, and they both stood a little taller, as though no longer bowed down by the weight of years and memories. Saxon looked like a different man, his face at peace for the first time since they'd met.

"It's like coming home," said Hawk finally. "Everyone's home."

"It reminds me of Hillsdown, and the Forest Kingdom," said Fisher. "Only more so. This is where we began, in the days before cities, when we all lived in the woods."

"I'd never pictured the afterlife as being so rural," said Saxon. "But then, I'm a city boy at heart."

"This is the animals' heaven," said Hawk. "It's shaped by their needs and natures, not ours."

"Heaven," said Fisher slowly. "Are we really dead? I don't feel dead. . . ."

"I remember dying," said Hawk, and for a long moment no one said anything.

"All right," said Saxon. "We're in animal heaven. What do we do now?"

Hawk smiled and shrugged. "Talk to the animals, I suppose. That's why we came here. All we have to do is find some that look as though they might listen."

He broke off as a lion walked slowly out of the wood towards them. Even at a distance it looked huge and majestic, the father of every lion that ever was. It walked unhurriedly among the gamboling animals and they gave way before it, but none of them seemed to fear the lion, or be alarmed by its presence. Hawk and Fisher and Saxon watched it approach, but felt no need to run or fight. It finally came to a halt before them, and the warm, sharp smell of cat washed over them. It stood a good five feet tall at the shoulder, its broad, massive head on a level with theirs. It sheer presence was almost overwhelming. Its eyes were a tawny gold, and full of all the understanding in the world. When it spoke, its breath was warm and sweet.

You can't stay here, growled a voice in their minds, low and soft like the wind that has within it the promise of a storm. *This is not your place. You don't belong here.*

"Where is here?" said Hawk tentatively. "Is this . . . the animals' spirit lands? The Fields of the Lord?"

No, said the lion, and there was amusement in the deep, calm voice. *You have not travelled that far. This is the place the slaughtered beasts made for themselves. Dying in pain and horror, they drew on the power in the place they came from, the magic that had been invested in that place long before the slaughterhouse was built over it. As more and more blood was spilled, so the many deaths awakened the ancient magic and made it strong again, and the beasts used it to build this place. Their bodies died in the slaughterhouse, but their spirits lived on, here. And here they stayed, down all the many years, nursing their fears and hatreds and planning their revenge, until finally the Unknown Door was opened in the only way it could be; from the other side.*

The lion paused, and looked briefly around him before returning his ancient, discomforting gaze to the humans before him. *Not all the animals have gone, despite the opening of the Door. The small and the timid have stayed, happy in their rest from the cares of the world. And some beasts with greater hearts would not go, having put aside thoughts of vengeance. Hatred has never come easily to the animal kind. It is not in their nature, though some have learned it from humans.*

"The ones who did go are killing people," said Hawk, his voice seeming small and insignificant after the restrained thunder of the lion. "We came here to try and put a stop to the hatred. If we can."

Why should they stop? They are only doing what you did to them.

"That doesn't make it right," said Saxon. "You can't put right a wrong by doing wrong yourself. I found that out. Vengeance feels really good while you're planning it, but in the end you've achieved nothing, and all you feel is empty."

"The soulstorm must stop," said Fisher. "They're killing the good along with the bad, the innocent along with the guilty, the caring along with the uncaring."

"And if they don't stop," said Hawk, "They'll become exactly what they've hated all these years, and then they'll never know peace."

The lion nodded its great head slowly. *You're right. The soulstorm has stopped.*

The three humans looked at each other. "Just like that?" said Fisher.

Just like that. Through me the beasts have heard your words and seen the colors of your hearts, and they have listened. You have shown them the darkness in their own hearts, and they are ashamed. The soulstorm is over, and the beasts are returning. They wanted blood and vengeance for so long, but having tasted its cold cruelty, they found it sickened them. Beasts may kill and even torture in the heat of their blood, but vengeance is a human trait, and they have turned their back on it.

"So, what happens now?" said Hawk.

The beasts will leave this place. It has served its purpose, and they are now free to go on to what awaits them. And you must go back to your own world.

"We can't," said Fisher. "We gave up our lives to get here."

And the beasts give them back to you, and all the other lives they took. Goodbye, my children. Until we meet again.

The lion turned, and walked back towards the woods. Hawk stumbled a step or two after it. He felt deep within him that he was saying goodbye to something great and wonderful, and part of him didn't want to go.

"Wait! Who are you?"

The lion looked back over its shoulder and smiled. *Don't you know?*

The spirit lands faded away and were gone.

Back in the cellar under Champion House, Hawk sat up slowly and looked around him. Fisher and Saxon lay beside him in a scuffed chalk pentacle, and as he watched, they began to stir and sit up. Hawk rose awkwardly to his feet and stretched slowly, feeling the muscles reluctantly unkink. The blood and the chains and the dark presences were gone, and the cellar was just an old stone chamber again. Fisher and Saxon got to their feet and looked around them. Hawk chuckled. They looked just as bewildered as he felt. He grabbed Fisher and hugged her to him, and she hugged back with a strength that threatened to force all the breath out of him.

"We're alive!" yelled Hawk. "We're alive again!"

Hawk and Fisher whooped and shrieked and staggered round in circles, still clinging tightly to each other, as though afraid that one might vanish if the other let go. Saxon moved quietly away, and crouched down beside Horn's body, still lying on the floor. He examined it carefully, and then moved over to Eleanour Todd's body. Hawk and Fisher finally broke apart, and went to see what he was doing. Saxon rose to his feet again, and there was a knife in his hand, dripping blood. Hawk looked quickly at the bodies. Both Horn and Todd had had their throats cut. Saxon met Hawk and Fisher's gaze calmly.

"I just wanted to make sure they stayed dead. Unlike Madigan and Ritenour and Glen, they didn't have a mark on them, and since the beasts are supposed to be returning all the life forces Ritenour stole . . ."

Fisher suddenly froze, and clutched at Hawk's arm. "Listen . . . can you hear movement up above?"

Hawk looked at Fisher, and then they both bolted for the stairs, with Saxon close behind. They ran through the House with broad, disbelieving grins on their faces, passing bewildered mercenaries who'd also apparently just risen from the dead. Hawk and Fisher knocked them unconscious again, just to be on the safe side, and then pounded up the stairs to the fourth floor, with Saxon right there at their side. They heard the clamour of voices from the main parlour long before they got there. Finally they stood in the doorway and watched as the two Kings and their fellow hostages milled round the room, talking excitedly and trying to figure out what the hell had happened. Apparently some of the hostages had shaken off their daze faster than the mercenaries, and had taken advantage of their captors' dazed state to get in the first blow. As result of which, the hostages were now in charge of a rather battered-looking group of disarmed mercenaries.

Take it easy, said Storm's voice in their heads suddenly. *I've alerted the Council as to what's happened, and they're sending men in to secure the House. And maybe then you'd care to explain exactly what the bloody hell has been going on, and how come you've all come back from the dead!*

Hawk grinned. *You'd never believe me. . . .*

6

Goodbyes

The Council sent a small army of men-at-arms into Champion House to mop things up, and the Guard sent in an equally small army of Captains and Constables, just to make sure they weren't left out of anything. Even in the aftermath of a disaster, there were still politics to be played. Also present were a hell of a lot of honour guards from the Brotherhood of Steel, watching the entrances and exits. They weren't really needed, but nobody wanted to be the one to tell them that. Their pride was still hurting from how easily they'd been brushed aside by Madigan's people. The Council carefully assigned them lots of busywork to keep them out of everybody's hair.

The two Kings and their fellow hostages were still in the main parlour, trying to get their wits together long enough to work out whether they should postpone the Treaty-signing for a more auspicious occasion, or sign the bloody thing now before anything else could go wrong. The raised voices could be heard on the floor below, but luckily most of those arguing were still feeling too poorly after their narrow escape from death to get really out of hand. Everyone else stayed well out of their way and let them get on with it.

The cellar was full of mercenaries, tied hand, foot, and throat, waiting to be carted off to gaol as soon as enough cells could be found to hold them all. Being a mercenary wasn't illegal in Haven. Neither was planning assassinations or a *coup d'état*. But taking part in one and losing was. Particularly when the intended royal targets survive, and are known for holding grudges. The rest of the hostages weren't too keen on the mercenaries either. At the moment they were taking turns using the cellar for a latrine. Some made several trips.

Sir Roland and his fellow traitors had already been escorted to Damnation Row, where special cells had been reserved for them. They were mostly Quality, after all.

With so many people in Champion House, the place was packed from wall to wall, and it was fairly easy for Hawk, Fisher, and Saxon to blend into the crowd and disappear. They finally ended up in the kitchens, where Hawk eyed a joint of beef uneasily.

"You thinking about turning vegetarian?" asked Fisher.

Hawk shrugged. "I don't know. Maybe. But I don't think that was what they were really mad about. Animals eat other animals on a regular basis, after all. I think it was more to do with the way they were treated. Maybe if the abattoirs were more humanely run . . ."

"You mean kill them in a nice way?" said Saxon.

"I'm going to have to think about this," said Hawk.

"While he's busy doing that, I think you'd better make yourself scarce," said Fisher to Saxon. "With everything that's going on at the moment, it's probably going to be some time before they get around to taking an interest in you, but . . ."

"Quite," said Saxon. "I think I've pretty much outworn my welcome here."

"I've got a question for you," said Hawk. "Why didn't Ritenour's spell affect you? It drained the life right out of everyone else. Isobel and I survived only because we were outside the House at the time clinging to some ivy. But you . . ."

"But I," said Saxon, "was back in the hidden passages again, and they're shielded against all offensive magics, by spells built into the walls themselves long ago. Simple as that."

"What will you do now?" said Fisher.

"Beats me. But I'll think of something. Maybe I'll start a society for the prevention of cruelty to animals."

"In Haven?" said Fisher.

Saxon grinned. "There are soft hearts everywhere, if you just know the right ways to approach them. You know, it wouldn't surprise me if there was a tasty amount of money to be made out of such a society. See you around."

He nodded quickly to them both, slipped out the back door, and was gone. Hawk carefully shut the door after him, and then he and Fisher sat down together on a bench before the open kitchen fire, leaning against each other companionably, and staring at nothing much in particular.

"As with most of our cases, we won some and we lost some," said Fisher. "Most of the SWAT team are dead, rest their souls, but at least we saved the Kings."

"Not just the Kings," said Hawk. "We put the beasts to rest, saved most of Haven from destruction, and prevented a war between Outremer and the Low Kingdoms. Not bad for one day's work."

"I just hope we're getting overtime," said Fisher.

"I've a strong feeling that will depend on whether we can come up with a story our superiors can believe. I don't even want to try and explain about the beasts' spirits and the Fields of the Lord. Never mind our part in it."

"Right," said Fisher. "Hawk, how much do you remember about the spirit lands? It seems to me the more I try to remember, the hazier things get."

Hawk nodded. "Same here. It's all fading away. Probably just as well. I've a feeling we got a little too close to things the living aren't supposed to know about."

"So, in the meantime, we just make up some comforting lies for our superiors?"

"Got it in one."

They both jumped guiltily as the kitchen door opened, but it was only the sorcerer Storm. He nodded to them both.

"It's all right, there's no need for you to get up."

"That's good," said Fisher. "Because we weren't going to. Anything we can do for you, sir sorcerer?"

"Just a few questions. I was most impressed by your fortitude in all this. Most people would have been driven insane by all you've endured, but you survived with all your wits intact. How is that?"

Hawk and Fisher looked at each other, and Hawk smiled at the sorcerer. "We've seen worse, in our time."

"You got that right," said Fisher.

The Immortal Warrior.
The Legend.

Conan